By Chris E. Saros

Semblance

Published by DSP Publications
www.dsppublications.com

Thank you to my family and friends who have always supported my ambitions. I love you all!

CHRIS E. SAROS

SEMBLANCE

CHAPTER 1

DRAKE WALKED toward the back of the club and leaned against the smooth, cool, tiled wall. The crowd, though small compared to on the weekends, was still a moving, organic mass of limbs and gyrating bodies that smelled of sweat. Each flicker of the strobe light showed a new form, unique from the one before it. Squinting against the light, Drake tried to make out the individual people on the dance floor, but the chaotic rhythm of the lights didn't make it easy to spot specific faces.

Willy never had been one to blend in, so Drake figured if he was around, it wouldn't be too hard pick him out. Willy seemed to think loud patterns were all the rage, no matter how much flack he took for it. Drake had to give him credit. The kid stuck to his guns, he would give him that.

However, tonight people weren't going to be giving Willy trouble over his lousy fashion sense. No, tonight the sharks were out, and they smelled his loud Hawaiian-clad blood.

Drake thought Willy would have bolted or at least gone underground for a while after being picked up by the cops, but sources had told him the kid was heading back to the club. Willy had long ago made his bed. He'd gotten himself in deep with some of the smaller sharks in the city. When he couldn't make good on his loans, he'd sought guidance from the larger predators in the pond.

In this town, only the Boredega cartel could get you out of trouble and bury you alive at the same time. The poor kid should have stuck with the small fish, but instead he started dealing for Boredega to pay back his loans. The thing about being higher on the food chain is that in order to stay on the top rung, you had to be pretty fucking badass. Unfortunately for Willy, he didn't have what it took to climb the ladder.

"Hey, Boss Man," a static-laden voice said in his ear. Drake put a finger to the radio so he could hear around the pounding bass from the DJ.

Drake huffed at the nickname. He had tried to break Frankie of the habit, one, because Drake wasn't his boss, he just happened to run the club, and two, because if anything, Frankie was *his* boss. However, no matter the argument, Frankie continued to use the endearment. *Keeping up appearances* was what he called it, making it so the club staff didn't get confused. As if they would suddenly turn into a chaotic swarm if Frankie didn't remind them who their boss was on a regular basis. Drake had fought the fight, but Frankie never backed down, and after a couple of years without there being any indication of change, Drake stopped making a deal of it. He'd sigh now and again, but he no longer commented on it.

"Yeah, Frankie? You got eyes on Willy?"

"Nah, maybe he grew a brain and decided to book it before Tony could find him." Frankie was a born-and-raised Chicagoan, which was clear by his rough accent. When Drake had first met him, he had thought Frankie was trying to put one past him, imitating an old gangster film or something, but as he worked with him, he found that it was truly his speech.

"Then why are you talking to me, Frankie?" Drake asked with a snort. He knew Willy wouldn't be smart enough to leave while he was ahead. He was one of those young kids who thought he could do no wrong.

"I thought you should know that I watched Natasha sashay her way into the club."

Drake pinched the bridge of his nose. It was Wednesday; why was everything going down on a fucking Wednesday? It was hump day, for God's sake! It was like the night world's day of rest.

"Is she working?" Drake asked hopefully. Maybe if she were distracted, she'd be in and out without bothering him.

"I didn't see a john with her, but that don't mean she ain't got one."

Ugh, just what he needed, another problem. Somehow, Natasha always seemed to know when shit was going to hit the fan or when something important was going to happen because that was always when she showed up.

"All right, thanks for letting me know. And hey, let me know if you catch sight of Willy."

"You got it, Boss Man," Frankie said.

Drake sighed. Well, today was already looking like it was going to be an interesting one. So much excitement wasn't unusual at the club, but Drake always held out hope for a quiet evening. He'd had his fingers crossed and his hopes high, so he should have known better than to think the night would go off without a hitch.

Breathing another sigh, he pushed away from the wall, making one last scan of the crowd, and then made his way to the bar. By the time he did a double tap on the counter, his notorious signal for *get me a drink, quick,* Scotty, the head bartender, already had his drink ready for him. Two fingers of scotch, neat.

With a grateful smile, Drake took a long swallow, letting out a whoosh of breath with the sharp burn the liquid left on his tongue.

"Rough night, already?" Scotty asked, popping the top off two beers for customers down the bar.

"Huh, you could say that."

"I could pull the fire alarm and we could call it a night."

Drake snorted into his glass. "You have no idea how appealing that sounds right now."

Scotty threw him a smile as he seamlessly made two mixed drinks and handed them off to two scantily dressed women. They giggled as he winked at them, and threw a couple of dollars' tip on the bar. Scotty nodded gratitude at them, sweeping the singles into his jar under the bar as he grabbed the top-shelf scotch to refill Drake's glass.

"Looks like you you're doing well for a Wednesday night." Drake gratefully took another sip of his scotch. He was going to nurse this one.

Sure he was….

"It's all in the wink."

Yeah, the wink and the perfectly sculpted arms that moved flawlessly around the bottles on the bar, completing their designated tasks. Possibly even the washboard abs that threatened to pop out of his snug white button-up. Or his sandy-blond hair that fell perfectly along his forehead enough to frame his sparkling golden eyes.

Drake huffed into his glass, trying to shake himself out of it. Yes, the man was good-looking, but he was his employee and therefore off-limits.

Didn't mean he couldn't watch, though, did it? Drake smirked to himself as he snuck another peek only to find Scotty back directly in front of him. Elbows on the table, Scotty leaned toward Drake, who felt his heart practically explode at the neared proximity. Just over half of the counter, Scotty dropped his chin onto his hands and batted his lashes at Drake. "It does help that I am absolutely adorable."

Drake coughed, trying to ignore the small tug in his stomach as Scotty flashed his goldenrod-brown eyes at him. He shifted uncomfortably in his seat as he felt a familiar heat start to warm his blood. Mentally shaking it off, he grinned.

"Yeah, a face only a mother could love."

"Then how do you explain the mountain of tips I made today?"

"Everyone knows you can't witness the freak show for free. I put a sign at the door."

Scotty grabbed his chest in mock pain. "Ouch. Okay, I concede on this one, but don't expect such submission next time."

"Maybe submission is exactly what I want from you."

Drake practically choked on his own words. Where the hell had that come from? Thank God it was dark enough that the flush heating his face was most likely hidden.

While the words had shocked Drake to his core, they didn't seem to faze Scotty, who leaned back, observing Drake with a cocked brow. "Well, I do declare, Mr. Clane, was that an invitation?"

"In your dreams, barkeep. Now, make yourself useful and get me a drink."

"And what pleasant dreams they are," Scotty said dramatically, fanning his face with his hand.

"I wasn't kidding about that drink, Scotty!"

"Aye, aye, Captain!" Scotty gave a mock salute, then went to put glasses away at the other end of the bar, blatantly ignoring Drake's request.

Scotty's predictability tugged a smile to Drake's lips. Scotty was the best damn bartender who had ever worked for Drake, but for some reason he always seemed to forget to refill Drake's glass. It was probably a good thing. Drake would be the first to admit that he probably drank just a little too much, but when you were doing the things that he was doing, sometimes you needed a little bit of an inhibition blocker. Sometimes you needed more than a little.

Drake propped his head onto one hand and spun his empty glass with the other as he watched Scotty confidently work his way around the bar. Scotty moved fluidly as he poured drinks and mixed cocktails; he smiled and winked, never missing a step between one patron and the next. And Drake couldn't help but notice how perfect his ass looked in his tight dark jeans.

Scotty laughed with one of the regulars, and Drake's lips quirked. Scotty was all sunshine and roses. Thinking back, Drake had a hard time remembering an instance when he had seen Scotty angry. Even when he was overwhelmed and overworked, he still kept his smile on. The way he easily struck up conversations was an asset, and Drake couldn't help but feel a little jealous at the ease with which Scotty flirted. Drake envied him his rose-colored glasses, glad that Scotty had been given a chance to still see the good, while Drake saw only darkness.

That innocence—that happiness—was the reason Drake hired outside staff to work the club. Sure, he could always hire some of Boredega's crew or bring his staff into the fold, but he didn't. He kept the dark of the club as far from the light of his employees as possible. It may have been easier to only employ Boredega's men, but even the darkest of corners needed some light for the shadows.

Scotty's full-throated laugh dragged Drake back to the present.

Jesus! he thought, pulling his spine up straight. He hadn't been drooling, had he? Shit. Drake shook his head at his ridiculous conduct, then quickly wiped his lips with the back of his hand, just in case.

Still deeply absorbed in his own thoughts, Drake started when Scotty set a glass of scotch on the counter in front of him. Drake raised a brow at the unexpected offering. Scotty tilted his head, using his chin to point behind Drake subtly.

"Incoming," Scotty warned with a wink as he turned to make his rounds.

Drake tensed at what was behind him. Shit, instead of sitting here daydreaming about his staff, he should have gone back to his office. Thinking quickly, Drake drained his glass in one gulp and moved to get up, possibly hide, when he felt a familiar hand caress his shoulder.

"There you are!" Natasha's high-pitched voice sent a chill down Drake's spine. He closed his eyes, preparing himself before turning around to face the dark-haired beauty.

She was exceptionally dressed this evening, which meant that she probably did have a john waiting for her somewhere around the club. But with Natasha, you never could guess. When sex was your business, you tended to forget that sometimes the store was closed.

She was what Drake had considered a onetime deal, but apparently, she didn't quite see it like that.

Natasha was what you would call multifaceted. It was amazing how little attention people tended to pay the whore. Prostitutes were objects, a means to an end, which left some nice wide-open doors for Natasha. Open doors, drawers, safes, and closets full of secrets. She was beautiful and seemed so innocuous. It was what made her good at her job. Sure, she was a prostitute, but she also had some of the best information sex could buy.

Drake had made the mistake of letting her get a little too close to him. He'd seen a young naive girl working the streets and had thought himself a knight in shining armor ready to save the damsel. Flaw with that was that the damsel had to *want* to be saved, and while Natasha did want to be saved, it wasn't in the way that Drake had expected.

He took it as a case of assumed identity. He'd assumed her innocent, and she had assumed him much more powerful than he actually was. It was a tale as old as time. Unfortunately, this story never seemed to end.

"Natasha, what a pleasure," Drake said darkly, crossing his arms over his chest.

Natasha brushed back her black curls to reveal more of her corseted, very squished breasts. Her definition of flirting, Drake supposed. That's what happens when you don't have the personality to back up the goods. You flaunt yourself and hope it is good enough. While it made her good at her job, Drake had given up trying to tell her that when guys weren't paying for the sex, they didn't necessarily want to see the whole package all the time.

Drake took a step back, leaning against the hard edge of the bar. "What brings you into the club on a quiet night like tonight?"

Accentuating her lusty curves with a roll of her shoulder and practiced tilt of her hips, she smirked at him with painted, bloodthirsty lips.

"A job." She stuck out her bottom lip to make a pouty face. "But he left me here so he could go meet with someone in the back. I figured you could enjoy my company in the meantime."

Drake shook his head at her words with a sigh. If her client was in one of the back rooms, that meant he probably worked for Boredega in one form or another. In this town, it was hard to find people who didn't work for Boredega in some way.

"He dealing or using?" Drake asked.

Natasha rolled her eyes. "He didn't tell me, and I didn't ask. I try not to make a habit out of interrogating my clients before they fuck me."

"Cute," Drake said, feeling a migraine start in his temple. He didn't know why he was letting her stress him out. It wasn't as if her line of work was a safe one. She sold her body, and she wasn't picky about her clientele. She had also made it clear to Drake that if her clients bought her drugs, she wasn't going to turn them down; she would simply raise the price. Something about it then becoming a "risk bonus."

"Aw, are you worried about little ole me, Drakeybo?" she asked, laying her body along Drake's. She brushed her lips along his chin.

Drake put a hand on each of her shoulders and pushed her back. "Hey now, you wouldn't want your john to get the wrong impression, would you?" She frowned as she was moved back, but the expression didn't last long before returning to its voluptuous sex goddess mask.

"I don't know, with his type, he might like it."

Drake snorted, turning back toward the bar for his empty glass. He looked for Scotty, but he was busy across the bar leaning against the counter and chatting with some young blonde sporting a low-cut shirt. Drake frowned as he spotted them and set his glass back on the counter with a sharp smack.

"You haven't seen or heard anything about Willy, have ya?" Drake asked, trying with difficulty to ignore the gnawing feeling in his stomach.

Natasha, completely oblivious to Drake's disinterest, pressed forward again, letting her curves mold to Drake's side. "You know, my client said it would only be a few hours tonight. Maybe you could come on over after the club closes. I could really make it worth your night." She ran her tongue along her full top lip.

"Um, yeah, I don't see that happening. I'm not into sloppy seconds."

The insult didn't faze her. She let her hand rub its way down the front of Drake's body, stopping at the top of his beltline.

"I could tell my date to hang around, and we could really make a night of it." The whispered words blew hot into his ear.

Drake shook his head. He didn't know why he had thought he could help her. She clearly didn't want it. She seemed quite content and comfortable with the life she led.

"That really didn't make the offer any more appealing. I'll pass, thanks. You didn't answer my question."

"You don't know what you'll be missing, Drake," she said, swinging around so fast that her hair slapped him in his face.

"Yeah, I think I do," he muttered under his breath.

Natasha made it about four steps before she turned around with a huge smile. She pointed a bloodred fingernail toward the dance floor and gave a "there you have it" shrug.

"Don't say I've never done anything for you, babe. Now you owe me one, and I plan to collect."

Drake's gaze followed the long stretch of Natasha's perfectly manicured finger.

Willy.

The idiot had come to the club. He was probably walking straight for the back, or dancing his way to the back, whatever, as if he didn't have a care in the world. As if Tony wouldn't have the entire crew looking for him. They knew his supplies would be low after the bust; they knew he would have to return to fill up the tanks. Unfortunately for Willy, he was too stupid to know better.

The least he could do was wear a less conspicuous shirt. Shit, the kid stood out like a sore thumb.

Drake turned a frown on Natasha. "I don't think pointing at a person counts as a favor."

"Hmm, maybe not for you," Natasha purred, "but I never sell myself short. See you around, Drakeybo."

Drake shook his head as Natasha departed, turning on his mic. He headed in the direction that he had last seen Willy. "Hey, Frankie, Willy's in the club. I saw him headed toward the back."

"What a stupid fuck. He should be halfway to Alaska by now."

"I am heading that direction now."

"Where? Alaska?"

Drake snorted. "Aha, ha ha, very funny."

"You want me to take point on this, Boss Man?"

Drake caught sight of Willy again, toward the back talking to a woman who looked like she desperately needed a savior. Drake shook his head. Not only was the man stupid enough to return to the club to get another fix, but he wasn't worried enough to not pick up women on his way. He was a fool, but in Drake's experience, those who got involved with Boredega usually were. Drake knew *he* was.

He should have let Frankie take point. He wasn't in the mood to deal with this shit tonight, but you didn't get anywhere sitting on your ass. If he wanted to take over Frankie's position, he needed to prove he was capable of handling these types of situations.

"No, I got this. I'll let you know if I need you."

"You got it, Boss Man. Keep your mic on so we know what's happening. I'll keep an eye on the club."

"You got it."

Drake approached Willy from behind. The woman's eyes darted to Drake as he moved toward them. She gave him an approving up-and-down before settling into a confident smile. However, as he approached, her once-approving invitation turned to wide-eyed concern, and she took a half step back, almost tripping over her own feet. Drake felt a self-satisfied tug curl his lips. Her reaction was from the expression on his face. Whenever he had to deal with one of Boredega's men or any jackass who made a scene in his club, he put his intimidation face on. It was a good look, a *mean* look. He knew it was. It had taken a lot of practicing to make it right.

The woman wasn't paying attention to Willy any longer, keeping her cautious eyes on Drake. He raised a brow at her as he put a hand on Willy's shoulder, fingers digging in tight. Willy turned at the touch, eyes wide.

Drake grinned, knew it wasn't pretty. "We need to talk."

"Hey, Drake," Willy began but stopped as Drake's look hardened even more. Willy tried to back away, probably just realized what type of trouble he was in and wanted to run, but Drake held him firmly by the shoulder.

"Excuse us, ma'am," Drake said to the woman, who was already quickly retreating into the pulsating crowd. Drake shifted his glare back to Willy, who visibly swallowed. "Come with me."

Drake didn't give Willy a chance to respond, to decline, to beg or plead; he dug his fingers in Willy's shoulder and shoved him ahead of him, pushing him toward the back of the club.

Stumbling, Willy trembled as he headed the direction Drake led him, past the bathrooms and storage rooms and down the narrow hallway that would take them directly to Drake's office. Willy didn't struggle against Drake's grip; he knew he wasn't going to get out of the club if Drake didn't want him to.

Drake pushed open the door to his office, dragging Willy in by his arm. Drake forced Willy up next to his desk and stopped, opening his top pencil drawer and pressing a button hidden at the top. A quiet snick let him know that the hidden door was unlocked. Willy watched the door open with wide eyes. He looked up at Drake, who, though he wasn't an exceptionally tall man, towered over Willy's smaller stature. Drake watched him swallow hard as he was led into the dank white room.

The room had many purposes, but the most common of them was an interrogation room for Boredega and his men. The walls were reinforced and had extrathick soundproof insulation. There were no windows and only the one entrance. The chair that sat in the middle of the room had cuffs attached to the arms and the legs. There was only one other piece of furniture: a tall cabinet containing a multitude of different instruments used to extract information from the room's guests. Drake made it a rule never to open that cabinet. Nothing from that cabinet would get him what he needed, but the stories told by those who *were* victims or witnesses to the cabinet made it a very effective tool.

Drake put Willy in the chair and clicked the cuffs into place. Willy looked at his restrained hands blankly, then back up at Drake, who closed the door with a loud clank.

"I don't know what you think happened, Drake, but it was nothing like that. I didn't tell them cops anything! I swear it!" Willy's voice trembled as he faced Drake.

Drake didn't say anything, just leaned back against the wall in front of Willy, letting him talk. He knew the silence was unnerving, and the threat of what could happen in the room created loose lips. While he waited in silence, he clicked the cord by his neck that kept his line of communication open. He preferred to do this type of thing radio silent, but Frankie rarely let him do anything without a presence in the room. Drake was lucky that he had allowed him to leave his radio on instead of coming into the room with him. It made his job a little easier. He could work around a sound device.

"I got picked up by the cops for a breaking-and-entering thing. I didn't even do it. That's why they had to let me go. Could only hold me for twenty-four hours. I had nothing to do with the house being busted. I didn't say anything."

Drake smirked. "If you had nothing to do with it, then why do you know that's what we are here to talk about?"

"Because! It happened when I was in the clink, man! I heard about it when I went to get my fix down in the Loop. They were low on supplies because of it. That's why I came here. Come on, Drake! You know me! You know I wouldn't say anything."

Drake shook his head. "You know that it doesn't matter what I think, Willy. It only matters what Boredega thinks. And right now, he thinks that you gave up the drug house to save your ass from more drug charges."

Willy shook his head adamantly. "No, no, I wasn't even in for drugs this time! It was on suspicion of a breaking and entering! I had nothing to do with it."

With no warning, Drake shot forward and punched Willy across the face. Backing up, he clenched and unclenched his fist. He hated the feel of flesh breaking along his knuckles. "You gotta give me something to work with here, Willy. If you didn't rat out the house, then who did?"

Willy hung his head, eyes blurry from the punch. Blood worked its way down from his nose. "I don't know. I don't know how the cops knew about it."

Drake punched him again, this time from the opposite side. "You gotta do better than that."

"*I don't know!*" Willy shouted. Drake punched him again and then again, switching it up. He would do two straight to the face, then one to the gut. It had to sound good, and gut punches always had a dramatic effect with the huff of forced air.

He paused every couple of swings to see if Willy had anything to add, but besides some whimpering babble and a spit of blood, he didn't have much to say.

Drake almost wished Willy would give him something. Some name, or some wild goose chase to send them on, anything to make the beating stop. But Drake had to hand it to the kid. He stuck to his guns. Another reason the kid was too stupid to survive this shark attack.

"Please, please stop," Willy whimpered from his chair. Drake backed up, tilting his head so the mic was close enough to Willy for his words to be heard clearly. The distance made it easier for him to see Willy, and he couldn't help but cringe as he looked him over. The man's nose was obviously broken, his lips cut, and eyes already swollen. Blood dribbled down his chin, his nose, and the side of his face.

He knew it didn't seem like it, but Drake was doing his best to keep Willy from becoming dead. He didn't know what would be happening if Frankie had been the one to bring him in, but he knew that Willy wouldn't have been walking out of the room after they were done, if walking again ever.

"You finally think of something?" Drake asked.

"I don't know who gave up the house. I don't know. Please, don't hurt me any more."

Drake sighed, "That's not what I was looking for, Willy. You gotta give me something." Drake willed him with his eyes. *Come on, kid. Give me something so this can all end. Give them a show so I can let you go.*

But for all the hard times they had given the kid over the past few months, for all the jabs the kid had taken about his choices in life and in fashion, he really did have moxie.

"I told you! I told you I don't know anything. I told you I didn't say anything. I don't know. Please stop. Please, please stop." His words leaked out of his lips.

Drake reached into his pocket and pulled out a syringe he had grabbed in his office as he dragged Willy through. He held it up so Willy could see what it was.

"You know what this is?" Drake asked, knowing full well that Willy knew exactly what it was. The man was hooked on it, after all. "Willy, look at me! Do you know what this is?"

Willy slowly lifted his head to look at the syringe. He eyed it with a mixture of fear and relief. He must have been jonesing after being in lockup. He nodded, then looked at Drake full on. "You gonna kill me, Drake?"

Instead of answering, Drake moved so he could crouch down by Willy at eye level. "You know what is very interesting about this drug? It was originally made by pharmaceuticals as a short-term anxiety suppressant. Kind of like a Xanax on steroids. *Selecure*, the magical elixir. They even sold it for a bit over the counter. It worked, I mean, it really worked. What am I talking about? Of course you know it works. You use it regularly." Willy's head lolled as Drake continued his lecture. "Weird thing about Selecure, though, if you take a small dose, the dose intended, you get high. High enough that people started driving off the road and hallucinating at work—that's why they took it off the market, you see. But if you take more than what's intended, then the drug does a jacked-up thing to your brain. It stimulates your pain sensors. Nothing can be happening to you, no physical harm, but your body will feel as if it's being torn to shreds." Drake paused dramatically, watching a thin stream of blood course down Willy's cheek to his chin. The putrid stench of fear filled the air as Willy's eyes followed any movement Drake made with the syringe.

"Add just a little bit more—" Drake tipped the syringe toward Willy, who unconsciously struggled against his bonds. "—like what I have here, and it signals your body to shut down, leaving you in intense pain but unable to move or scream. All you can do is wait it out or hope for death."

Willy eyed the syringe warily. Drake watched his face carefully, searching for any sign that he knew who sold out the house or that he had any information that would be good enough for him to stop.

"I'll give you one more chance, Willy. What do you know?" Drake watched as Willy debated what to say. His face changed from calculating to formulating, then returned to resigned complacency.

"I told you I don't know. Just get it over with," Willy said, then turned his head away.

Drake paused to blink. Well, that was unexpected. They had all underestimated him. He was stronger than they thought. Drake had brought many men into this room, and not many of them left without telling him everything they knew or making something up to get them out of there. An iron will like that, the guy could be useful.

Drake looked thoughtfully at the syringe he held. It held enough to cause Willy some serious pain. But he knew he didn't need to get any information from him anyway. Willy didn't know anything.

Holding the syringe up to the light, Drake depressed the plunger, letting a stream of liquid jet to the floor.

Reaching up to the collar of his shirt, Drake clicked off his mic. He knew it was loud in the club, and he hoped Frankie wouldn't notice the radio silence. Grabbing Willy's wrist, Drake ignored his pained whimper as he pushed up Willy's sleeve so it was tight around his upper arm, cutting off blood flow. Drake tapped the crease Willy's elbow. "It's your lucky day," Drake said, wringing another pained moan from Willy.

Drake readied the needle against Willy's skin and then used his free hand to hold Willy's chin up to him. Willy was beyond panic, eyes rolling in his head.

"Willy, look at me," Drake demanded, pressing his fingers roughly into Willy's chin. "Hey, hey, look at me."

Willy's swollen, bloodshot eyes met Drake's. Drake just stared at him for a moment, making sure he was there and that he was listening.

"I am about to do this," Drake said, nodding toward the needle. "It's not enough to do anything but give you a nice high, all right? But I need you to do something for me, okay? When I put this needle in your arm, I need you to scream. You hear me? Scream, okay?"

Willy's wide, panicked eyes narrowed slightly before he gave a small nod. Drake released Willy's head and turned his mic back on. Then before he could think about it anymore, he pushed the needle under Willy's skin and depressed the plunger.

Willy stayed true to his word, letting out a strangled scream as the liquid flooded through his system. He moaned loudly and then let out a short cry.

Drake could tell the moment the drug fully took over because Willy's head dropped back and his eyes drooped to half-lidded. He worked his jaw, trying to speak, but no words came out, just garbled sounds.

Covering the mic with his hand, Drake knelt close to Willy, their heads only inches apart. He spoke in a low voice so the mic wouldn't pick him up.

"You're going to be okay, all right? I'm going to put you in the back storage room and lock it from the inside. As soon as you feel able, get the hell out of here. Go out the back door at the end of this hallway. Don't talk to anyone, or stop to see anyone, and definitely do not get any more drugs. Got it?" Drake waited for Willy's loose nod. At least he thought it was a nod and not just a fall of the head.

"Once you get your shit, get out of here. Leave and don't look back. Get out of the city, hell, get out of the state. Just fucking go. You got it?"

Willy nodded again, this time more clearly. Drake clasped him on the shoulder and then undid the cuffs to release Willy's hands. Drake pulled him up, supporting his dead weight as he opened the door into his office. He half dragged, half supported Willy as he walked through the office. As soon as he opened his office door leading back to the club, he glanced out into the hallway to see if anyone was around, then quickly pulled Willy to the first storage room available. He lowered him to the floor and then covered his mic.

"Remember, don't go home…. Leave. Got it?"

Trying to push himself up into a sitting position but failing, Willy collapsed so he was flat on his back. "Why?"

Drake licked his lips. Why what? Why didn't he kill him? Why didn't he torture him more? Why did he make him scream?

Drake had lots of reasons. Because he had never killed anyone. Because he didn't like the look or smell of blood. Because he wasn't the bad guy everyone thought him to be.

Because he was the one who had given up the drug house.

But he couldn't tell Willy any of that.

"Because it's your lucky day," he said instead, glowering down at Willy. "I never want to see your fucking face again." With his last words, Drake locked the door and closed it behind him.

Fucking Wednesdays, Drake thought as he headed back to the bar.

CHAPTER 2

THE CLUB was finally starting to clear out as Drake sat at the bar nursing another scotch. He'd had a few since he'd locked the storage door behind him. It wasn't unusual for him to imbibe when there was shit going down, so he wasn't worried about seeming especially nervous and antsy. At his third scotch for his second round at the bar, Scotty came to sit beside him.

"I think now is a good time to put the brakes on, don't ya think?"

Not turning to look at him, Drake drained his glass. "Aren't you supposed to be working?"

Scotty didn't even twitch at his boss's jibe. He pushed a glass of water to Drake. "Eh, it's starting to slow down. Workday, ya know? Julie can handle it."

Eyeing the water with distaste, Drake spun his empty scotch glass. "Business seemed good today."

"Hm, yeah, it wasn't bad for a weeknight. But are we going to talk about business, or are we going to talk about how you're downing a bottle of Black Label all by your lonesome?"

"I don't see how what I'm drinking should be concerning you. Your job is to pour it, not ask questions."

Scotty raised a surrendering hand. "Hey, sorry. I didn't mean to overstep."

Drake let his head fall. He hadn't meant it how it sounded. Well, he guessed it was more like he didn't mean what he'd said. He'd had too much on his mind. Between dealing with Willy, his apparent lust for Scotty, and Natasha throwing him glowering looks all evening, he was starting to feel like the canary the cat ate.

"Hey, stop, I'm sorry," Drake said, putting his hand on Scotty's arm before he could leave. "I am having an off day is all."

Scotty glanced down at Drake's hand on his arm and then looked back up, golden eyes meeting Drake's dark ones. Drake shivered at the look but hid it by removing his hand and shifting on his stool.

"Yeah, I can tell," Scotty said, settling back on his own stool. "You want to talk about it?"

Drake picked up his water. "You know that I'm going to want more scotch before the night is over, right?"

"Who am I to tell you what you can and cannot drink? I thought slower coasting would be better than full speed with cut brakes."

Snorting, Drake cocked his head at Scotty. "It's much more fun this way. You should try it."

"No, thank you. I watch plenty of people go from sophisticated to unintelligible mess in one night. I'm not fool enough to join them."

Scotty stopped suddenly at his words, holding his hands up. "I didn't m—"

"I know what you meant. Don't worry, I've drunk enough that your insults just bounce right off."

"Really? Well then, there have been a lot of things I have been meaning to tell you...." Scotty laughed as Drake punched him in the arm. "Hey!"

"I'm not that drunk!"

"Good," Scotty said with a smirk before a shadow fell across his face as he spotted something behind Drake.

Drake turned to see Frankie heading for him. Uhhh, that brought everything all back to the surface. *This day has truly sucked. Hump day or not, it sucked.*

For some reason, Scotty and Frankie didn't hit it off. Frankie was probably the only person who Drake had seen Scotty not take a liking to. He wasn't sure if it was the rough exterior, interior, or both that Frankie projected or the fact that Frankie was a tough guy who shoved people around when things went squirrely.

To help keep up appearances at the club, Frankie masqueraded as a bouncer. That way it didn't look suspicious or odd to see him drag somebody out the door or down the hall to the back office. But it was as if Scotty could sense there was more to it than bouncing. Whenever Frankie was around, he made himself scarce.

"Uh-oh, looks like the big bad wolf is seeking an audience."

Nodding, Drake took a sip of his water. He cringed, putting the liquid back on the counter. "Yep, looks like. You mind, uh?" He wiggled his empty scotch glass.

Scotty raised a brow disapprovingly, but after returning behind the bar gave Drake a refill.

"Thanks," Drake said.

Nodding stiffly, Scotty went back to his duties as Frankie took his now vacant seat.

"Hey, Boss Man," Frankie said. "You ain't looking so good today. You want me to close up?"

Drake sipped his scotch and motioned for Scotty to get Frankie a beer. "Nah, I'm just settling in."

"What do you think about Willy?"

"Poor kid didn't know which way is up. You know how it is with these junkies."

The ice clinked in Drake's drink as he slowly spun his glass. He wouldn't show it, but he preened a bit inside as Frankie spoke to him. If Frankie was asking his opinion, it meant his opinioned *mattered*.

"So, ya think he did it?"

Frankie reached over the bar to grab some nuts. He put a handful into his mouth, chewing noisily as he watched Drake. Drake cleared his throat, not entirely comfortable with the inquiring look he was getting, but still silently pleased with the question. He swallowed before answering. "Eh, who knows? Kid's tougher than we give him credit for. He took everything I gave him and didn't even try to make anything up. He stuck to his story. Even pumped full of Selecure, he didn't have anything to say."

Frankie nodded. "Right."

"You heard it. He didn't seem to know anything. I got him pumped full of drugs and sleeping it off in a back room. I figure we scared a few years off his life. He won't be making any waves after this."

Frankie popped another handful of nuts in his mouth, chewed them, and swallowed before replying. "Tony ain't going to be happy with that. We can't go back to him without some sort of answers. We have to give him something."

Shrugging, Drake ran a hand through his hair. "I guess we gotta keep looking, then. As far as I could tell, the kid didn't know anything."

"Oh, we'll keep looking, but we are going to give Tony something too. Just cuz the kid don't know, don't mean that he can't be a lesson and a warning to the one who did talk to the cops."

Shit. Not good.

"I'll have Tony's guys come pick him up and see what they can get out of him."

Drake's stomach twisted at the words. "You think that's necessary? I mean, Willy's just a kid and a junkie. He would have talked if he'd known something. And if he did know something, man, that kind of sealed lip could be a good thing to keep around."

Frankie's dark gaze met Drake's, and it took everything Drake had to keep his expression cool and composed.

"This life ain't for the weak at heart, Boss Man. You gotta break some eggs if you want an omelet. It's all part of the job. Sealed lips can be paid for and wagging lips dealt with. All we have to worry about is making sure Tony feels satisfied."

Drake covered his frown with a cough, putting a hand to his mouth, nodding. He had thought he could get the kid out of it without too much trouble, but he should have known better. The loss of the drug house had been a big one, and there was no way Boredega could let that go. The coincidences with Willy were too high to let him walk. Drake should have known better than to hope they'd let him walk away.

Now the kid had some fuel about Drake too. Shit. Maybe he should have killed him….

What?

No, what was he thinking?

Frankie watched Drake take another swig of his scotch, his eyes narrowed in a way that made Drake shiver. "Why don't you head out? You look like you need an early night. Besides, I gotta wait for the club to clear out so I can take out the trash."

Drake tried to hide his flinch but wasn't sure if he pulled it off. He tilted his glass, tossing the remainder of his scotch to the back of his throat, then grabbed his jacket from the stool next to him.

"Yeah, fine, that sounds good. I guess I'll head home, then." Drake took an unsteady step back.

Frankie watched him with a cock of his head and threw him a smug smile. "The boys said that Natasha is still hanging around if you want me to grab her to take you home."

"Oh, God no," Drake groaned and made himself stand a little straighter. The mere thought made him feel instantly sober. "I'm fine. I'll be in early tomorrow to look over the books. Can you make sure the bar finishes inventory so I can place an order tomorrow?"

"Sure, sure," Frankie said, taking a swig from his domestic longneck.

Drake turned to walk away but stopped when Frankie called him back over. "Tony wanted me to tell you that he's got a new kid coming in tomorrow."

Drake smirked. "New errand boy?"

"New errand boy," Frankie confirmed. "Apparently, the kid is on the fast track to move up in the ranks, so Tony thought he could start as the runner for the club and see how it goes."

"Fast track, huh? He someone important?"

"You could say that. He's Tony's nephew or some shit like that. Has an ego on him too from what I hear."

"Great. Another kid to babysit. So, what? He only a runner or can I utilize him too?"

Frankie snorted. "He wants to tend bar."

"Perfect, exactly what I need. Another thug behind the bar." Drake shook his head. Scotty was going to kill him. Whenever Tony brought in a new face, they always ended up behind the bar and very rarely were they trained enough to be a decent bartender. He wasn't going to be happy to learn about a new head to train.

"From what I hear, he is a pretty boy, should be perfect for behind the bar."

Drake laughed. "Yeah, I'll tell Scotty you said that. All right, I'm outta here."

"Night, Boss Man," Frankie called as Drake exited the club.

CHAPTER 3

"Dammit!" Drake's fists ached with his repeated pounding on his steering wheel. "Dammit, dammit, dammit!"

How did he let that happen? How did he go from saving the kid's ass to putting him on the chopping block? He'd been able to get people out before. He had only had one or two opportunities but as far as he knew they had been successful.

Willy would probably have been better off if Drake had just given him the full syringe. Right now he was sobering up, thinking that everything was going to be fine, that he was going to make it out of there. Instead, he was going to be tortured and killed.

Fuck! Nothing was working out as it was supposed to. Drake hadn't counted on Willy's release being so close to the raid. Damn stupid cops! They should know better than let a known criminal with ties to Boredega go after a bust. They basically signed his death warrant.

Shit!

He dropped his head into his hands and drew a deep breath. He knew there would be lives lost in this battle. He knew the consequences of his actions could end up killing him and most likely those around him. But it felt like such a waste. Willy was a Selecure junkie, but he wasn't a bad guy. He was more like the token low-end mob kid. He wore ugly Hawaiian shirts and hit on women he had no chance of getting with. He was harmless.

"I should have waited! I should have waited an extra day," Drake muttered with another punch to his steering wheel.

He'd had the opportunity to leave an anonymous tip about the new drug house that had been set up on the south side. He didn't usually know the exact locations of the Selecure houses, but this time he'd gotten a first-class ticket to see it. Frankie had taken him on a job. It was a double plus for Drake, because not only did it mean he was working his way into the big guy's trust, he'd found another way to hit the cartel where it hurt—their revenue stream. It had to be done. It had to. If the drug house had still been operational, then there would be more of the drug on the streets and more bodies piling up. Sometimes you have to sacrifice the one to help the many.

As much as Drake wanted to blame this one on the cops, he knew Willy's death was on him. Collateral damage—it was a means to the end.

Drake clenched his head in his fists before collapsing to lay his forehead on the wheel.

"I don't know if I can take much more of this."

Knock knock.

The sound was so loud in the silence that Drake nearly jumped out of his skin as it vibrated through him. Involuntarily jumping away from the door where the sound originated, he reached for the gun he had mounted under his seat.

"Hey, Drake, you okay in there?" Scotty called through the glass.

Drake blinked, letting his surroundings settle back around him before dismissing the instinct to grab his gun, and instead slapped his hand to his chest. He shook his head, trying to regain some of the air he had lost.

"Jesus, Scotty, you scared the shit out of me!" Turning the key to on, he rolled down the window.

Scotty peered into the car with a smug grin. "I got a change of pants in my locker if you need it."

"Ha ha." Drake rolled his eyes, "What the hell do you want?"

"I was takin' the trash out when I saw you sitting in your car. You had quite a few drinks. You probably shouldn't be behind the wheel."

"What are you, my mother? I'm fine." Drake shook his head at Scotty's cocked brow. "I am! I'm fine! I can handle a few glasses of scotch."

"A few glasses? Try most of the bottle!"

"It wasn't that much."

"Uh, yeah, it was."

"What business is it of yours anyway?"

Scotty raised his hands in a sarcastic shrug. "Like all my business. I pour the damn drinks. I know when someone should or should not be driving and you, *Boss Man*, should definitely not be behind the wheel."

Drake took in Scotty's rant, letting the air settle around them. Scotty was right; he'd had a few drinks tonight. Not enough to squash his riptide of guilt and overwhelming emotion, but enough that he probably shouldn't be driving home. That would be all he needed. To end up causing an accident that killed another innocent person.

Giving in, Drake nodded. "All right, okay, I hear you. I'll call a cab."

The smoldering grin that broke across Scotty's face caused goose bumps to prickle along Drake's arms. Damn, that man had no idea what he could get away with using that face.

Scotty, smile still in place, shook his head. "No, I'll give you a ride."

"What? The hell you will! You're still on the clock! I'm already paying you to stand out here as a useless blob. I am not paying you to take me home."

"Because you would rather pay a random taxi driver outrageous fees than let a friend give you a lift. Besides, Julie can handle it. It's a Wednesday night. It shouldn't be too bad."

Drake went to protest but closed his mouth. Scotty was right. The taxis in this city did have outrageous rates. It would probably cost him more than an arm and leg to get to the other side of town. Besides, he and Scotty had never spent time together outside of club business. It might be good to get to know him a little better.

Drake shook his head, distilling those thoughts. Nope, there wasn't time for that. It didn't matter that Scotty was like a walking Calvin Klein model. Drake was neck-deep in shit, and he didn't need any bedfellows.

"Okay, stay here. I'm going to grab my stuff," Scotty said, already walking back toward the building.

Just because he couldn't touch didn't mean he couldn't look, right? Drake's lips curled as he appreciated Scotty's smooth gait. The events of the night returned to him as Scotty ducked through the back door of the club, disappearing from view.

What the hell was he doing? Not only had he sat out in the parking lot long enough to get spotted throwing a fit in his car, but he was letting his mind get clouded with thoughts of sex. Probably mind-blowing sex, by the looks of those arms and firm ass, but—dammit!

Drake mentally scolded himself for letting his thoughts get carried away by his lewd imagination. Just because Scotty had a nice ass was no reason to think he could fall into bed with him. Sure, Scotty had hinted that the gender of his partners wasn't an important issue, but it definitely didn't mean he wanted to sleep with Drake.

Drake was his boss. If anything, Scotty definitely should not want to sleep with him.

Or more to the point, Drake shouldn't want to sleep with him. He couldn't screw an employee! He had enough trouble on his plate dealing with the club without adding another person to the mix. Besides, when shit went down, there was no telling what was going to happen or who would get hurt. He'd thought he would be able to get Willy out of there alive, but that hadn't happened. He couldn't risk Scotty. No, he needed to keep his distance.

But as Scotty trotted back toward his car carrying a small bag, Drake couldn't help but think of the possibilities. Drake's eyes glued to Scotty's figure as he moved quickly through the parking lot toward Drake's car. His lithe body maneuvered between the parked vehicles gracefully. Drake licked his lips.

Okay, maybe he'd had too much to drink. He should be able to watch an employee and friend walk to his car without his pants getting tight.

Scotty walked directly to the driver's door, pulling it open. He leaned in with a cocked brow. Waving a hand to indicate that Drake should scoot over into the passenger seat, he tossed his bag into the back, then slid in, shutting the door.

"Oh, it's a stick shift," Scotty said, sliding his seat forward so he could reach the pedals and move the mirrors.

Drake watched him in horror. "Yes, it's a stick. What the hell are you doing?"

Scotty shot him a quick look. "What do you mean?"

Drake gestured frantically at Scotty, who was still messing with the seat. "You're changing all my settings. Do you have any idea how hard it is to get your seat in exactly the right spot?"

"I have to be able to reach the pedals and use the mirrors if I am going to drive you."

"You don't touch a man's seat settings! Now it will never feel right again."

Scotty rolled his eyes, shifting the rearview mirror a touch more, mostly to get more of a reaction out of him, Drake figured, before turning the key in the ignition. "Oh, you'll get used to it again, just like you did the first time."

Drake sat back in a pout, arms crossed. "I can't believe that you did that."

"Get over it. I'll change it back, and you'll never even know that it was moved."

"Of course I'll know it's moved! I just watched you move it. And there is no way that you could possibly get it back exactly how I had it."

Scotty tilted his head toward Drake with an amused smile, "Jeez, are you always this whiny?"

Drake's frown deepened. "No, I save it for annoying pricks that mess with another man's seat settings."

"Did you call me a prick?"

"I believe I did, yes."

Letting out a laugh, Scotty shook his head. "I don't think I've heard that one in a while."

"Really? I can't be the only one out there calling you a prick, when you so obviously radiate the characteristics."

"So, this is the kind of treatment I get for driving you home?"

Drake sat back, enjoying the banter. "Hey, I didn't ask you to. You volunteered all by yourself."

"What was I thinking?"

"That you can't get enough of me."

"Ha! You wish that were the case."

"I know it is."

Scotty sat quietly for a moment, his eyes on the road. The silence, such a difference from the bickering banter back and forth, was unsettling, and Drake shifted so he could watch Scotty covertly from the corner of his eye.

He was as handsome and alluring driving his car as he was pouring drinks. Not that it mattered. As much as Drake wanted him, longed to touch him, to feel his skin ripple under his fingertip, his heat sink into his flesh, Drake had to remember that his life was not conducive to relationships. He didn't have the right to bring anyone into this life. That's why he'd always stuck with one-night stands, and most of those he'd had with people already involved in the dark underbelly. It was too dangerous to bring in an innocent bystander.

"Hey, you have to turn here. Go right at the light," Drake directed, and Scotty followed his instructions, flicking on his turn signal.

The silence stretched, making Drake squirm in his seat. He didn't like long silences. Especially awkward ones. He could feel his nerves getting the better of him.

"So," he said, letting his voice trail off. He hadn't actually thought of anything to say before he opened his mouth.

Scotty's lips curled. "So," Scotty repeated, his eyes never leaving the road.

Drake turned back to face the windshield, fingers drumming restlessly on his leg. He tried to think of something to fill the silence.

"Silences make you uncomfortable?" Scotty asked, making the next turn to head to the outskirts of the city.

Drake looked up and met Scotty's golden eyes briefly before Scotty turned his gaze back on the road. "Enjoying the peace and quiet, actually."

"Some say that they find my voice melodious."

Drake snorted. "Melodious? Really? Where did you pick up that ten-dollar word?"

Scotty shook his head. "Can I ask you a serious question?"

"Um." Drake fidgeted. "I guess so."

"Why do we always fight when we talk?"

Drake looked up in surprise. "Fight? I didn't realize that was what we were doing. I thought we were just—"

"Joking, I know."

"Flirting, actually," Drake said before he could stop himself. He felt his cheeks redden at his admission, and he barely contained his impulse to bury his face in his hands.

Scotty laughed abruptly, making Drake jump. "You are absolutely adorable when you get flustered, d'ya know that?"

Drake hadn't known it was possible, but his cheeks burned even hotter. He tilted his head back against the seat. "No, I wasn't aware of that."

"Oh, you are. It's one of the reasons I pester you so much."

"Oh, okay, so the truth comes out. You are the reason we fight so much. Good to know it's not just because I'm an easy target."

"You're a very easy target. Sometimes you almost make it too easy for me." Scotty winked at Drake. "Don't worry, it's icing on the cake."

Drake watched Scotty as he drove. He was beautiful. He had all the qualities that always threw Drake over the edge. He was funny. He had a nice wit on him and was always ready with a comeback. He was serious about his work. As long as Drake had known him, he hadn't once been late to the club. And this may only have been the first time he ever left work early and it was to help Drake get home, so technically, still working.

Sometimes you meet people and you feel like you've known them forever. Like you feel more relaxed around them than you do other random strangers. Scotty was like that for Drake. But Scotty was a friendly guy. He emitted an approachable vibe, whereas Drake had always given off a "stay the fuck away from me" vibe. But somehow Scotty had managed to ignore Drake's unpleasant ambiance and now... who knew what could happen?

Scotty's golden gaze landed on Drake's, and he shifted, realizing he was staring.

"What are you brooding about?" Scotty asked.

Drake thought about how to answer. He decided to stick with truth. "I am trying really hard to talk myself out of asking you in when we get to my place."

"Damn, I thought that might be what you were thinking."

A smile broke along Drake's face. "Yeah?"

Scotty answered Drake's smile with one of his own. "I would be lying if I said that the possibility hadn't crossed my mind."

"It would be a mistake, though, wouldn't it?"

"Would it?"

"I am your boss...."

"If anything, it would look really bad at work."

"Not that anyone would need to know." Drake groaned, rubbing his brow. "What am I saying? It would be a horrible decision. Besides, I have too much going on right now to add another factor."

Scotty nodded. "Okay, so we know the attraction is there, but we aren't going to act on it."

"Right."

"Right."

The silence stretched around them again. Much like last time it was uncomfortable, but this time it had a new awkward tinge to it. Fidgeting, Drake tapped his fingernails on the car door handle. Also, his knee had apparently developed a mind of its own because it was bouncing up and down, and he hadn't even noticed until it knocked against the dashboard.

The conversation seemed to awaken something in him, and he was more aware of Scotty's presence than he had ever been. Suddenly the car was filled with his very essence. Drake couldn't take a breath without smelling the musky cologne Scotty wore. And it was as if Scotty was radiating his body heat toward him.

He couldn't have gotten closer to the car door if he tried. No matter how far away he moved, he could still feel Scotty there. Keeping distance between them became pertinent. It was almost impossible to stop himself from reaching out to touch him.

"Shit," he growled, putting both hands on his knees and trying to contain them.

Scotty didn't glance over at him. He didn't acknowledge him at all. Instead, he jerked the steering wheel to the side harshly.

"What are you doing?" Drake questioned as Scotty pulled the car over to the shoulder and hit the brakes.

Flinging the gearshift to first and turning the engine off, Scotty launched himself over the console between the seats to press his warm lips along Drake's in a hard kiss.

It happened so quickly that it took a moment to process, but it didn't take him too long to realize that Scotty's lips were pressed to his with a command for reciprocation. It took even less time for him to react. Without thinking, not wanting thoughts to get in the way of this moment, Drake reached up to pull Scotty closer, opening his lips so Scotty's tongue could flick along his lips and teeth.

Drake groaned at the sensation and shifted to get a better angle. Nothing mattered more than deepening the kiss. Nothing existed outside him, Scotty, and the car. All that mattered was that he press himself as close to Scotty as possible.

He didn't know how long they stayed that way, locked together, but all too suddenly Scotty pulled back. Teeth grazed along Drake's bottom lip as they hesitantly drew apart.

They stared at each other, light golden eyes meeting dark brown ones, chests heaving.

"Hi," Scotty said, his breath hot on Drake's lips.

Drake licked his own lips, tasting the remainder of Scotty, and smiled. "Hi."

They stayed like that for countless seconds. Bodies hot against each other, their breath mingling between them. Reluctantly, Drake pulled farther away, automatically feeling the cold distance.

"So much for not acting on it."

Scotty laughed, ducking his head. "I have wanted to do that since the day I walked into my interview at the club."

"What a coincidence, I have been thinking about that since about the moment you walked into your interview at the club."

"Now what?" Scotty breathed, still close enough that his breath was hot on Drake's lips.

Yeah, now what, Drake? How was he supposed to stay away from Scotty with the taste of him on his lips? How was he supposed to walk away with the memory of his trim, firm body pressed against his? He shouldn't have allowed it to happen. Because now that he'd had a taste, he was hungry for more.

"As much as I want to do that again, I don't know if on the side of the road is the best place."

"Hmm," Scotty moaned plaintively, chastely brushing Drake's lips once more with his own, before settling back into the driver's seat.

As soon as the car was moving again, Drake let out his breath. That had been unexpected. Even more unexpected was the scorching heat still flaring through his body and his frantically beating heart. Jesus, he was reacting as if it had been his first kiss. He hadn't felt his heart pound that hard since he'd kissed Brittany Seller in sixth grade. The only other time he could remember feeling this much anticipation and excitement with a single kiss was when he had shared his first stolen kiss with a shy boy after lunch behind the cafeteria when he was fifteen.

"That…. Uh…," Drake said, clearing his throat, but he couldn't continue. He had no idea what to say. He turned back to face out the front.

Scotty kept his gaze fixed on the road, but his hands tightened on the wheel "My place is up the road here." Drake tried to form the words around anxious lips. "Those condos up on the left. Turn in the first drive, then park anywhere."

Scotty followed Drake's instructions and parked in an empty spot closest to the door. As soon as the car was parked, Drake was across the console. This time he quickly unbuckled his seat belt and lunged across to capture Scotty's mouth with his. Squirming his way over, he fought for space, struggling to fit himself tight against Scotty, the steering wheel jabbing into him as he found himself practically cradled in Scotty's lap, both his hands back in Scotty's silky hair.

A warm, eager hand slid up his back, and Drake groaned as Scotty's fingers splayed along his torso, exploring the muscles while at the same time pressing Drake closer. Scotty rubbed up and down hungrily, and then when he found the hem of Drake's shirt, he hesitantly lifted it to press his hand to Drake's skin.

"Oh God," Drake murmured, shifting so Scotty could pull his shirt up farther. Tilting his head, Scotty trailed his lips along his neck, nipping at his skin.

Needing to get closer, Drake removed one hand from the soft tangle of Scotty's hair to brush his own hands along Scotty's chest. He let his fingers wander down the front of him. Enjoying each curve of hard muscle, he grazed down, down, past his stomach, past his belt. He kept his hand moving until he could cup the hard bulge.

Scotty gasped as Drake fondled him through his jeans. Pulling back slightly, Scotty reached so he could once again press his lips to Drake's. Almost involuntarily, Scotty pushed his hips up, rubbing himself on Drake's hand.

It had been a long time since Drake had messed around with someone in a car. He'd forgotten how uncomfortable it was to try to maneuver around all the obstacles. But it added a challenge as well. Drake grinned against Scotty's lips as he moved to get a better grip on him.

Now it was Drake's turn to gasp as his own bulge was grasped through thick material. Using his teeth, he nipped softly at Scotty's lips and tongue, making him groan in pleasure.

Drake tilted his head back at the pressure of his dick being rubbed through his pants. His hips moved with the sensation, pushing at Scotty's hand. Needing more, Drake squeezed himself between Scotty and the steering wheel. Keeping their mouths pressed together, he blindly searched for the lever to push the driver's seat back. Scotty scooted up the seat back, giving Drake enough room to move until he was straddling Scotty. It allowed them both easy access, which they took advantage of without hesitation.

Scotty's mouth sought Drake's as he bucked under him, grinding his bulge along Drake's. At the touch, Drake growled and pushed Scotty's hips down so he could rub himself along him. Scotty fought Drake's hold, but Drake held fast, not letting the other man move, only subjecting him to exactly what he wanted him to feel.

"We should... get... inside," Scotty managed to moan.

Drake pulled back, blinking. He had totally forgotten they were in his car. He had lost track of everything around them. All he had been able to focus on was the feel of Scotty's body around him, under him. It had clouded his head, made him forget.

Forget.

Shit! What the hell was he doing? He wasn't supposed to be making out with Scotty. He was supposed to be getting a ride from him and then finding a safe passage for him to get home. But here he was, straddling Scotty, who didn't seem to mind, in the middle of his parking lot. How could he do that when a few miles away a kid was being killed for something that *Drake* had done? No, it wasn't right. As much as an empty head and Scotty's warm skin wrapped around him felt fantastic, he couldn't allow himself the luxury.

Shaking his head, Drake pushed back into the passenger seat. "I'm sorry."

"You're sorry?" Scotty breathed. "Trust me, you don't have anything to be sorry for."

"We weren't going to act on it. I totally jumped you."

Scotty laughed. "If I recall correctly, I believe I jumped you first."

Drake couldn't drag his eyes away from Scotty, who on a regular day was beautiful enough to keep your attention and was now still writhing from the throes of desire. He was still leaning back in his seat awkwardly, as if Drake were still straddling him, his eyes half-lidded and filled with a burning fire.

It wasn't a good idea. Drake was bad news, especially for someone as close to the fire as Scotty. He worked in the damn club. There was no telling what could happen to him if for some reason, Frankie, Tony, Boredega, or any of the guys caught wind of what Drake was doing. He would be putting Scotty directly into the crosshairs if they got close.

The thought of Frankie getting ahold of Scotty cooled Drake's blood. Even though the only thing he wanted to do at the moment was drag him inside to have his way with him, he couldn't do it. It was far too dangerous.

Scotty's contented face fell into a frown as he watched Drake's internal struggle. He sat up slowly, his frown deepening.

"We aren't going to do this, are we?"

Taking a deep breath, Drake answered, "No, we aren't."

"Does this have to do with you being my boss? Because I can look past that. It really doesn't bother me."

"It does have to do with that," Drake said, holding up a hand when Scotty began to protest. "But that's not all of it. I wasn't lying when I said I have a lot going on right now."

"It doesn't have to be anything serious."

Drake closed his eyes, shaking his head. "Did any of that feel like it was going to lead to something that wasn't serious?"

Scotty searched Drake's face, surprise evident in his eyes. His gaze finally landed on Drake's with glum resignation. He shook his head and said in a reserved, almost blank-sounding voice, "No, it definitely felt like something."

Drake nodded, swallowing hard. "I think it would be best if we left it at this for the time being."

"Okay," Scotty said a little breathlessly as he fumbled with the car door. He pushed it open and got out, slamming it behind him. Drake opened his own door and exited the car. He glanced over at Scotty, who, much to his surprise, was pacing with his hand in his hair. He didn't even seem to register that Drake was watching him as he went through his own inner turmoil. Drake let his gaze follow him for a couple of moments before clearing his throat.

"I can call you a cab. I don't know how far you are from here, so I will definitely pay your way."

Scotty looked up blankly, as if he hadn't even heard him speak. "Hmm, oh, no, it's not necessary. I, uh, don't actually live too far from here. I can catch the train, or, er, get a ride. No biggie."

"You sure you don't want me to call an Uber?"

"Um, no, like I said, it's not far from here," Scotty said, backing up toward the sidewalk. "So, I think I can make it. I, uh. I'll see you at work tomorrow."

Scotty turned quickly and basically ran from him. "Hey, Scotty," he called. Scotty turned back to face him. Drake smiled sadly. "Thank you for driving me home. I really appreciate it."

Scotty gave a quick salute before turning back around to walk quickly away. Drake watched his retreating figure and couldn't help but feel sad at the sight. He wasn't exactly sure what was wrong with him, but it hurt to watch Scotty leave, especially leaving it the way they were. Ignoring the fluttering in his stomach, Drake forced himself to turn away from Scotty's diminishing figure. But he couldn't help but feel as if he had just made a mistake.

CHAPTER 4

THERE WASN'T enough scotch in the world to make Drake feel any better. It was as if the door to his condo was the entryway to a different dimension, one where there was nothing but the nagging, condemning voices in his head. While turning Scotty away was the smartest decision he could have made, it meant he was alone, in the quiet, with nothing to do but drink scotch and nothing to think about except Frankie disposing of Willy's body.

Everything about the last couple of days came flooding back into focus, overwhelming him. The images, the stress, and the guilt plagued him as he paced in tight circles in his walk-in closet.

His clothes were tightly squished on their hangers, bunched close together at the front of his closet where he had shoved them to open a space on the wall at the back. A whiteboard was bolted to the closet wall, with pictures, newspaper articles, and notes plastered on and around it. Drake frowned at the board as he paced.

He had been gathering information on the cartel since he was a teenager, and in order to understand it at its fullest, he had needed to lay it all out. Much like a crime board you could see on any procedural drama TV show, he had pictures of people and places stuck around with black lines spiderwebbing them together. Each picture told a story in and of itself, but placed on the board, it shed a new light on the complete and ever-evolving tale.

Everything Drake knew about the Boredega operation, every bit of knowledge he had been able to learn or squeeze out of his contacts was arranged in the detailed collage. The pictures and lines told a story, created a world, one that was invisible to the average person, but once you saw it, it was everywhere. That world had its own solar system, and like a solar system, it all centered around one point of power.

Boredega.

The cartel had connections everywhere and with everything. At least, that was how Drake saw it now. The cartel had fingers in the local governments, the state governments, and possibly in the federal government. Boredega could function practically in invulnerability because there wasn't a department that was willing to try to take him down. He had connections that went up the ladder as well as connections with the lowest of the underworld. It went as far as no one knowing for certain who the actual Boredega was, besides the few men who worked directly with him, or so Drake assumed.

The man was a ghost.

Boredega was able to function openly because according to most reports and any evidence Drake had gathered, he didn't exist. There were multiple occasions when all the signs pointed toward a particular person, and in the end, that person would end up dead. But the Boredega cartel lived on.

Nineteen years ago, the police had finally gotten the drop on a man they believed to be Boredega. They had taken him in, and within moments he'd been hauled away by the federal government. Soon after the agents had walked the man down the police department steps, a sniper had taken out the alleged Boredega. Both agent escorts had also been lost in the attack.

The sniper had left no trace. Not even shell casings were left behind. All that remained were the three bodies, a single hole in the wall from the one bullet that went through and through, and three fragmented bullets that had absolutely nothing unique about them that could be traced anywhere.

The precarious situation left the police in a state of disorder, and like with most agencies, it became about saving face rather than finding the bastard behind everything. Boredega was safe to function again behind a smoke screen of bureaucracy.

The cartel was nothing if not tenacious. And while the feds and the local PD tried, albeit half-assed, to piece together their case and come up with new theories, Boredega struck again. Within the next month, every officer and detective to work on the Boredega case was silenced. Two officers were killed in freak accidents, and a detective lost his life while on duty, while another suffered a massive heart attack. The lead detective was murdered in a home invasion, which also resulted in the death of his wife and daughter, and left his eight-year-old son in a coma for eight months.

Nothing tied the deaths together except for the fact that each one had been directly involved in the Boredega case. Each had played a vital role in bringing in the alleged Boredega, and they were also the only ones on the case who'd had any direct contact with the man while he was in custody.

But that coincidence wasn't enough to run an investigation on. *Circumstantial evidence* was what the investigators had agreed upon before quickly closing the book on each unfortunate *accident*. Allowing the Boredega case to fall through the cracks.

The streets ran rampant with the results of that negligence. The Boredega cartel basically ran the city. More drugs were out than ever before, and with Selecure being so readily available and easy to cook, the death tolls were rising.

The city was a black lagoon of crime and chaos, and there wasn't anything anyone could do about it. The cartel had grown so huge in the last decade that it was even more difficult to tell whose money lined whose pockets and where loyalties lay.

That left people like Drake to do the dirty work.

Drake paused his pacing in front of his board and eyed a newspaper clipping showing the smiling face of a decorated middle-aged detective. His chest rising as he dragged in a breath of air, he gazed at the smiling face, then exhaled, letting his fingers drag along the edge of the photograph.

He would do it. He would make his way into the cartel and take it down from the inside. He would continue to earn their trust by doing the despicable tasks expected of him. He would launder money and rough up junkies, and he would use the credence to climb up the ranks, gaining more and more control, all the while covertly dismantling their operations until the bigwigs started to panic. Then as soon as they showed their face, as soon as Boredega made himself known, Drake would end them. Even if it meant he had to go down in the process.

He had a better motivator than justice. He didn't want to bust the cartel because it was the right thing.

Turning his back on the newspaper clipping, he faced the opposite wall and let his eyes settle on a framed photo hung there. He gazed mournfully at a family photo taken at the beach. The sun was hot and bright, casting a solar flare in the top left corner. The family radiated smiles of happiness and content, holding each other close. The detective and his wife each had an arm around a child, pulling them all together.

It was the perfect example of a happy family. By looking at the picture, you would never have guessed that only a few months later they would be struck by such tragedy.

No, Drake wasn't in it for justice. He could care less about doing the right thing. He was in it for revenge.

CHAPTER 5

"No, NO, no, don't flip—" Drake couldn't help the small smile that came over his face as he listened to Scotty's frustrated shout over the scrape of chairs along tile floors as his early crew started their day by cleaning up the evidence of last night's business. Some had found it odd that he used his crew to clean up in the morning rather than the night before, but he found that it worked better for morale if he did it this way. Not to mention it was better if the staff left as soon as the club closed to keep them out of Frankie's way.

The resounding crash of shattering glass that followed Scotty's shout drew a small snicker from Drake as he finished counting the tips from last night and dividing them between the staff on duty. Pausing momentarily, he shot a glance behind him at the bar, where Scotty was very agitatedly swiping a cloth over the counter as Frankie's new recruit swept the glass into piles.

"Oh, sorry, Scotty. I really thought I had it that time!"

Scotty had to take a moment to collect himself before replying. Drake could see the effort behind his deep breath to keep cool. "Jacob, I told you not to try to flair anymore. It takes a long time to learn how to do it. You need to focus on mixing drinks right now."

"We've been working on mixing drinks for days now. I want to try something new."

Drake listened to the conversation as he split the cash into six piles.

"We've only covered half the drink menu at this point. Let's try focusing on that, shall we?"

"Yeah, whatever," Jacob murmured, obviously not thrilled that his bartending training wasn't as exciting as what he'd expected.

"Finish sweeping up that glass, and then make sure there are plenty of glasses prepped for tonight. I'm going to check the stock in the back." Scotty turned to leave at Jacob's nod and then turned back to face him, pointing a stern finger in Jacob's direction. "Don't break anything while I'm gone, okay?"

Drake didn't even try to hide his amusement as Scotty walked out from behind the bar. Scotty shot daggers at Drake as he started to pass him, but then seemed to think better of it and crooked a finger at him. "Can I talk to you for a second?"

Drake's smile broadened. "Yeah, give me a sec." Scotty's glare scorched him as he passed, but he couldn't help the amusement he found in the man's irritation.

Drake hadn't been sure how things would be between him and Scotty after their short make-out session. Much to his surprise, not much had changed. He'd been expecting at least tense awkwardness, but Scotty had continued as if nothing out of the ordinary had happened. Of course, that could have had more to do with the fact that Scotty and he had hardly had a moment to talk to each other the last few days, between it being their busy part of the week and Jacob starting without a lick of bartending experience.

It didn't help that Drake continued to wallow in guilt and self-pity over the mishap with Willy. The mere thought of the kid sent bile burning in the back of Drake's throat. He didn't know what it was about Willy's death that bugged him as much as it did; he'd been involved in plenty of other people's "disappearances." He'd never been so close to getting any of the others out before either. Also, while he had been involved, he had never before played such a direct role. But that was done and over with. Now he had to focus on Jacob and getting the kid to a level where Scotty didn't want to bash his head in with a broken bottle. That was one death he could definitely prevent.

Jacob was a piece of work. The kid thought himself pretty big stuff. Both Drake and Frankie had had to give him the lecture before he started that most of the staff was unaware of the business that went on behind the curtain and he had to keep up appearances by working at the club. It didn't matter to the bar staff that Tony was his uncle or that his job was just a front. He'd been told that for all intents and purposes, Drake was his boss, and while he was behind the bar he was to listen to Scotty.

So far, the kid wasn't doing such a great job of keeping up the charade. In fact, it seemed like he was being intentionally annoying, especially to Scotty, because he had no interest in the pretense of Semblance and was wholeheartedly into the goings-on in the underground of Semblance.

Unlike other people Frankie or Tony brought in, Jacob was put to work doing some odd jobs here and there right away. Usually they had the new kids work the bar for a while first and become a familiar face around the area before utilizing them for their extracurricular projects. Drake hadn't a clue what most of the kid's jobs were, but he could almost taste the relief that came over Scotty when the kid was handed some task that took him from behind the bar.

Drake picked up the piles of money, keeping them separated in his fingers. He walked to the bar and held out the smallest pile toward Jacob. "Here, this is from last night."

Jacob took the small pile of bills with a frown. "Why is mine smaller?"

"Those broken bottles don't pay for themselves," Drake said with a smirk, patting his own pocket.

The kid glowered but didn't say anything, returning to sweeping up his mess. It may have been a stupid thing to do to the kid, who had a blood tie to Tony, but when he was behind the bar he was Drake's employee, and it didn't matter that the kid had connections to the largest drug cartel in the city. He would get the same treatment as any other employee. Drake chuckled as he put the rest of the cash under the register for the others to grab as they left for the night. Closing the drawer with a tight snick, he turned to go find Scotty.

He found him in the back room leaning over a shelf, reading the labels on a couple of bottles. Drake took a second to admire the scene, drinking in the long powerful legs and the nice tight ass showcased by the black pair of slacks that pulled snugly in all the right places. It took everything he had in him not to reach out and touch Scotty. The lure to do so was strong, but he squelched his temptation. There wasn't time for such distractions.

Clearing his throat, he stepped into the room and leaned back against the wall, crossing his arms over his chest. Scotty quickly stood at the sound and picked one of the bottles he had been reading.

"Yes, my liege?" Drake asked. He couldn't keep the amusement from his voice.

Scotty's brow shot up into his hairline. "Are you really going to act like there isn't a big problem hanging out behind the bar?"

"Big problem?" Drake said, playing dumb.

Scotty's glum look didn't lighten at all with Drake's humor but instead darkened a degree. He took a step toward Drake and pointed the bottle at him like a large scolding finger. "That kid shouldn't be behind the bar! He doesn't have the first clue about what's going on. He's never mixed a drink before in his life, and he thinks he's Jerry Thomas."

"Who?"

"Jerry Thomas! Blue Blazer? He used to…. No, never mind. It doesn't matter. The point is, the kid shouldn't be behind the bar. He should be out waiting tables or something."

"Aw, give the kid a shot. He's only been at it a few days. I'm sure he'll catch on. Besides, I don't foresee him staying on the job for a long time."

"Great! So he's another one that I get the pleasure of training and as soon as they start to catch on, they up and leave? Really?"

Drake shrugged. They always did fine even with Tony's boys cluttering up space. He made sure to schedule an extra hand while they were working to pick up any slack.

Scotty sighed at Drake's shrug. "If you were just going to hire whatever crazy wackadoos that wanted a job, why did you take all the time and effort to interview me?"

"Wait," Drake said, holding up a hand, "can we take a minute to appreciate the fact that you used the term 'wackadoo' in a sentence?"

"Drake!"

"Okay! I'm sorry. I am. But I told Frankie that I would give the kid a shot. Besides, he has been helpful on the busy nights at least busing. He's only broken about six bottles and four glasses. And I took half his tips to pay for those. So, I'm sure he will start to get the picture."

Scotty let out another drawn-out sigh and grabbed another bottle to go with the first.

"I took so long interviewing you for a couple of reasons, but mostly because I wanted someone who had excellent skills behind the bar and would be able to handle any crazy 'wackadoos' that may end up back there with them. I needed someone with both a great disposition and work ethic to handle whatever problems may transpire. You fit the bill. I have faith that you can handle any piece of work that comes trotting into this club."

Scotty's face slowly lost the tight lines creasing his forehead as Drake spoke, his glare lessening into more of a frown than a full-on glower.

"Fine, I'll put up with him for a while longer."

"Okay, good, because I wasn't really giving you a choice," Drake said, a teasing lilt to his voice. He started to head back out front to make sure everything was set for the day but turned when Scotty said his name. "Yes?"

Scotty was looking down, kicking at a piece of paper or some other speck on the floor. He looked like a small schoolboy playing innocent. After a moment of silence, Scotty lifted his head just enough to peer through his bangs with a face that belied any innocence Drake might have seen in him. The look was pure seduction.

"Don't think that I don't remember about our unfinished business."

"Un-uh." Drake had to clear his throat before continuing. Man, he had the most beautiful eyes. He could get lost in them. Scratch that—he was already lost in them.

What was going on? Oh, right. "Unfinished business?"

Walking close enough to put a hand on Drake's chest, Scotty smiled. "You know exactly what I'm talking about. You said you had a lot on your plate, so I'm giving you time to work through it, but we'll finish what we started."

Drake's mouth seemed to fill with cotton. His jaw worked like it was on a hinge, and his tongue was too dry to form any intelligible sound. He tried to say something. He tried to form a snippy comeback—he wanted to say something about how Scotty wasn't the boss around here—but he couldn't make the words come out.

Scotty's eyes taunted him. He knew exactly what effect he had on Drake, and he was enjoying it. His smile morphed into a confident smirk, and he patted Drake consolingly on his shoulder, dimming Drake's mind while simultaneously tightening his pants.

"I'm going to go back to babysitting. But we'll talk soon."

Drake, still unsteady, not really knowing what the hell was going on, could only nod his agreement. At this moment, he would have done anything, agreed to *anything* Scotty said.

Blinking rapidly, trying to pull himself out of the mind-numbing haze, he watched Scotty walk back toward the bar.

His pants, now a very uncomfortable fit, forced him to shift. He would have to stay back in the storeroom for a couple of minutes while his body recouped. Jesus, he was in much more trouble than he had thought if Scotty could effectively pull that reaction out of him with a single look. He needed to get his shit together.

Priorities, he had to think of his priorities. He wasn't here for sex or a relationship; he was here to take Boredega and the whole damn cartel down by any means necessary. Even if that meant he had to go down with it. He was on a mission; he had to keep his head in the game and his lower head in his pants or more innocent or misguided people were going to end up dead because of him. The death count was already too high for his liking, and he didn't know if he would be able to handle it if one of those casualties turned out to be Scotty.

CHAPTER 6

"HEY, BOSS Man, Jacob have time to take a trip to the store tonight?" Frankie asked, shoulder propped on Drake's office doorframe.

Drake didn't look up from his inventory list. "A trip to the store" was his way of saying that the kid was going to do some odd task during work hours. "Frankie, there will always be time for Jacob to do anything that doesn't include working the bar."

Frankie snorted a laugh. He was aware that Scotty hadn't taken a liking to him. Drake was pretty sure that Frankie always asked him to place the new kids behind the bar for that reason. He knew it would get a rise out of Scotty. Apparently, he thought it was fun to get the usually tolerant man riled.

"Now, he ain't that bad. Last I saw, last night he was raking in quite a few tips."

Drake tapped his pencil on his notepad, marking where he was in his process before finally looking up. It sure was an image, Frankie standing in the doorway. He made a very menacing presence, dressed in a tight white wifebeater and dark jeans. His muscles rippled the fabric in a way that was more about showing the multitude of power underneath rather than the beauty of a built body. Nothing about Frankie was alluring. Sure, women hit on him and liked to run their hands over his taut muscles, but mostly people were wary of him.

He was definitely someone Drake would have crossed the street to avoid if he saw him coming at him. There wasn't a warm and fuzzy feeling connected to Frankie in any way. The man had a job to do. He was the muscle of the cartel, and he looked the part.

"Yeah, sure, he can bring in some good tips with those baby blues of his, but by the way he keeps breaking glasses and bottles, he's definitely going to be spending more than he's making. I'm pretty sure Scotty is going to kill him the next time he tries to flip a bottle before mixing the drink."

"Well, the job I have for him is gonna take a while. So, he probably won't get back for his shift tonight."

"Scotty is going to be heartbroken."

"I bet."

Drake chuckled and turned back to his books.

"Also, you should get a deposit together for tonight. I'm gonna have one of Tony's boys come and pick it up at close."

A "deposit" for Tony was one of the ways the cartel kept themselves in business. Every week, each business cooking the books gave Tony a rundown of the money, everything coming in and everything going out. It was a way for Tony to keep track of everyone individually and make sure there wasn't anyone skimming. It also helped to keep tabs on everyone who owed the cartel money.

From what Drake had gathered, each book was delivered on a specific day to a specific place and only with the most trusted of carriers because each book held enough information to bring to light a portion of the cartel. Drake had only ever seen his own book and had never had a chance to see where it was stored. When he did a drop, it was to one of Tony's boys, or if picked up, one of Tony's boys would come to collect.

Those books were an important part of the operation. If they were to fall into the wrong hands, then vital parts of the inner workings of the cartel would be exposed. Drake desperately wanted those hands to be his.

Drake pursed his lips. "We usually do deposits on Thursdays—what's going on?"

"Nothing to worry about. We're going to have a larger than normal shipment come in tonight, so we should make an extra-early deposit."

Drake stilled at the news. A larger than normal shipment coming in? What was happening that they were going to be bringing in more money than usual? He hadn't come across any large operations; he hadn't heard anything about it. That wasn't good. If Frankie wasn't talking to him, did it mean his trust was slipping? Maybe they were keeping things tight because the of the house bust.

It was strange that they had extra money coming in. After the cops shut down the lab, Drake would have expected less money to come in, not more.

Besides, usually when something big was going to go down they would make sure to plan something at the club, some sort of big event so the extra cash could be explained away. It was unusual for there to be a large amount coming in without warning. Something must have happened. It bothered Drake that he wasn't in the know. He had really thought he was making leeway with Frankie.

Using his inventory books as a distraction, Drake looked down and added a few numbers to the pages, pretending the news didn't mean anything to him. He jotted down a couple of random notes. He wasn't even sure if what he wrote was English for the amount of thought he put into them. He needed to get some more information. Thinking quickly, he schooled his expression to look back up at Frankie.

"Am I going to need to bring in a few extra helping hands? I can book that DJ to come back again. Last time it brought in a large college crowd. Or we could do another ladies' week. That always seems to go over well."

Frankie crossed his large arms. "No need to worry about it. We aren't going to be doing nothing that would draw attention."

"Okay, I just want to make sure I can explain it with the accounting. We had a lot of business over the weekend, so it shouldn't be a problem. Let me know if I need to plan any extra activities for the next few weeks. I don't want to have too much cash flow without any specials."

"Yeah, you got it. But like I said, we ain't doing anything that will draw attention. Just an extra drop tonight."

"All right." Drake turned back to his books, jotting down a few other numbers. He was going to have to go back through everything again because he was not paying attention to a single figure he was jotting down.

Nonchalance was all he had to portray right now, like he didn't care what was going on and he had no vested interest in deals that went on outside his club except for the deposits when they came through. It wasn't his business to know.

"'Kay, we're leavin' in ten. We'll be over by Chinatown, so we'll be back right at close if not a little before that so I can help lock up later."

"Eh, don't worry about it. We have plenty on staff tonight, plus without Jacob making a mess behind the counter, there shouldn't be a problem." Drake grinned.

Frankie laughed and tapped the doorjamb twice in farewell before heading out to whatever dastardly task he was issued today. As soon as he was out of sight and Drake's door was closed once again, he sat back with a sigh. Running a hand over his face, he made a new plan for the day. He had a broad location, and that wasn't much to work with. Chinatown covered a lot of ground. If he was going to make a dent in whatever business was going down tonight, he was going to have to do some digging to see if he could figure out what the hell they were up to.

CHAPTER 7

DRAKE LEANED back against the wall in his usual spot, scanning the thin crowd on the dance floor. They were busier than usual for a Monday night, but the crowd was still sparse. Most of the people Drake could recognize as regulars, many of them part of Boredega's crew. The traffic in and out of the back rooms was pretty steady, maybe a little busier than usual but not enough for Drake to question it.

If it hadn't been for the fact that Frankie had pulled Jacob from behind the bar, much to Scotty's relief, and the early deposit, Drake wouldn't have thought anything of it. But as soon as Frankie and Jacob took off, Drake started to notice that things were moving a little differently. It could have been because the drug house had been busted leaving plenty of dealers dry and some of them playing catch-up, but it didn't feel right. Something was up, but Drake didn't know what.

It was unusual for this much action in the club without Drake hearing about it in advance. Maybe the extra money would make up for the loss on the house. But it didn't seem right.

Drake stood, scanning the crowd for someone he knew he could get information from without it seeming strange. He was almost ready to give up the hunt for a familiar face when Natasha stumbled her way onto the dance floor tangled around a young kid who Drake recognized as a regular at the club but not of the back rooms.

Drake caught the eye of the wandering waitress and signaled for her to grab him a drink before he headed toward the dance floor. He approached slowly, watching the couple move with the music. The kid had Natasha pulled close, pressing her large and scantily covered breasts along his chest and her groin tight to his. Even though the pair looked intimate, Drake could see a fine line of distress distorting Natasha's usual bravado.

With closer inspection, he noticed that she had a hand pressed between them, pushing herself back as far as she could get as he held her to him. The kid's face was pressed into her neck. If this was any other type of story, Drake would have thought he was a vampire by the way his head moved along the crease above her shoulder, but this scene was in the wrong genre.

Something happened to make Natasha jump. She tried to break away but was held captive by strong arms. Drake scowled. Sure, she was a prostitute, but that didn't mean that she couldn't say no.

Ugh, he was definitely going to need that drink before he went over there. From the look on the kid's face, he didn't think the two were going to last on the dance floor very long.

As if on cue, Jenny, the wandering waitress, approached with his drink. Drake took the glass from her, downing the bronze liquid in one gulp.

"Hey, can you find Paul and Tank and tell them to watch my back? I might need backup."

Jenny's pleasant face creased with worry as she glanced around. "Do I need to call the cops?"

Drake shook his head, handing her his empty glass. "Nothing that drastic and most likely nothing I can't handle, but I left my earpiece in my office, and I want them to be prepared. Just in case."

"All right," Jenny said, hastily backing away.

"Oh, and Jenny?" Drake said. "I'm going to need another as soon as I'm done here."

"You got it, Boss," she said with a mock salute as she hurried off on her mission.

Drake pulled in a deep breath to prepare himself and then confidently sauntered across the dance floor.

Dragging in another breath, Drake quickly glanced around to see if Paul or Tank had received the message, and after a quick subtle nod to each of them, he tapped the kid on the shoulder.

The kid turned with a dark, surprised look at the interruption. He looked Drake up and down, sizing him up. On closer inspection, Drake probably shouldn't have been describing him as "kid." He was young, there was no question about that, probably in his early twenties, but what he lacked in age he definitely made up for in size. The kid was wide. And not a "he's kinda stocky" wide; he was built like a brick house. He could have been a linebacker. Actually, he probably was one at the local college, and if he wasn't, he should have been. In fact, Drake was certain that Frankie probably would have loved to hire him on as some extra muscle. The kid was intimidating. Too bad Drake had too many threats in his life to worry about some punkass kid.

Drake smirked. "May I cut in?" he asked formally, complete with a slight bow of his head. Nothing exuded as much raw confidence and nonchalance as a healthy dose of sarcasm.

"Get lost, man," the kid said in an alarmingly deeper voice than what Drake had imagined. He turned back to Natasha, who was jerked hard back against his body. She didn't fight him but let herself be groped and manhandled into position. But her eyes darkened as the kid's hands ran over her body.

Drake could barely contain his sigh of exasperation as he tapped him again. This time the kid spun around, aggressively puffing his chest out, but Drake remained unimpressed. He glanced behind the kid to Natasha.

"You okay, Natasha?" Drake asked, checking her over quickly.

The kid's deep voice growled, "She's doing fine."

Drake clucked his tongue. "I don't believe I asked you. I was talking to the lady."

"The lady," the kid sneered with the word, "is doing just fine."

Drake kept a close eye on the kid but addressed Natasha behind him. "Are you doing 'just fine'? Because it didn't look like you were fine from where I was standing."

With the last of his words, the kid gave another one of his growls. He had tried vampire earlier, and now he was working on werewolf. The guttural sound was Drake's only warning that the kid was making a move, and he barely moved before a fist swished past his face, almost grazing him. Then the kid's other hand slammed on Drake's shoulder in a crushing grip. Drake almost swore he could hear his bones grinding together, but he didn't react on impulse. Instead, he calmly reached up and pried the kid's middle finger up off his shoulder, and then in a quick turn, he spun around, yanking the finger up with a twist and forcing the kid to follow his movements. Before the kid knew what had happened, Drake had his arm behind his back, his finger and wrist turned so all it would take was a slight movement to snap bone.

Holding the kid immobile, he noticed that the dance floor had cleared very suddenly. Now the only ones left standing were him, the kid, who was hunched over quivering with pain, Natasha, who was watching gleefully, and Tank and Paul, who were both approaching, chests out and arms at the ready.

Drake caught Paul's eye and shook his head minutely as he increased pressure on the kid's arm and wrist. Both Paul and Tank stopped but held their position just in case something was to happen.

Bringing his full attention back to the matter at hand, Drake brought his lips close to the kid's ear.

"As the owner of this establishment, I reserve the right to refuse service to anyone. You ever put a hand on Natasha, me, or anyone else in my club again, we will have a problem, and next time you won't be dealing with just me." Drake used his chin to indicate the two massive structures staring them down a few feet away. The kid barely glanced up, but Drake was sure he was getting the message. "Now, I want you to get the hell out of my club."

Drake released the kid's limb with a light shove that had him moving back a few steps before he could recover. With a last glowering look toward Drake and a hesitant glance at Paul and Tank, the kid spun around to make it toward the exit.

"You okay, Boss?" Paul asked as the kid made his way off the dance floor.

Drake nodded. "Follow him out, would ya, and make sure he keeps his hands to himself."

The men both nodded and followed the kid.

Drake let out a quick puff of air, letting the adrenaline rush slither through his body. Now he needed that drink. Hopefully Jenny hadn't forgotten about that part of the plan, in all the excitement.

"Wow," Natasha said, hands on her hips to accentuate her curves. "You just keep getting hotter and hotter."

"Um, thanks, I think," Drake said. He guided Natasha to the side of the dance floor and, as cautiously and inconspicuously as possible, rolled his shoulder forward and back. Damn, that kid had a grip.

"You can try that move on me anytime. That was hot. What other tricks do you have up your sleeve? What else have you been keeping from me?" Natasha spun around, pressing her front along Drake's, her free arm running down his back.

Drake rolled his eyes as he pushed her away gently before her hand could go any lower.

"Not much, I can promise you."

Natasha's teeth dented her bottom lip as she raked him over with hungry eyes. "I really doubt that."

"What was that all about anyway?"

Natasha shrugged. "With that lug you get exactly what you see. I was going to make a pretty penny off of him too. He likes it rough, and I charge extra for rough." Drake cocked an eyebrow at that.

So, she wasn't in trouble.... He should have known it was some sort of rape fantasy. He knew that she was more than capable of taking care of herself.

At the look, she sighed. "Don't ask questions you don't want answers to, Drakeybo."

The seductress façade faded momentarily at that small admission, and a jaded woman stood before Drake. But the vulnerability didn't last long before the pretense was back in place, concealing any misgivings the lady of the night may have.

Her lips puckered as she morphed back into her provocative posture. She flipped her hair, eyeing him.

"You finally taking me up on my offer, Drakey?" asked the spider to the fly.

"Nothing as extravagant as that," Drake deflected.

She arched a brow at him and tutted. "Then what were you doing interrupting me while I was in the company of a young gentleman?"

"Don't worry, I won't take too much of your time."

A small smile quirked her lips. "Honey, now you can take all night if you want to, but I'll have to charge you by the hour since my meal ticket was just escorted off the premises."

"Listen, I wanted to see if you knew what was up or if you've heard of anything going on. Frankie ran outta here dragging one of my boys with him. Usually he gives me a heads-up before he takes off during club hours."

Natasha took a step back, contemplative. She cocked her head, looking Drake over, brow arched. Drake fidgeted under her scrutiny. It was a look he hadn't received from her before. It was more speculative than he had anticipated. Maybe he shouldn't have brought it up to her, but he figured of anyone, she was probably the safest bet.

Natasha ran her tongue over her bottom lip, but this time it wasn't in an act of seduction but one of deliberation. "Do you think it's wise to ask questions?"

Drake didn't say anything at her inquiry. He figured it was more of a hypothetical because of course it wasn't wise to ask questions. It wasn't wise to let the cartel run drugs and launder money through his club, and it also wasn't the smartest idea to try to take them down, especially since anyone who had tried before wound up dead. So, yeah, Drake took it as a hypothetical because he wasn't in the business of doing anything wise. He waited for her to answer his question.

Natasha's lips smacked and her normal flirty tilt of her hips was back. "Well, I haven't heard any news since Willy ratted out the drug house. That made quite the little mess."

"Okay, I figured I would check." Drake let out a little breath he hadn't realized he had been holding. "Well, I guess I'll let you get back to... whatever it is that you do." He gestured toward the dance floor, which had been slowly refilling with people since he and Natasha moved off to the side and all the fighting seemed to be over.

"Hmm, yeah. I am sure I can scrounge up some new business." Natasha scanned the crowd with hungry eyes.

Drake backed away slowly. He didn't want it to seem like he was running away, but yeah, he was making a getaway. "Well, I'll let you get to it."

Natasha batted her eyelashes at him with that damn smirk of hers, and then as soon as it was there, the seductive façade was gone. Seriousness shone through her pale eyes. "Hey, Drake." Even the teasing lilt was out of her voice.

Drake frowned as he watched for the second time as her entire demeanor shifted before his eyes and she once again morphed back into the confident huntress she played herself out as. With an exaggerated wink, she blew a kiss at him, and then with a sashay of her hips disappeared into the crowd on the dance floor.

Uncertain, Drake stood and watched the spot where Natasha had been standing. That had been weird.

Everything about the exchange, from Natasha needing a rescue to the final words that had seemed almost like a warning, was strange. He flipped back through his mind, going over all the occasions he could think of when he had interacted with Natasha. Generally, it had been a quick exchange packed full of flirting and ignored invitations but usually not anything serious. Something about her wasn't panning out.

Or he was looking further into it than he should have been. There had to be more to her than thoughts of money and sex.

Dismissing the notion, at least for the time being, he headed toward the bar. There were a few people standing around it, but for the most part, it was empty. Even so, Scotty moved around the small area as if they had a large crowd. He pulled a beer from the tap, wiped the counter, pocketed tips, and refilled the condiment trays with ease and a content smile.

Taking a stool, Drake dropped his chin on a fist and watched the man do his work. It was enough to take his mind off whatever that had been with Natasha.

The ease with which Scotty laughed and communicated with the customers while simultaneously mixing beverages and keeping his area in order was like a form of art. Or it could have been the abs contouring the front of his tight-fitting white T-shirt that was the art form. Either way, Drake liked what he was looking at, and for just a moment, he let himself watch. He watched and imagined what it could be like to come into work and be able to only run the club. To be free to sit and watch Scotty without worrying about what was happening in the back rooms or what the next big tip he was going to give the cops would be. He imagined what it could be like to walk right behind the bar and take Scotty into his arms and kiss him without wondering what type of danger that could put him in.

But the truth of the matter was, it didn't matter how much he wanted the freedom to be with Scotty and be free of the cartel; he wasn't free and he wouldn't be until he had taken their organization down. As much as he wanted Scotty, which was obvious with each shift he made to readjust himself, he couldn't go down that path.

"Sorry, Drake! I couldn't find you!" Jenny said from behind him. As Drake turned toward her, quickly drawn out of his daydream, she set a tumbler of scotch in front of him.

"Oh yeah, thanks."

Jenny smiled, shifted her tray, and started to turn but then stopped. "Oh, I almost forgot, Tank told me to remind you that you should be wearing your earpiece. Frankie called and said he would need help in the back in about ten minutes."

Drake subconsciously touched his empty ear. He hadn't even thought to grab his earpiece today. Something with Frankie being out of the club made it seem less necessary. "Yeah, I wondered why I could hear myself think today," he said. "Thank you, Jenny. How's it going today? Getting good tips?"

She shrugged. "It's not great, but it's not horrible. Yesterday was better."

Drake nodded. Yeah, it was what he expected of a Monday night. "Well, I won't keep you from it. Thanks for remembering my drink." With a small toast of his scotch, he dismissed Jenny.

As soon as her back was turned, he frowned. What the hell was going on? Frankie had said they wouldn't be back until around close, and they still had at least an hour before last call.

Drake swirled his scotch before draining the glass in one go. It burned just right, warming his body and settling his nerves all at once. With a sigh, Drake gave one last lingering glance at Scotty, who returned his gaze with a wink, making Drake's heart jump, before making his way toward his office. He probably should grab his earpiece before Frankie came in. Who knew what kind of trouble was coming.

CHAPTER 8

THERE WAS too much blood. Drake had thought that maybe his sensitivity toward blood and broken flesh had diminished after so many interrogations, but now, seeing the puddles of blood, too much blood for a single person to lose and keep breathing, curdled his stomach. It took all his willpower to swallow back his bile as he pressed down on what used to be a white T-shirt, now saturated in deep red.

Hyde, the large man lying barely conscious on the table with three bullet holes in his chest, struggled to breathe. Drake didn't really know the man. He had seen him around. Every once in a while the guy had come to the club, utilizing the back room for a sale or sometimes just for the soundproofing. He recognized him as one of Frankie's guys, but he wasn't one of the regulars. But now he was dying practically in Drake's arms.

Using all the strength he could muster, Drake tried to staunch the blood coming out the two holes he was in charge of keeping under control, but the flow was too heavy.

"Oh God, oh God!" a kid Drake never met before cried as he leaned, nearly collapsed, against the wall. His face was plaster white, his chest moving in and out quickly with his frantic puffs.

"Jacob! We need those towels!" Drake called out, surprised at how calm his voice sounded. He didn't sound like he was about to lose it at all. Keeping up appearances, he turned to face the hyperventilating kid. "Hey! We could use a hand here!"

The kid pushed off the wall on visibly shaking legs and approached slowly. His Adam's apple bobbed wildly as he swallowed, hopefully keeping whatever was threatening to show at bay.

Drake pointed with his chin, directing the kid to put pressure on another wound on Hyde's shoulder, but the kid collapsed before he could get close enough.

Frankie shook his head. "Useless," he murmured under his breath before hovering over the wounded man, checking him over. He used his fingers to pull open Hyde's eyelids, studying him. Apparently, he didn't like what he saw because he took the man's face in his fingers.

"Hey, stay with me, Hyde," Frankie said, slapping his face lightly to get his attention. "Keep your eyes on me, okay? Doc is coming."

Hyde tried to obey. His head lolled to face Frankie, his eyes squinting, but just when Drake started to think that maybe things weren't as bad as he had thought, Hyde jerked in his arms and spat dark blood.

"Shit, man! It must have hit a lung or something!" Jacob yelled, rushing forward with a handful of towels used behind the bar.

Frankie grabbed a towel from Jacob and used it to wipe up some of the dark fluid on Hyde's face.

"Oh, shit, man! Shit, it looks bad!" The fallen kid had managed to regain his feet, but his voice still held a quivering panic. Frankie glared at the kid across from Hyde's body.

"He's fine," Frankie growled. He looked back down at Hyde. "You're fine, Hyde. Keep your eyes on me, okay. Doc will be here soon." Drake had no clue how Frankie was able to keep his voice so calm and smooth. His accent wasn't even all that noticeable as he spoke.

"He's not okay, man. He's not okay! It's bad. It's really, really bad." The kid's wobbling voice broke through Frankie's soothing one.

Jacob spun suddenly, weapon held in his bloodstained hand. The kid cried out, jumping backward and hitting the wall he had earlier been leaning on.

"Jacob!" Frankie shouted, never taking his eyes off Hyde. "Go see if Doc's here."

"But I—" Jacob protested, wagging his gun at the now-blubbering kid.

"Just go!" Frankie shouted, and this time his tone demanded action.

Jacob's jaw clenched and unclenched before he dropped his arm back to his side. His heavy gaze rested on Frankie, who was still busily staunching Hyde's blood, and then he finally turned and walked out the door.

Drake winced. "Hopefully he went toward the back and not into the club." That would be all he needed—a blood-soaked, armed kid running around and freaking everyone out. They definitely didn't need the cops coming around.

"He knows Doc only comes in the back." Frankie wiped away the blood from Hyde's lips before taking his head in his hands so the man could focus on him. "Stay with me, Hyde."

"What the hell happened?" Drake asked. He switched out the soaked T-shirt for a couple of towels. He would have to remember to put those on the inventory list. There was no way he could wash these enough times.

The blood absorbed into the towel quickly. The warm liquid practically squishing under his fingers made the bile rise in the back of his throat. He tried to swallow it back, but it refused to budge, and he coughed to try and cover the gagging noise he desperately needed to make.

"Goddamn cops! That's what happened!" Frankie said through clenched teeth. "The fuckers were staking out the park. When Hyde went to make the sale, they surrounded him. Somehow, the bastard was able to get out of the park but not before taking a couple of rounds. I took Jacob with me because it was supposed to be an easy in and out. It was a good way to learn the ropes. Fucking cops!"

"Shit," Drake said. "Who's this?" He nodded toward the still-blubbering kid.

Frankie's face darkened. "The buyer."

"I didn't know, man, I didn't know! I had nothing to do with it!"

Frankie's snarl snapped the kid's protesting mouth shut. "Shut the hell up!"

The kid whimpered and opened his mouth as if to speak again, but the entry of Doc, the only doctor on the cartel payroll as far as Drake knew, cut his dissent short.

Drake held his position as the doctor was debriefed on the situation by Frankie and then gratefully traded off with one of Doc's assistants as they started to take control. Drake watched them work for a series of moments. The men and woman surrounded Hyde, each faced with a specific task. They moved around the body, using tools and disinfectants to try to remove the bullets and stop the bleeding.

Everything seemed to be moving along smoothly when suddenly Hyde's body started to thrash on the table, knocking a couple of the men away before they were able to rush back to try to hold him down. Doc yelled something that Drake didn't understand and then the body stilled, releasing a loud gush of air.

Slowly the people around the table backed away. Doc shook his head and started to remove his gloves. Hyde didn't move, didn't take a breath.

"Oh God," Drake whispered around the ocean swimming in his head.

It was hot in the office. Was everyone else sweating? He couldn't breathe. There was absolutely no air. Maybe that was why Hyde couldn't breathe. Maybe they had to open a damn window. No one was going to be able to breathe in here.

"You okay, Boss Man?" Frankie said, standing shoulder to shoulder with Drake. He had a bottle of Jack in his hand and took a long swig. He offered it to Drake, but Drake couldn't tear his eyes away from the body lying on his table.

Drake swallowed hard a couple of times before jerking his head in a nod. Yeah, sure he was okay. He just had a dead guy on a table behind his office, but you know, other than that it was business as usual.

"Is he dead?" The kid's wail echoed in Drake's ears. "Oh God, he's dead!"

Jacob, who had stayed near the door, brought his pistol back up, his eyes hard.

"Jacob," Frankie scolded, dragging Jacob's gaze back toward him. "No, that's too loud."

Pulling his own gun out in a quick motion, he shot the kid twice in the chest, watching in calm silence as the kid flew back from the close-range shots, his chest erupting into starbursts of red. The kid's body fell along the wall, sliding down in an unceremonious heap, blood trickling out the corner of his mouth.

"You should start carrying a silencer." Drake watched in shocked silence as Frankie, cool and even, holstered his weapon, then took another swig from his bottle of Jack. "Someone get this pile of dead shit outta here."

Drake stood blankly, trying to move forward to comply with Frankie's commanding tone, but his legs wouldn't obey him. In fact, he couldn't really feel his legs. He looked down to make sure they were attached. They were. That meant he probably still had fingers as well. Drake tried to flex his fingers and thought maybe a drink would do him some good, help him get his head back on straight, but as he folded his fingers, he realized his skin felt tight. Too tight. Glancing down, Drake remembered, to his horror, that he was covered in blood. His clothes were spotted in large patches of wet red, and his hands were encased in what looked like brownish gloves.

"Jesus." Drake gagged at the sight and lost all confidence in his ability to hold in any of the contents of his stomach.

"You okay, Boss Man?" Frankie asked, voice low. He held out the bottle of Jack to Drake, who took it with trembling fingers. Frankie watched him closely, eyebrow cocked. "Don't worry, you get used to it."

Numbly, Drake nodded at Frankie's bleak words. He lifted the bottle of Jack to his lips, but the coppery scent of death stopped him short, and he gagged as he saw the smear of red along the dark bottle. With fumbling fingers, Drake thrust the bottle back to Frankie, who took it with a laugh, watching Drake's struggle.

Staggering in a rush, Drake barely made it to toilet outside of his office. It had been a close call, but he made it in the nick of time. He let his head hang for a while longer, just in case he wasn't as empty as he thought he was, but then finally feeling like it was over, he sat back against the door. Raising a hand, he went to wipe his mouth but remembered at the last second the reason he had been sick in the first place.

Jumping to his feet, he dashed to the sink and turned the hot water all the way on. He scrubbed at his skin, working the blood away, trying to rinse it off. He grabbed the soap, but it only made the blood foam in a red lather, causing his stomach to flip again. He probably had some more bile in his system to dispose of, but he worked it back, focusing instead on cleaning his hands.

He let the hot water scald him. It didn't matter. All that mattered was getting the blood off his hands.

After a couple of minutes of frantic scrubbing, the only red left on his hands was skin rubbed raw and burned. He looked in the mirror, ignoring the bloodstains on his shirt. He met his own eyes in horror.

This was what was happening out there. Every time he gave up some piece of the cartel to the cops, someone ended up dead or dying. He wouldn't have had as much of a problem with it if it were the actual people behind the cartel, if it were Boredega, Tony, or even Frankie. He wouldn't have been able to shed a tear, but with these random guys—the ones who maybe made a few bad choices here and there and ended up in a bad spot—these deaths and injuries seemed useless. Wasteful. Wasteful use of police operations. And useless losses of cartel assets. Sure, they kept the business going, but these people were expendable. They were just a gear that would be oiled and replaced. It created a hitch, but it was definitely not a deterrent.

Even though he hadn't been the one to set the cops on them this time, he quite literally had blood on his hands. He knew there were casualties involved. He had a whole section of his crime board devoted to them. He was going to have to find a picture of Hyde to put on there. He didn't even know if the man was involved enough to be on his board. But he deserved to be commemorated along with the others lost to the cartel.

A hysterical laugh escaped his lips as he thought of everyone who had lost their lives to the cartel. The list was long, and good people were on it. His family was on that list. He had to remember that. Sure, Hyde didn't deserve to die, but he had made his bed when he joined the cartel, and now he had to lie in it.

Drake pushed himself back from the mirror. He had to man up. He was in this for the long haul. And if he was going to be who was needed, if he was going to earn Frankie's and then Tony's trust, then he had better get used to it.

Taking a deep breath, Drake readied himself to go back out into the office. He had two dead bodies and a change of clothes that he had to deal with. It was just another day at the office.

CHAPTER 9

"So, what are you fine-looking ladies up to tonight?" Jacob leaned against the bar, definitely invading the two blondes' personal space. He dropped his tray to the side so he could run a hand through his short-cropped dark hair, then posed against the bar, leaning back and lifting his chin, shooting them a cocky smile.

Drake smirked as the girls gave Jacob a quick, disinterested, verging on repulsed look before turning back to face each other to talk. Drake couldn't help but shake his head at the kid's overinflated ego. He had been working the bar for over two months, and not once had Drake seen him succeed in truly impressing anyone. Somehow, the kid still managed to have an ego; it must have been the byproduct of privilege, being a child of the cartel.

At the blatant rejection, Jacob's face darkened. Drake watched as a muscle in his cheek twitched. Instead of walking away like most spurned men, the kid stood staring, his eyes narrowing as he inched closer so that he was only a hairsbreadth from the first blonde.

The second blonde pursed her lips as she eyed Jacob distastefully. The first blonde's fingers clenched around her clutch, and her shoulders tensed at Jacob's close proximity. Drake watched amazed as the two seemed to have a full conversation with their eyes that spoke volumes louder than the completely separate conversation they were having with their mouths.

"I haven't seen you two around here before," Jacob said, his tone light despite his determined look.

The blondes ignored him, Blonde One rolling her eyes, then tilting her head to indicate to Blonde Two that they should leave. Blonde Two put her hand on Blonde One's arm and stood, pulling her friend with her, but stopped short when Jacob's own hand snapped out, clasping Blonde One's upper arm. Blonde One's entire body stilled at the intrusion. After the passing of a few tense moments, Blonde One attempted to shrug off

Jacob's grasp, but his fingers only tightened, marking Blonde One's tan skin with white.

"Get the fuck away from her!" Blonde Two shouted, drawing quick looks from other patrons nearby, but no one paid much mind.

Drake held his breath as he watched. He took a step forward, ready to intervene. He couldn't have any of his staff, even if that staff was not necessarily *his* staff, assaulting guests. He clenched his jaw as he opened his mic to ask for assistance. He started to call for Paul or Tank, who he knew were watching the door and the dance floor, but stopped before he did, eyes widened in amazement.

Blonde One jutted her free arm's elbow back, nailing Jacob directly in the ribs. The woman was slight in build, but any sharp elbow to the chest was enough to distract an aggressor, especially if the aggressor wasn't expecting it. Jacob doubled over, releasing Blonde One to put both hands to his chest, his breath expelling in a surprised whoosh.

Drake couldn't help his smirk as Blonde One didn't stop there but added well-deserved insult to injury by spinning around and slapping Jacob across his cheek, leaving a splash of red in her wake. Jacob's head turned with the force of the slap. Slowly, as if stuck in molasses, Jacob turned back to face the two blondes, eyes narrowed, chin jutted forward. Drake's breath caught as he took in Jacob's dark gaze. If he hadn't watched him almost cold-bloodedly murder a kid days earlier, he would have thought the look to be that of a petulant child. But instead the glint in Jacob's eyes sent a chill down Drake's spine. The blondes, unaffected by Jacob's violent past, turned up their noses and walked away.

Drake plastered a smile on his face as the girls started to walk past him.

"Ladies," Drake said, stopping the blondes just before they exited the lounge area. Blonde Two looked about ready to claw Drake's eyes out, but Drake settled her with a calmly outstretched hand. "I couldn't help but notice what happened at the bar." Drake winked at Blonde One. "That was a wicked jab. I'm impressed." Blonde One opened her mouth to protest Drake's praise, no doubt ready to spout out a number of insults in Drake's direction, but again Drake silenced them.

"As the owner of this establishment, I just wanted to let you know that your drinks are on the house for the remainder of the evening. Please enjoy yourselves and make sure you call a cab for your trip home."

Blonde Two tilted her head to the side, eyeing Drake with skepticism. Looking for the other shoe to drop, Drake was sure. But there was no other shoe. Giving the girls one last amused smile, Drake turned back toward Jacob, who was still standing at the bar, one hand absently rubbing a circle along the bottom left side of his ribs.

Drake glowered at Jacob, who, true to form, didn't show any remorse for his actions, instead glowering right back at Drake. Shaking his head, Drake fought back a sigh. Drake could honestly say that Jacob was fitting into the underworld of Semblance quite snugly. His ability to work the bar, however, had not much improved. When he wasn't breaking dishes or mixing up orders, he was flirting with pretty much any girl he came across. He had a complete lack of respect for the rules of the club, and because of who his uncle was, there wasn't a damn thing Drake could do about it. And Jacob knew it.

On numerous occasions, Scotty had cornered Drake to discuss Jacob. He'd asked him to fire him or, if not fire him, at least put him into a position less demanding and not under Scotty's watch. Drake had laughed him off, because what else could he do? But then other staff members had started to make comments.

Now Jacob was accosting customers, and that was the last straw. All they would need was for some woman to go to the authorities with an assault charge, or heaven forbid, a rape claim. That was not the type of publicity the club needed.

"Jacob, table three is still waiting on their drinks," Scotty shouted over the commotion at the bar, instructing Jacob with a nod. He indicated with his chin to where the drinks he had made sat, ice melting.

"Yeah, yeah, yeah. I'll get to that."

"No," Scotty said, sliding the drink he had just made to its waiting recipient and then slapping his hand on the counter to bring Jacob's attention back to him. "You won't just get to it whenever you damn please. You will do it right now!"

Drake continued to move to the bar. As much as he loved to see Scotty's face flush with anger and the way his movements became tense, as if taming his raw muscles under his skin to keep from punching the kid in the face, he had to step in. Jacob's expression was still set in a menacing glower, and his gaze followed the two blondes, who had wandered out toward the dance floor.

One thing was for sure, Jacob was a loose cannon, and Drake couldn't be sure when he would go off.

"Hey, Boss Man," Frankie crackled in Drake's ear.

Sighing, Drake belatedly remembered he had his mic on.

"What's up, Frankie?"

The mic crackled again before Frankie spoke. That meant that Frankie wasn't actually in the club but in the office or the hidden room behind it. Drake felt ice trickle through his bones at the thought. He hadn't been back there since Hyde died. He wasn't sure if he was ready to go back in there yet.

"I'm gonna take Jacob out tonight. We got some shit we gotta handle."

"When?"

"Now is good, if the bar is covered."

Drake snorted. "Yeah, like he ever actually works anyway. Listen, we need to talk about something that went down tonight with Jacob."

"I know that he's a pain in the ass—"

Drake spoke over Frankie. "The kid manhandled some chick at the bar, Frankie."

The radio crackled. "He what?"

"A girl didn't want to have anything to do with him, and instead of walking away, he grabbed her. Fortunately for her, she knew how to handle herself."

Drake listened through the static.

"Goddamn fucking kid," Frankie snarled. "What is he thinking?"

Drake shrugged and huffed into the mic. "I don't know if he does think." Drake shook his head and eyed Jacob and Scotty still arguing at the bar. "Now he and Scotty are fucking getting into it."

Frankie cursed again, sending a cacophony of static to blast in Drake's ear. "I'll talk to Tony about it."

Sighing, Drake ran a hand through his hair. "Okay. Yeah, well… I gotta split these two up, and then I'll send Jacob your direction. You in the back?"

"Yup, your office."

Drake turned his mic off and pushed through the dense anger that surrounded Jacob and Scotty at the bar. It looked like the already rigid conversation had steadily become more heated since he'd stopped paying full attention. If he didn't know any better, he would have thought Scotty was poised and ready to strike, and he didn't even want to think about what Jacob's reaction would be to that, especially after his encounter with the blondes.

All the while Scotty had been working at the club, Drake had never seen him so fired up. Even rowdy and rude customers he'd handled with a smile, but something about Jacob, and rightly so, brought the fight out in him. And while Drake did enjoy the way Scotty's muscles rippled and his eyes flared with fire, he couldn't have a brawl break out between his staff members. Especially after one had already assaulted a customer.

Drake approached from behind Jacob so he had a clear look at the fury on Scotty's face. He only caught the back end of what Jacob was saying.

"—be interested in a couple of girls anyway, would you?"

Scotty visibly tensed even further, although Drake wouldn't have thought it possible, and Drake thought Scotty was going to jump the bar right then and there. But before Drake could even jump between them, Scotty's enraged eyes met his over Jacob's shoulder, and he relaxed a degree.

Drake cleared his throat, gaining the attention of both men. Jacob spun around as if surprised to find Drake so close behind him. Drake eyed them both before first meeting Scotty's eyes, giving him an apologetic smile, then directing his attention to Jacob. "I don't know what kind of club you think this is, but in this establishment, we don't expect our customers to wait for their drinks."

Jacob scowled at Drake. He knew he had to put on the pretense of Drake being his boss, but he also knew Drake didn't really hold any power over him. "I had other tables to take care of."

Drake raised a brow. "Yeah, I saw how you took care of those tables. I pay you to serve drinks, not assault women."

Jacob gritted his teeth, clenching and unclenching his jaw. Drake had to give the kid a little credit—he wasn't just blatantly telling Drake off. He had enough sense to at least keep up the charade that Drake was in charge here.

"Frankie needs some help in the back. Go see what he needs and get the fuck out of my club," Drake said, thrusting his thumb over his shoulder.

Jacob didn't move at first, just kept his eyes glued to Drake's, challenging him. But Drake didn't back down, didn't look away. Kept his gaze calm and steady as he stared back, and finally Jacob shoved past Drake to go to the back. Drake held his position as Jacob knocked his shoulder, and he sent his eyes heavenward as soon as the kid was past.

"What the hell does he have to do to get fired?" Scotty asked, still all worked up. He flung his hands in the air just to slam them back down on the counter.

Drake glanced at the customers waiting around the bar. Jenny and Julie were both back there working, but they were starting to get backed up without Scotty's help. Plus, Jenny was supposed to be waiting the tables and the dance floor, so they were probably even more backed up than what it seemed.

"I need you to relax, okay?" Drake said, leaning closer to Scotty and speaking calmly.

Scotty made a noise that sounded close to a hiss at Drake's words. "So, he gets to be a complete jackass and do absolutely nothing but be a jackass, and I have to calm down? What the hell, Drake?" Scotty's voice deepened with anger.

Drake ran a hand through his hair. "I get it, okay? I get it. I know he sucks. I know he is terrible at his job and that he was very close to doing something that could have ended us all in hot water, but I can't do anything about that right now because he's a relative of one of my backers. Okay? That's why I haven't fired him. I can't let them pull out. I would lose the club. So, will you please calm down and help Jen and Jules at the bar so we don't create an angry mob?"

Scotty stared at Drake for a moment before releasing a breath. The tension he had been holding dissipated as if it had never existed, and his eyes lightened back to the soft golden brown. He nodded. "Sorry. I shouldn't have yelled at you. I handled that whole situation badly. I've had a couple of rough days, I guess."

Drake nodded too, releasing tension he hadn't even realized he had been holding. "It's okay."

Scotty started to move toward the crowd, but Drake called him back. "Yeah?"

"As soon as the crowd dies down, can I get another scotch?"

Scotty frowned his disapproval but gave him a short nod as he returned to work.

Well, one crisis was averted. Now all they had to do was wait for the next storm to hit.

CHAPTER 10

DRAKE RUBBED his eyes and glanced at the clock. Four a.m. It was way past go time. He was still sitting at his desk, looking at his books. He had done the inventory earlier, and he had shifted the numbers to account for each deposit that came in a little above what was expected. Then he had twiddled his thumbs and waited. He assumed Frankie and Jacob would come back to the club after they were done with whatever the hell they were doing but so far, he hadn't heard anything.

If he stayed much longer after close, it could look suspicious to Frankie as well. He didn't usually stick around once the staff was on their way out. He wanted to get home so he could get back in before the rest of the staff came in the next day to make sure there were no telltale signs of the club's after-hours events.

Stifling a yawn, Drake poured himself one last glass of scotch. He'd had quite a few throughout the evening. He blamed it on the tension with Jacob working the club and the stress of not knowing what was happening when Jacob and Frankie went out.

He could probably add a bit of sexual frustration in there too. It had been a while since he had taken someone home. Not that one-night stands were a common thing for him, but he usually took care of the craving before it got out of hand. But now he couldn't seem to be bothered by anyone except for one toned blond who really knew his way around a bar.

Ugh! He couldn't get the guy out of his head. He had never had that trouble before. Usually there was some attraction and he either did something about it or he didn't, but the thoughts didn't linger. With Scotty, it was near impossible to get over it. He saw him every day, and each time he found himself explicitly enthralled. Either his perfect physique, or the way his hair would sweep across his forehead just enough to frame his captivating eyes, or his firm muscles as they flexed and contracted under his tight clothes.

Drake was practically drooling on the table thinking about it. Since when did he turn into one of those ridiculous old-school cartoon dogs? He had never drooled over anyone before. What was his problem?

Always want what you can't have. Drake snickered to himself and finished off his glass. He pushed his cup and his bottle to the edge of the desk. He would take care of it tomorrow when he came in. He didn't feel like putting them back in kitchen.

Stretching as he stood, Drake took one last quick look around his office and then headed for the door. Grabbing his leather coat from the hook by the door, he turned out the light, double-checked to make sure the door was going to lock behind him, and headed to the parking lot in the back of the building.

"I told you I am *not* going with you!"

The angry shout coming from the far side of the lot piqued Drake's attention. That was Scotty's voice. What the hell was he still doing here? Drake tried to see what was happening, but the parking lot was just dark enough that he could only make out two figures in the distance and not much else.

"No! You said you wanted to talk and you did." Drake picked up his pace. Scotty definitely didn't sound like he was okay. He wished he could see them better. The city was supposed to fix those damn lights weeks ago. Guess you had to wait for someone to get killed before they actually fixed anything.

"Craig! Stop! Let go of me!" At that, Drake broke into a run.

Drake could see them better now, and he didn't like what he saw. Scotty struggled with a big guy about twice his size as he tried to pull him toward a car. Scotty twisted his arm around, trying to break free, but the other guy was too strong.

"Hey!" he yelled as he approached. "Scotty, you okay?"

Both men stopped their struggle to look over at Drake as he got closer. The big guy dropped Scotty's wrist but didn't move away from him. Scotty quickly snatched his arm back and rubbed at his wrist where the guy had been pulling.

"We're just fine. Why don't you move along?" the big guy, Craig, said, making a shooing gesture.

Drake stopped next to Scotty. "Hey, I didn't ask you. I asked him." He motioned toward Scotty, who looked like he was trying his best not to look at him. "Do you need a lift?"

"If he needs anything I can get it for him," Craig said, this time making another move like he was going to grab Scotty again.

That was so not going to happen. Before Drake thought about it, he moved between Scotty and Craig and grabbed Craig's arm right above the wrist, pulling him forward while swinging around to take him to the ground.

"Again, I wasn't talking to you."

"What the—" Craig groaned as he fell on his stomach on the asphalt. The man was bigger than Drake, but Drake knew he could keep him down with a quick arm bar. He put pressure on Craig's upper arm right below the triceps, keeping his shoulder locked. Any movement he made would only cause him more pain. Craig tried to regain his feet, but Drake added more pressure and knelt hard into the guy's back.

"Stop! Stop!" Scotty's voice finally reached Drake. When he was in attack mode, he was very good at tuning out the surrounding noise, but finally Scotty's demands that he let Craig go sunk in. Letting go of Craig's arm, he gave one last jab with his knee for emphasis before standing back up.

"Jesus, Drake!" Scotty yelled, reaching down to pull Craig up off the ground.

Craig regained his feet and made as if to lunge at Drake, but Scotty pulled him back. "Knock it off!" He pushed Craig over toward his car. "It's done! We're over, that fight is over, everything is over. Get in your car and go home!"

Craig glared at Drake with malice, but Drake just smirked in return. He could take him. He was up for it. He was also in a foul enough mood to relish a chance to practice his hand-to-hand. It had been a while since he'd had an actual person to tango with. Punching bags and mats at the gym were not the same thing.

"Shit, man. You better watch yourself!" Craig yelled, pointing at Drake, but Scotty pushed him back once more toward his car.

"Just go, Craig," he said and then turned back to face Drake with a shocked look. Taking a few steps toward Drake, he spread his arms up and out in an exaggerated shrug. "What the hell?"

Drake shrugged. "The guy was trying to drag you to his car. What the hell was I supposed to do? Just let him force you?"

"I can take care of myself!"

Drake laughed. "Yeah, it was super obvious with how well you were able to get away from him. Sorry I tried to help. Next time I'll let you get manhandled."

With a shake of his head, Drake spun on his heel back toward his car. His shoes crunching over some broken glass echoed through the darkness. Jesus, what the hell? You try to help someone. Someone who was obviously in trouble. Someone who you had thought was totally into you, someone who you had wet dreams about regularly but was apparently not available to be in said wet dreams.

Drake hissed in frustration as he dug in his jacket pocket for his keys. What a stupid fucking day. First, Jacob grabbed a woman, then Scotty and Jacob practically broke out into a fist fight, then Frankie took off with Jacob to who the hell knows where leaving Drake completely in the dark as to what was going on, and then Drake found Scotty in the parking lot with some 'roided-up dude. He was finished with the day. It was *past* time to go home.

He finally dragged his keys out and hit the button to unlock the car. He was about to open the door to climb in when he heard footsteps approaching from behind.

"Wait!" Scotty said, jogging up to Drake. Once he reached him, he stopped and put both hands on his knees to catch his breath. "I am way too tired to be running."

Drake just stood and stared at him. Scotty may be too tired, but Drake was just too annoyed. He couldn't even find the cabinet in his brain that housed the snappy banter and comebacks that usually fueled their conversations.

Scotty rasped in a few more gasps of breath and then stood tall again to face Drake. "Hey, I'm sorry. I just didn't expect that from you. I mean, I've seen you pull a few moves like that in the club with some dumbasses, but I guess it just surprised me is all."

Drake didn't say anything. He just let Scotty talk. Scotty faced him in silence for a couple of seconds and then fidgeted nervously. "I guess I'm trying to say sorry for freaking out. I really did need the help. Thank you."

As much as he didn't want to soften up, as much as he wanted to stay mad so he could go home and maybe think about some other hot body to star in his dreams, he couldn't do it. Scotty looked so humbled in front of him. His golden eyes twinkled with the light from the club door, and his usual crooked smile was back on his face. Not to mention all the action in the parking lot, then jogging over to Drake had left Scotty a touch sweaty. Jeez, he really needed to get laid if sweat was turning him on. Well, groveling and sweat.

Fine, he gave up. He was over it. He was back to wanting to get in Scotty's pants. "Are you going to tell me what that was about?"

Scotty gave a slight lift of shoulders. "Not much to tell really. But um, I will tell you if you would be willing to maybe give me a lift home?"

Drake laughed and indicated the passenger door. "You missed the last train, huh?"

Scotty smiled in relief and went to the passenger door. Then he stopped and met Drake's eyes over the top of the car. Drake lost his smile as Scotty's eyes narrowed on him.

"What?"

"How much did you have to drink when you went to your office?"

With a shrug, Drake lied. "I don't know, one or two more glasses."

Scotty put his hand out on the roof of the car and wiggled his fingers in a "come on" gesture.

"What?" Drake asked, looking from his hand back to his face, then back to his hand.

Scotty just kept his hand held out while walking back over toward the driver's side. "Give me the keys. I'm driving."

"What? No, I'm fine!" Drake said, closing his hand around his keys tightly. He could handle his liquor. He could handle it scarily well now. That should probably bother him, but it didn't. It was a vice he was allowing himself.

Scotty dropped his hand back to his side and reached for his pocket. He pulled out his phone and scrolled through his contact list.

"What are you doing?" Drake asked.

"Calling a cab. I am not riding with someone who's been drinking. You might not care if you kill someone or yourself, but I don't have to be a part of it."

Drake didn't know what to say but then sighed. "Fine, here." He threw the keys to Scotty, who caught them midair with a big smile. "I guess you remember how to drive it."

"I sure do!" Scotty said with glee. "I even remember how to move your seat how I like it," he quipped as he dropped into the driver's seat.

Groaning, Drake plopped down next to him and slammed his door shut. "Do you have any idea how long it took me to get the seat back the first time?"

Scotty pushed the button to lift the seat up and grinned. "Nope, and I don't care."

"Of course you don't." Drake rolled his eyes, then let his head drop back to the headrest. He smiled as Scotty situated himself and relaxed back into his seat.

"There, all set." Scotty put the key into the ignition and turned on the car. After pulling out onto the main street, he coasted to a stop at the first streetlight. "What made you think it would be a good idea to buy a stick shift in the city?"

Drake lifted a shoulder. "I didn't really think about it. It has better gas mileage, and I liked the way it looked."

"Really, that's all it took to get you to buy the car. Gas mileage and the look?"

"It's all I cared about. It gets me from point A to point B, and it looks good doing it. I don't have much to complain about."

"Huh, I don't think I buy anything that quickly. I have to go price shop and compare different brands, then you can't forget the reviews. You should never buy something before checking the reviews."

Drake exhaled a laugh as Scotty shifted, pulling onto the entrance ramp for 90 and merging in with traffic. Somehow, even in the earliest hours of morning, the roads were still busy. They rode in silence for a couple of miles. Drake wanted to keep up the lightheartedness, but he was too tired to keep up a sunny disposition. Besides, he had too many questions. Like, what the hell had that been with the guy in the parking lot? Who was he? And when Scotty said it was over, did he mean it or was he still thinking about him, even while driving Drake home?

Drake shifted his eyes so he could watch Scotty. Even though he looked tired, Scotty didn't seem any more or less frazzled.

"So, what was that about? With Craig, I mean."

Scotty chewed on his lip before answering. Drake thought maybe he was going to avoid the question and turn it around, but he didn't. "Craig and I were together a while back. Well, at least we were friends and had an on-again, off-again relationship on the side. But then he got a job over in Cicero and I started working at the club and our hours shifted, and it was too hard to try and make it work." Scotty thrummed his fingers on the steering wheel. "So, I decided that we should just end it, but Craig wanted to try and make it work. When I told him that it was more than just having inconvenient schedules, he asked if we could talk. I told him we could, and so he met me in the lot after work. We talked, but I guess I didn't say anything he wanted to hear."

Drake nodded, letting Scotty continue.

"He was hurt and angry. That's all. He wouldn't have hurt me. But—" Scotty slid his eyes so he could see Drake. "—thank you for stepping in anyway. I mean, I don't think he would have hurt me, but you never know."

"You don't think he might come back to the club and try to get you again?"

Scotty snickered. "Well, I don't think he will anymore, now that he's seen the moves my boss has! Where did you learn to fight like that?"

"Self-defense, jujitsu, and martial arts. I started when I was in middle school and kept up at it all through college and beyond. I like to keep up on it, and I figure it's a good skill to have at the club. It comes in handy every once in a while."

"No kidding. Kind of like that kid a while back. The one that you took down who was messing with Natasha. That move was hot." Drake lifted his brows and looked over at Scotty, who had a smug look on his face as drove. "It took about all the willpower I had not to run over and jump you right then and there."

Laughing, Drake shifted around the tightening bulge in his pants. "I didn't think you'd even noticed. You hardly looked at me afterward, you were so busy keeping up with the bar."

"Yeah, I did that to distract myself. Because otherwise we would have just been a tangle of limbs on the dance floor."

Drake laughed again and shifted in his seat to try to find any loose fabric that might be left in his pants.

"You know, one of the things that Craig wasn't so happy hearing about was that I was interested in somebody else." Drake felt a hitch in his breath as Scotty continued. "I told him that I couldn't see him anymore because there was only one person I could think about and it wasn't him."

Drake met Scotty's eyes for a brief hot moment and then coughed and looked away. He didn't want Scotty to see him blushing. Because he was. Man, he was flattered, embarrassed, and incredibly turned on. He didn't let himself think; he just spoke before his brain could catch up.

"Come over?"

The satisfied smile that stretched Scotty's face did not help the growing anticipation in Drake's pants. In fact, it seemed to have an adverse effect, making the ride even more uncomfortable.

"I was hoping you would ask that," Scotty said and then pressed his foot down harder on the gas.

CHAPTER 11

IT FELT like one of the longest car rides in the history of car rides. Drake only lived about twenty minutes away from the club, but with Scotty sitting so close but not touching him and the expectancy of things to come, it seemed to stop time dead in its tracks. Time slowed, and roads elongated. He had never been so happy to see his condos come into view.

Scotty had barely had a chance to get the car into park before Drake dragged him by the collar to his lips. The kiss was feral, one that demanded action now. It was rushed and forcible, teeth nipping and tongues battling. Breathing suddenly became a nonissue because it didn't seem important enough to stop. Nothing felt as good as Scotty's arms wrapped around his neck and Scotty's lips wrapped around his tongue.

Too soon, Scotty pushed back, and with gulping breaths, they gazed into each other's eyes. Drake licked his lips, tasting Scotty on him. Scotty pushed him back into his own seat, and Drake moaned in protest until he realized that Scotty was quickly undoing his seat belt so he could get out of the car. Drake, having already removed his safety belt before the car had pulled into the lot, shot out the door.

Scotty hurried next to him, shoving the keys into his hand. "I don't know—" He had to stop for a breath, his voice deep with arousal. "—which key to use."

"I don't know if I can tell either," Drake said with a laugh and with shaking hands flipped through his keys until he finally found the one he needed.

It took too long to get the door open. It took even longer to get them both ushered inside. But then finally they were pressed together again, this time with Scotty's body grinding his into the wall. The kiss was wild but now less rushed. Drake let himself explore the contours of Scotty's mouth. He brushed his tongue along the line of his teeth and nipped at his lip. And then with untamed desire, he kissed along Scotty's jawline, down to his neck. Once there, he took in a deep breath and savored the natural smell of Scotty. A hint of spicy aftershave and the lingering scents of alcohol and disinfectant from behind the bar all mixed with the pure organic masculine scent of Scotty.

This time Drake pulled back, but when Scotty made a plaintive whimper, he smiled. He didn't plan on going far. No, he just wanted to explore. He let his hands roam down along the front of Scotty's shirt, barely touching, just the hint of fingertips along abs. But as his fingers reached the hem of the shirt, he delved under, letting skin glide along skin. He soaked in the hot flesh, following each hard line of Scotty's abs. Once he reached as far as he could go, he stopped and tweaked his hard nipples, and Scotty let his head fall back with a moan.

Smiling, Drake claimed Scotty's lips as his once again. But this time the kiss was more relaxed. They didn't need to be in a rush. They were finally going through with it, and there was no reason to make it end too soon. So, Drake let the kiss soften and enjoyed the feel of Scotty pressed against him, the way his muscles quivered under his touch as his hands continued to discover his body. Once he had his fill of exploration with a cloth boundary, Drake pulled Scotty's T-shirt up and over his head.

While Drake had been exploring Scotty, Scotty had been holding tight to Drake's shoulders, every once in a while rubbing along Drake's chest but for the most part holding on. But now Drake had something different in mind. With a quick move, he spun them around so Scotty was now pressed up against the wall. With firm hands, he clasped Scotty's wrists and pushed them up over their heads. He held them there, sealing their position with a kiss, letting his hands glide down Scotty's arms over his shoulders. Then dropping his head down, he explored his body with his mouth.

Each flick of his tongue and sucking of his lips drew a gasp from Scotty, who had left his arms up where Drake had placed them. His fingers clenched into tight fists. Drake couldn't help but smile in satisfaction as Scotty submitted to his whim. Giving Scotty's nipple one last light tug with his lips, he pushed back and just took in the view.

"Damn, you are beautiful," he managed. And that was the truth. If Scotty was beautiful behind the bar, he was beyond stunning pinned up against the wall. His blond hair now disheveled and his eyes hooded from passion, he looked like a god. A god served on a platter just for Drake. Heaven knew he didn't deserve him, but at this point, he was too weak to turn back. He'd had a taste of the elixir, and now they were past the point of no return.

"Want you," Scotty gasped. "Wanted you for so long."

Drake felt a growl in the back of his throat, and as he unleashed it, he yanked his shirt over his head and undid his belt.

Scotty reciprocated, letting his arms drop. The only reason Drake allowed it was because Scotty was undoing the clasp of his pants. Excitement shot through him as Scotty quickly and without preamble jerked his slacks and his boxers to the ground.

Drake dragged in a breath, soaking in the sight. It was almost more than he could handle. They had gone too long, had let the anticipation last for so much time, that now that the prize was in front of him and it was everything and more than he could have hoped for, he could no longer control himself.

"Shit." Drake pulled the now naked Scotty into his arms, attacking his mouth with his own, grinding his still-pant-ridden cock into Scotty's leaking naked one. Scotty gasped and moaned, but he didn't pull away. He pushed closer and fought back with his mouth eagerly.

"What—" Drake tried to get the words out, but Scotty nipped at his lips. "What do you want?"

Scotty moaned into him before responding, "You. I want you. Please."

"Are you sure?" Drake asked. He didn't want to do something wrong. He didn't want to risk moving too fast or assuming too much, and he didn't want to do anything that would make their progress so far screech to a halt.

"God yes, I am sure. So fucking sure," Scotty breathed, pushing his hand between their groins to grab at Drake's cock, tenting through his slacks. "Oh my God, I want this. Now!"

Drake gasped and pulled back, tugging Scotty with him. "Condoms and lube in the bedroom. Come on."

Somehow, they managed to make it to his bedroom. He hadn't even thought about how he left it. He wasn't the cleanliest of people, but he couldn't be bothered with wondering what clothing they stumbled over as they made their way to the bed. He couldn't even care about the towel they collapsed on as they rolled onto the mattress. No, all he could care about was the fact that he was still wearing pants.

Groaning, he sat up and kicked off his shoes and with hurried fingers fought with the button of his pants. Then with a little help from Scotty, finally they were pressed back together, this time skin to hot skin. Drake groaned as Scotty's erection bumped his own, and he gasped as they moved their bodies to rub them together.

"So much better than I imagined," Drake said, reaching between them to wrap a hand around both their erections. He used the precum leaking from them both as a lubricant and pumped them once, twice, three times.

Scotty writhed with each stroke, letting out strangled gasps. "I'm not going to make it," he moaned into Drake's neck. He ran his teeth along the stubble on Drake's chin. "Please, hurry, I am not going to make it."

Drake took one more second to kiss Scotty hard and deep and then rolled so he could get to his bedside table. Opening the drawer, he sighed with relief when both the condoms and the lubricant were right where he thought they were. He hadn't used either in so long, he thought maybe he might have moved them or gotten rid of them. Thank God he hadn't.

After moving back up the bed, he pulled Scotty up so he was on his back alongside him. Putting the condom wrapper corner in his teeth, he held the lubricant with one hand while adjusting himself between Scotty's legs. He pulled one of Scotty's legs so it was on his shoulder, then took the condom from his teeth.

"You still sure about this?" he asked one last time. As much as it would be hard to stop, they didn't have to go through all of this tonight. He was close to getting off already.

Scotty shifted so he was closer, tilted his hips up so that Drake could reach him. "I am sure. Fuck me. Please, fuck me."

Drake didn't need to hear any more. He tore the condom wrapper with his teeth and rolled it on, then flipped open the top of the lube and drizzled some into his hands. Then he quickly rubbed his hands together, warming up the lube before taking one hand to run along his own length. With the other hand, he pressed along Scotty's hot opening. Scotty shivered as his finger pressed but didn't enter him. His whole body quaked with need, but Drake just massaged, letting Scotty get used to him being there.

"Oh God, please. I can't—I don't need…. Shit," Scotty whimpered and then moaned as Drake pushed one finger in. He moved his finger in and out slowly, letting the muscles relax around him. Then he pressed in a little deeper and curled his finger to hit that spot and Scotty jerked and cried out.

"You like that?" Drake asked, doing it again because he wanted to see the way Scotty's eyes rolled back as he lost all inhibitions.

"I do. You know I fucking do," Scotty breathed.

Drake added a second finger, following the same pattern. He pressed in and out, then back in and curled his fingers to massage along Scotty's prostate. Scotty cried out again, his hands clawing at the sheets at his sides. He reached like he was searching to drag Drake toward him, but Drake was out of his reach. His body shook with his need and quivered in desire, and when Drake thought maybe he couldn't take any more, he pulled his fingers out to line his aching cock up to Scotty's hole. And with a small slow thrust, he pushed in.

The sound Scotty made as Drake pushed in almost undid Drake altogether, but he kept it together and slowly worked his way in past the tight muscles and deep into the heat of Scotty's body. He pressed until he was sheathed as far as he could go, and he paused. Leaning forward, he claimed another kiss; then with a jerk of his hips, he thrust forward hard.

Scotty cried out and whimpered around his lips, and Drake continued to snap his hips forward, fucking him hard. Nails scratched at his back, bringing him down closer, and one of Scotty's legs wrapped around his waist to press them even tighter together, while the other used Drake's shoulder as leverage so they had an even better, deeper angle.

Drake moaned as Scotty flexed and tightened around him. Dragging his teeth along Scotty's skin, he moved his hips even faster, drawing even louder sounds from Scotty. "I'm not going to last much longer."

Scotty wrapped his arms around Drake's neck, pulling his head down so he could capture his lips. "Neither am I."

Letting the overwhelming sensation take over, Drake pumped his hips until his orgasm ripped from him. He continued to thrust until he was finished, and then with a quick breath, he collapsed on Scotty.

"I've been having dreams about that since the last time you drove me home," Drake grated out, almost too exhausted to move, but he pushed himself up. They weren't done yet. Holding the end of the condom, he pulled out, then ran to the bathroom. He hurried back, bringing a washcloth with him. He smiled at Scotty, then threw the cloth to the side. "For later," he said and crawled back on the bed.

Scotty hadn't moved the entire time Drake was gone and now he lay with his legs still spread and one hand lazily rubbing up and down along his straining erection.

Drake crawled until he was back between Scotty's legs, but this time he let himself collapse down so that his lips were at just the right point. Just to tease Scotty, who was still so aroused he was practically out of it, he blew along the sensitive cockhead and smiled as the member jerked in response. Then licking his lips, he took Scotty into his mouth.

"Oh shit." Scotty moaned, lifting his hips off the mattress and pushing farther into Drake's throat. Drake relaxed his muscles so he could take Scotty deeper and swallowed around him, loving the sound of Scotty cursing under his breath as he squirmed. After a few twists of Drake's tongue and a torturous glide of teeth along sensitive skin, Scotty cried out and came. Drake pulled back so only some of the fluid went in his mouth. Another shot landed on his chin and another on Scotty's chest.

Smiling, he swallowed the cum in his mouth and let Scotty watch as he wiped the cum from his chin and licked it from his fingers. Scotty shivered as he watched, and Drake dropped down to once again seize Scotty's lips. This time he did so with the taste of Scotty still fresh on him.

Totally sated and exhausted, Drake fell back to his side so he was facing Scotty. He couldn't help the smile that tugged at his lips. He hadn't felt this satisfied in a long time. They lay in contented silence for a while, and then Scotty shifted so that he was facing Drake.

"That was way better than I had imagined it," he said, reaching over to brush some hair off Drake's forehead. Then he let his fingers softly caress his face. Drake tilted his chin to nuzzle into Scotty's fingers, enjoying their soothing strokes. "And trust me, I imagined it pretty fucking good."

"If this was that good when we were rushed, and let's face it, a little desperate, imagine what it will be like when we take our time," Drake said with a lethargic smile.

"Hmmm." Scotty sighed, then pressed their foreheads together. "A repeat of the same wouldn't be a disappointment either."

Drake laughed. "I think I would be satisfied with a repeat performance."

They lay that way for a while, fingers softly caressing exposed flesh, exploring each other's bodies, totally content to just lie there, no need for conversation, no haste to get back at it. Drake hadn't realized how much he would like having someone in his arms as he was drifting into sleep. Usually his guests didn't stick around long enough for sleeping to even be an issue, and considering the life he led, he had always been fine with that. But something about Scotty's lithe body twined with his ignited a desire deep within himself. A desire to belong to somebody. To have something to care about more than revenge. A need to have someone who wanted to be with him.

As crazy as it was to think those types of things, Drake couldn't help but once again fall into the fantasy. Letting his lips curl into a relaxed smile, he tilted his chin to press soft lips to Scotty's in a quick chaste kiss, then tucked his chin and enjoyed listening to the even, soothing sounds of Scotty's breath as it lulled him off to sleep.

CHAPTER 12

DRAKE WOKE with a start. What was happening? What woke him?

A small noise came from outside his room, and Drake tried to clear sleep from his head as he pushed himself up in time to see a light flash off down the hall. He tensed, ready to roll off the side of the bed and grab one of the guns strapped under his nightstand for just this occasion. He let instincts take over and held his breath as he waited for the moment that action would begin. His palm itched, his hand ready for the strike, but as a dark figure materialized into view, his tension eased.

Scotty tiptoed into the room, highlighted by the morning light glittering through the curtains covering the window. He quietly shut the door behind him, moving stealthily as if trying not to wake Drake. Drake's breath left him in a single rush as he let himself relax back into the soft pillows.

He definitely wasn't used to someone being in his house when he was asleep. Generally, he made it a rule never to entertain overnight guests at his place, but as he watched Scotty sleep-stumble back toward bed, Drake smiled. He definitely could get used to someone staying the night. A very specific someone.

Scotty pushed back the covers to crawl in next to Drake. His now chilly skin just barely brushed Drake's.

Drake blinked at him as he settled into bed. Their eyes met.

"Hi." Drake smiled, scooting closer and letting his body's heat encompass Scotty.

Scotty returned the smile, then shifted even closer so they were wrapped together. "Hi."

"Comfortable?"

Scotty hummed a pleased little sound, snuggling deeper into the pillows. "Yeah." His eyes drifted closed.

"Good."

Drake enjoyed the feel of warm skin pressed against his under the sheet. He reveled in the fact that he could run his fingers up and down

Scotty's arm, memorizing his contours and shape. He enjoyed the feel of coarse hair mingling with his as their legs touched. More than anything, he relished the contented lift of Scotty's lips as he slowly drifted back into restful sleep in Drake's arms.

Damn, he could get used to this.

Listening to Scotty's even breaths, Drake studied his face. Yeah, he liked what he saw. Even more than that, he liked how he felt. It was nice to be wrapped around someone who wasn't just another warm body. So many of his partners had been someone to take the edge off, someone to help him forget the world he lived in, even if only for a couple of hours. Lying next to Scotty, Drake realized how much he savored having someone who he actually cared about and who might actually care about him. Scotty seemed to give a damn about his well-being. He concerned himself with Drake's drinking. Not that that was a sign for a good relationship. Just the fact that Scotty needed to be concerned about his drinking was an omen for future problems. But Drake couldn't help but live the dream, at least for the night.

Sleep was just beginning to reclaim him when a soft buzzing followed by a soothing harp playing harmoniously broke into his consciousness. Groaning, Drake used one hand to search for his phone, trying to silence the damn alarm while still keeping his eyes shut.

His phone wasn't where he usually stashed it. With another groan, he opened his eyes, trying to follow the sound.

"What the heck is that?" Scotty moaned plaintively from his side of the bed, covering his head with the sheet.

Finding the source of the jingle, Drake sighed. He'd left his phone in his pant pocket, and he could see the cloth jiggling where it vibrated. Pulling himself up into a seated position, he rubbed his hands over his face.

"It's my damn alarm," Drake said, pushing the blanket and sheet to the side so he could silence the damn machine.

"What time is it?" Scotty's voice came muffled from under the sheet.

Drake pushed to his feet. "It has to be about nine thirty. That's when my first alarm goes off."

Scotty groaned again. "Nine thirty? Are you kidding me? We went to sleep like three hours ago!"

Finally hitting the small button on the top of the phone, Drake returned it to silence. Drake collapsed back on the bed. "Don't remind me." He pushed his phone under his pillow.

"Why in the world do you have an alarm set for this ungodly hour?" Scotty asked again, head still covered.

Drake slithered back under the covers, letting his legs wrap with Scotty's. "It's when I usually attempt to get up. I don't actually get up until about ten or ten thirty, but I start the day with good intentions."

"Why?"

Drake snorted. "It's important to start every day with good intentions."

Scotty moved as if to smack Drake, but the sheet hindered his arm and he gave up. "You know what I mean."

Nestling closer, tucking his chin into the sheet where it was indented from the crevice from shoulder to head, he breathed softly, feeling the heat soak into the fabric. "You don't expect me to have a body like this by sleeping all day, do you?"

"Oh God, you run, don't you?" Scotty's muffled exclaim sounded morally offended.

Laughing, Drake snuggled in, wrapping his arms around Scotty and pulling him in, enjoying the feel of the man relaxing against him. "Among other things. Don't you?" Drake couldn't imagine that Scotty could keep his lithe figure without doing something.

"Only when I have to. Now, shhh, time to sleep." Scotty's voice was already light with slumber.

Drake held in his laugh, although it did take some effort. This was a part of Scotty that he hadn't known existed, the lazy and tired side. Drake smiled.

The silence lasted approximately eight minutes before, once again, Drake's alarm started its sweet song.

Drake choked on his laugh, digging under the pillow for his phone as Scotty threw the sheet from his head with a frustrated but amused groan.

"You have got to be kidding me. You hit snooze?"

Drake chuckled, finding the phone and going through the settings to turn the alarm off. "There, it's off."

Scotty huffed, staring up at the ceiling. "Well, I'm up now."

"In that case, do you want to go for a run?" Drake pursed his lips, holding back a grin.

Turning on his side so that he was facing Drake, Scotty scooted a little closer, dipping his head so they were practically nose-to-nose. "Hmm, I think I can think of a better way to get that morning burn in."

Drake pushed up and turned, pressing Scotty down onto his back on the mattress. He kept their faces the same distance apart. "Yeah?"

"Yeah," Scotty said breathlessly, before closing the distance between them.

CHAPTER 13

DRAKE COUNTED out the tips from the night before and separated them into piles. As he divided the bills, he glanced up to watch Scotty on the other side of the bar setting up his station. He smiled as Scotty turned around to shoot him a quick glance and caught him looking. They smiled stupidly at each other before both going back to what they were doing.

"Hey, Drake," Julie said, leaning against the counter. She had a moist towel in one hand and the spray bottle in the other from cleaning off the tops of the tables.

"Jules." Drake nodded at her. Julie had dark features and almond-shaped eyes she accentuated with black eyeliner. Where on some, the dark lines could be taken as overuse of the eye product, on Julie it helped to contrast against her eerily light blue eyes.

"Jenny called and said that she might run a little late. Her sitter called in sick and she has to find someone else."

Drake nodded. "Does she need the night? I could call in Ethan, or heaven forbid, we could make sure Jacob is around tonight."

Julie shook her head. "Nah, she said that if she doesn't make it on time, that she would only be about twenty to thirty minutes late."

"Okay, thanks for letting me know." Drake picked up one of the stacks of cash and handed it to Julie, who took it graciously.

"Thanks!"

Drake watched her walk to the back where the staff stored their stuff and then picked up another stack to take to Scotty. With the cash in hand, Drake leaned against the counter and watched Scotty as he moved fluidly around the small space behind the bar. It was a sight Drake was pretty sure he would never get sick of.

The last twenty hours had been some of the best times that Drake could remember. He couldn't remember a time when his main focus, his only reason for breathing, wasn't Boredega. His life had revolved around the cartel; everything he had done had been to get to this point, but now....

Scotty had opened his eyes to the possibilities. The blinders Drake had to everything but the cartel were starting to widen, and thoughts he had never believed possible were beginning to peek through. Somehow, Scotty had managed to burst into his world and spread a light in his world of darkness. Obviously, he still needed to take down the cartel, and he wasn't stupid. He had done and risked too much to back out now. Besides, he couldn't walk away at this point without getting a bullet to the head. But maybe...

Maybe Drake had finally found another reason for living.

Lips turned up in a lighthearted smile, Drake walked up behind Scotty. He took a glance around to make sure they were mostly alone, or that at least no one was paying attention to them, and then he leaned the front of his body against Scotty's back.

Scotty jumped but quickly pulled himself together. He faced Drake with a warm smile that made Drake's heart miss a beat and leaned forward, giving Drake a quick chaste kiss.

"Hi," Scotty whispered as Drake pushed back so they could look at each other.

Drake took a deep breath, breathing in the soothing scent of Scotty, a tangy aftershave that smelled as if he had spent the morning on the beach and the underlying smell of simply Scotty.

"Hi," Drake repeated, lost in the encompassing atmosphere that Scotty emitted. But then at the sound of a stool being pushed to the side, scraping against the floor in a jarring whine, he jumped back.

Biting his lip, Scotty looked down, holding back a laugh. Drake snorted as he turned to make sure no one was paying attention still and held out yesterday's tips for Scotty.

"Um, here are your tips," Drake said stupidly.

Scotty's eyes glistened amusedly as he took the offered money. "Thanks, Boss."

Drake didn't move as Scotty folded the bills and shoved them into his pocket to deal with later. They watched each other for a couple more minutes before Drake realized they probably looked like lovesick fools gazing at each other like that and stepped back, clearing his throat. He glanced around but only saw Julie in sight, who was busily wiping down tables.

"I'll, uh," Drake spluttered. Why in the hell couldn't he form a sentence?

Laughing at him, Scotty patted Drake on the cheek. "I have to grab some bottles from the back."

"Right, yeah, of course." Drake rolled his eyes at himself. What the heck was wrong with him? It wasn't like this was the first time he and Scotty had spoken. Hell, they had spent the better part of the morning together talking. Er, well, Drake supposed there hadn't been that much talking. But they had spent the entire morning and afternoon together before splitting up so they could get ready for work.

"You want to help me?" Scotty asked, a deviant glint in his eye.

Drake swallowed. Holy hell, did he ever. But—and man did it pain him to even think it—he couldn't let it go this far at work. He had already let it go further than it had any right to go, and now he needed to pull his shit together. Not only was their relationship not at all professional, but it could be dangerous if the wrong people were to know about it.

Letting regret show on his face, Drake shook his head. "I have some things I have to do in my, uh, office."

Scotty shrugged, then winked at Drake. "Maybe next time."

Swallowing, Drake took another step back before he did something stupid like change his mind. "Uh, yeah. Next time," he said and spun on his heel to go hide in his office.

What kind of bumbling idiot was he? Drake mentally kicked himself as he walked to his office. He had sounded downright stupid out there. It was as if his IQ had dropped ten points because Scotty was within touching distance of him. Sex had never done that to him before. Of course, he had never felt as attracted to anyone as he did to Scotty.

Jesus, he was all off-kilter. He'd only minutes before admitted to himself that he may have found something more important to him than stopping the cartel. But that was impossible, wasn't it? You couldn't discard something so fantastical so quickly, could you?

Drake needed to put a tether on this. Everything was spinning out of control. The sex was good—hell, who was he kidding, the sex was fucking fantastic, pun intended. But that's all this was. He was thinking with a sex-addled brain. Once he got some space between him and Scotty, he would be able to function more clearly.

Pushing open his office door, Drake stopped short when he saw Jacob sitting at his desk, feet propped up in total disregard for the paperwork Drake had strewn across the top. Frowning, Drake continued through the door, making sure to shut it behind him.

What the fuck was happening now? He needed to get his head sewed back on pronto.

"What the hell do you think you're doing?" Drake demanded, striding confidently up to his desk where Jacob continued to lounge.

Jacob spread his arms out in a welcoming shrug, his malicious grin belying his gesture. "Waiting for you."

Drake stood, legs spread, arms crossed, glaring down at Jacob, who chortled lightly. Jacob lowered his feet to the floor and pushed back in the chair to regain his feet. He stood to his full height, and Drake noticed for the first time how tall the kid was. He wasn't a big guy, he didn't have a wide build, but was instead tall and thin, and his arrogant stance and self-righteous vibes gave him a dangerous appearance. Also, the fact that the kid didn't seem to think twice about acting on his senseless violent nature only added to his malevolence.

"Well, here I am. What the fuck do you want?"

Drake let his crossed arms drop to his side. He wished he was wearing one of his weapons. If the kid made a move, Drake knew he could take him in hand-to-hand combat without breaking a sweat, but he didn't trust that the kid would play fair. And he was 99 percent certain that the kid was packing.

"What the fuck do I want?" Jacob asked, taking the few steps that were between him and Drake. He stopped with the toes of their shoes practically touching. "What I want is for you to fucking mind your own fucking business."

Drake fought the urge to step back. As much as he liked his personal space, giving Jacob the satisfaction of seeing him back down wasn't worth the comfort.

The kid couldn't be serious. He wanted Drake to mind his own business? What did he think Drake was doing? This club and everything that happened in and around it was his business.

"Aw, did someone get in trouble?" Drake asked, feeling a pleased smirk contort his face.

Jacob smiled back at him, showing teeth that Drake would swear were razor-sharp. "You think you're special because you own a building?"

Jacob asked, leaning in even closer. "You aren't special. You're a bug. An insect. Someone like you disappears, poof." Jacob made a puffing gesture into his hand, his fingers spreading as if blowing dust from his palm. "The cartel finds someone else to take your place. You cause too much trouble or get caught doing something you shouldn't, you're dead. People like you are a dime a dozen. I think it's best you remember your place when you stick your nose where it doesn't belong."

Drake held his smile in place, although he could feel the cool edge of the threat tingle down his spine. He made sure to keep any unease to himself. "You think you're in a much better position?" Drake asked, proud to hear his voice come out steady and sure.

Jacob leered at him, his eyes shining like he knew more than he let on. "I know that I am. So, I will only say this once—mind your own fucking business, and stay the fuck out of my way." Jacob shoved past Drake and headed toward the office door in a cool, confident swagger.

"Or what, you're going to kill me?" Drake called to Jacob's back because, obviously, he couldn't keep his fucking mouth shut.

Turning back to face him, Jacob grinned, and it reached his eyes. "Everybody has someone they care about." And with that final chilling comment, Jacob opened Drake's office door and left.

CHAPTER 14

THE POUNDING bass of the music and the distorted confusion of hundreds of conversations going on at once was a soothing distraction from Drake's panicked inner monologue. Ever since Jacob had walked out of his office, he hadn't been able to shake the prickling dread crawling through the murky trenches of his consciousness. Drake knew he shouldn't let the kid's threat bother him, but he couldn't help it.

If Drake was an upstanding violent criminal without an inch of worry or care for himself or anyone else, then he might have been able to walk away from that incredibly tense conversation with a shrug. But he wasn't an upstanding violent criminal. In fact, the more he thought about it, the less he wanted to be a criminal in any capacity. Sure, he had gotten into this life with good intentions, but everyone knew where paths of good intentions led. Sure enough, he was on the right trail.

The worst part of the whole thing was that ever since Jacob had said that, as soon as Drake had heard the words "care about," he'd finally realized that he had done the one thing he had told himself he would never do. Not only had he started to care about someone, but he had put that someone in the crosshairs of the fucking cartel that had taken everything from him in the fucking first place.

Drake tilted his glass to his lips, letting the smooth liquid warm him. He took a small sip, thought better of it, and drained the glass. After setting the tumbler down firmly on the bar, he spun it expertly so it moved across the counter, stilling only once it reached the edge, ready for a much-needed refill. Drake tapped his fingers on the speckled bar top, waiting for Julie to finish her current rounds so she could replenish his goods. She was taking her damn time, but he couldn't begrudge her that; she was doing her job.

Patience is a virtue. The thought floated through his mind, and he closed his eyes on the intense outpouring of emotion it brought to him. He could almost hear his mother saying it as she calmly worked around him while he continued to pester her in the way children did.

How was it that he could hear her voice, but he couldn't picture her face? Would there be a day when even the memory of her voice would disappear as well?

Dispelling the unwanted memory, he searched for the refuge of a distraction and took that moment to glance farther down the bar at the still busily working Scotty, who was fulfilling his drink orders.

One thought of misery leading straight to another.

Unable to face Scotty after the whole Jacob incident, Drake had decided to forgo sitting in his section and instead opted for Julie's portion of the bar. The act had earned him a couple of curious glances from Scotty, who gratefully had remained too busy to come over and talk to him, but Drake had tried his damnedest to not notice. He needed to think and he needed to drink, and Julie was much more likely to continue to serve Drake drinks after he'd reached his limit—unlike Scotty, who would have probably already cut him off.

"Got a lot on your mind, Drakeybo?"

The soft sound of Natasha's soprano voice grated through Drake's skull, and he dropped his head into his hands. This was it. This was the proof that the world was fucking with him. He must have been a serial rapist or something in a past life because it was the only thing that explained why his life was the way it was.

"You have got to be kidding me! Are you always here?" Drake managed through clenched teeth. The music was still loud and the crowd's ambiance overpowering, but Natasha's raised perfectly manicured brows let him know that she could hear him. "Don't you have a life outside of this club? Shouldn't you be working, or something?"

Natasha pursed her moist red lips as if waiting for a kiss and cocked her hip against the bar facing Drake, too close for his comfort.

"What makes you think that I'm not working?" She tilted her chin up, her curly hair falling back from her face in seductive waves.

Slanting his eyes toward the back room, Drake sighed. Of course. Sex and drugs, the only things people cared about anymore.

Who was he to talk? He'd had sex on the brain ever since he'd hired the gorgeous bartender he was trying his damnedest not to ogle and failing miserably. He couldn't say drugs weren't on his mind either, considering he worked for a cartel.

Speaking of drugs, he really needed a refill on his drink. What the hell? Drake eyed the bottle of Black Label staring at him from the mirrored bar. Unfortunately, Julie was still working with some customers at the end of her station. She probably wasn't going to come fill his glass anytime soon. Of course, Drake owned the bar. There really wasn't a reason he couldn't just go get the drink himself. Or a better option would be to go into his office and hide out for the rest of the evening. That way he wouldn't need to converse with anyone, and he wouldn't be able to publicly yearn for a guy who he had no business yearning for.

A warm body pressing against his brought Drake back to the present to find Natasha sidled up against him. Drake felt a repulsed tingle work its way through his spine as Natasha slid her hand up his arm. She leaned close, her hot breath moist against his ear.

"We could go somewhere a little more private, and I bet I could make you forget all about that drink you're waiting for." She paused. The air was warm and sticky against the skin on his neck. "Or that bartender you're drooling over."

A chill ran over Drake's skin at Natasha's words. Those words confirmed what Drake had thought. Not only had he let someone get close to him, but he hadn't had the decency to keep it under lock and key.

Not wanting to bring more attention to the fact that Scotty meant anything to him, Drake rolled his eyes and pushed back from the counter. "Are you fucking serious?"

Natasha maneuvered to keep her body pressed against his even as he tried to move away. One corner of her mouth tilted up in a brash smile.

"Honey, I am always serious." She licked her lips in invitation as a warm hand landed on Drake's inner thigh and slithered upward. "I guess this explains why you suddenly have no interest in me. I don't have the right—" She brazenly clasped his cock in her grip. "—anatomy."

Drake hissed in outrage, his breath hot as fire. Using one hand to stop the obtrusive grope, Drake pushed off his stool hard enough to send the metal-and-cloth contraption clanging to the floor. Although the bar was loud and was in a constant wave of change, the violent movement caused the people directly around Drake to jump out of the way. A little red-haired girl squealed in surprise as the stool slid by her high-heeled feet.

Drake straightened to his full height, Natasha's arm grasped firmly in his hand. He could feel the bones under her skin, and he had to stop himself from squeezing hard enough to cause real damage. Natasha's cocky smile faltered with each second of Drake's staunch grip, but the curve never left her lips. He edged forward, towering over her smaller frame, meeting her dark daring eyes. "Get the *fuck* out of my bar." The words seethed through his teeth.

Natasha's smile, though dulled, never left her lips and she faced him head-on. Dripping in dark seduction, she said, "Aw, Drakey, you don't mean that."

"I mean it," Drake growled. "I want you out. You so much as show your face in here again, I will have you thrown out."

Natasha pulled her arm from Drake's grasp roughly. Her confident gaze returned to Drake's. "It's cute that you think that you have enough control to keep me out of here." She licked her lips. "Did you think I came here to see you? Oh, honey, you may think you're something, but you are just a speck of dirt in the grand scheme of things."

Drake's voice deepened. "I'm getting tired of people threatening me."

"I haven't even begun to threaten you. When I do threaten you, Drakeybo," Natasha said sweetly, tapping Drake's cheek with her open palm like speaking condescendingly to a child, "trust me, you will know it."

Drake jerked back, attempting to avoid her touch, but she just laughed before turning on her heel to walk back toward the dance floor. He watched her go, his face still hot with anger. Swallowing hard, he let out a deep release of breath, dispelling a modicum of the pent-up heat, and the red around the edges of his vision started to clear.

"Here, Boss, I thought you might need this," Julie said, setting a glass down on the counter. Drake picked it up and slugged it down before sending her a smile of gratitude.

"Thanks, Jules." Returning the empty glass back to Julie, he fought off the urge to have her pour him another. If he wanted more, which he definitely did, then he had a bottle with his name on it in his office.

"I'm going to do inventory. Find me if you need me," Drake said, then went to find a bottle to drown his nerves.

It took longer than Drake had thought it would for Scotty to find him. He had made a bet with himself that Scotty would have followed him to his office, especially after all the questioning looks he had been receiving, but that hadn't happened. Then he'd thought Scotty would follow him to the storage room after Drake clearly avoided him while doing a quick stock inventory of the bar. Not that Drake was complaining about not being followed around like a puppy, it was just that he had prepared himself for the confrontations in the moment. He had worked himself up to be able to push Scotty away, which obviously was something he had to do, because he wasn't in a position to care about anyone. He wasn't in a position to *protect* anyone. He couldn't think about anyone but himself, and Scotty deserved so much more than that.

So, when Scotty did show up, Drake was fully unprepared. He'd gone into the storage room under the guise of doing inventory, but who was he kidding? He didn't have the ability to focus on anything but his inner monologue. He had spent the hour in the storage room pacing and randomly picking up bottles. He had looked over a few, reading their labels, but if anyone asked him what they had stored, he wouldn't have had a clue.

He was looking blankly at a bottle of white rum when Scotty's voice, though quiet, shook his very foundation.

"What in the world are you doing in here?"

Drake jumped, almost dropping the bottle but catching it clumsily in his arms at the last minute. He also made a startled squeak, which he would go to his grave denying.

"Jesus," he gasped, putting the bottle back in its spot on the shelf. "Don't sneak up on me."

Scotty's amused expression became even more snarky as an eyebrow rose into his hairline. "Sneak up on you? Really?"

Drake caught his breath and quickly schooled his features. Looking around him for his drink, he found his empty glass sitting next to an equally empty bottle of Black Label. He huffed, then crossed his arms over his chest.

"What do you need?"

Scotty came farther into the room, the bright light illuminating his concerned features. "I'm looking for you. What's going on?"

"What do you mean, what's going on?" Drake shrugged. "I'm doing inventory."

Scotty glanced around, eyeing Drake's empty bottle with a disapproving frown. "Inventory, right."

As Scotty moved closer, Drake moved back. "Yes, inventory. I wanted to get it done early so I don't have to stay until close tonight."

"You're leaving early?" Scotty said, his voice thick with something Drake didn't want to think about. Instead he picked up his empties and the inventory notebook he had neglected.

When he turned around to make a hasty exit, he was stopped by the crestfallen look on Scotty's face. Closing his eyes, Drake shook his head.

"Look," he said.

At the same time, Scotty breathed his name. "Drake."

They both stopped. Drake looked everywhere but at Scotty. He had to do this. He had to push him away. His life wasn't one meant for this; he wasn't supposed to find love and happiness. He was broken, and there was no way to fix that. The only thing he could do was get his revenge, and he couldn't do that with another innocent life on the line.

Hardening his expression, Drake finally met Scotty's lost gaze. "Look," he repeated. "We both knew this wasn't a good idea. Right? We knew that it wasn't going to be able to go anywhere, so I suggest we end it now before it can go any further and one of us gets hurt."

"Before one of us gets hurt, right," Scotty said, his voice flat. "Might be too late for that."

"I told you I had a lot going on. I told you that I couldn't do it." Drake swallowed hard. "I was weak and I let this happen. I shouldn't have, and now I'm correcting that. You are better off, Scotty. I promise you."

With an annoyed grunt, Scotty said, "Why are you the one that gets to decide what's better for me? What if I don't want what's *better* for me?"

"Just… trust me," Drake breathed.

Scotty's saddened expression morphed into one of anger. "Trust you. Because you tell me so much? Because you are so honest with me?" He closed the distance between them, Drake surprised enough about Scotty's anger to delay any reaction. "The thing is, Drake, I do trust you. You don't seem to trust me."

"Scotty," Drake began, but his voice broke.

Scotty's expression softened. He put a cautious hand on Drake's shoulder. "I know, okay?" he said, squeezing lightly. "I know that you're involved in something. I know that the club is just a front. I know that you aren't who you say you are."

Drake's blood surged at the confession, his spine snapping up. "What?"

Drake had attempted to step away from Scotty's grasp, but Scotty traveled with him, keeping their bodies the same distance apart, although they were no longer touching. "It wasn't that hard to figure out." Scotty pushed his hand through his hair, sweeping the light locks from his goldenrod eyes. "I've known that you were involved in something for quite a while. I mean, you have rooms in this building alone that me and other staff can't go to. Frankie gives more orders than you do, not to mention he and the never-ending rotation of punkass kids are hardly ever actually working at the club."

Drake's mouth worked like a fish out of water. He tried to speak, but he couldn't come up with anything to say. What Scotty said opened a floodgate of panic, relief, and various other emotions he couldn't quite comprehend. Scotty *knew*. He knew, and he still wanted to be with Drake. He knew, and he still pursued him.

Scotty knew! Oh, Jesus fucking Christ, Scotty knew. How much did he know? Did anyone else know that he knew? Oh God, what if Frankie found out? Worse, what if Jacob found out and then killed him? Because not only would he be disposing of a potential risk, he would also be able to use the killing against Drake.

He had done it—exactly what he had wanted to prevent. He had done it, and now he had to fix it. He had to do something, anything to make it right. This was murder and drug smuggling. This was twenty-five-to-life-type stuff on his shoulders.

Drake rolled his head on his shoulders, feeling the tension underneath. He could already feel the alcohol starting to ebb, the inevitable headache growing. He would need another drink soon or else his muscles would continue to tighten, dragging out a migraine. But he just stood there. He didn't have the energy to get a drink. He let his gaze meet Scotty's again.

"How are you so calm about this?" Drake asked. He let his hands settle at his sides. "How can you walk into this room, this small, enclosed room with only me, the guy who you *know* is involved in a cartel, and be calm?" He gestured to the confined space where, if Drake wanted to, he could do anything to Scotty and no one would be the wiser. Surprisingly, Drake's voice wasn't nearly as rattled as he thought it would be. All his words came out calmly, maybe even a little unnervingly. The tone certainly frightened him, but he couldn't let that show. Scotty had to know what he was dealing with.

The air stilled around them as Drake waited for Scotty's answer. It was like neither of them were breathing, both tensed and ready for anything. Drake didn't move, didn't twitch. He watched Scotty's face as he debated how to answer. He raised a brow pointedly, showing his impatience with the continued silence.

Scotty shrugged loosely. "I don't think you'll hurt me."

Drake felt a cruel smile spread across his lips. "Are you willing to take that risk?" Moving quick, hardly thinking before he acted, Drake closed the distance between them, his right hand shooting out, fingers wrapping around Scotty's neck. He tightened his hold so the grip was firm, but he didn't cut off any of Scotty's air.

Scotty gasped at the sudden movement but didn't fight back. He reached up one hand to grasp Drake's wrist, but he didn't try to pull him off. His eyes had widened, but he didn't look away from Drake.

"I could do anything I want to you. I could kill you right here, and there isn't anything you can do about it."

Scotty had both hands on Drake's wrist now, but he still didn't fight. His eyes were wide, but he didn't look frightened, more like reserved.

"I trust you," Scotty choked out as Drake let his grip tighten a little more. "Drake, I trust you."

Drake let the words tumble over him, through him. With a curse, he shoved Scotty away. Scotty fell back, clutching his throat where Drake's fingers had been.

"Goddammit, Scotty!" Drake yelled. Scotty jumped at the sound but didn't move any farther away. Instead he stayed the few paces away, one hand still rubbing his neck while the other hung at his side, his twitching fingers the only sign that he was nervous. Drake raked his hands through his hair.

"I've been trying to keep you out of all this since the moment you walked into the club. I've been holding myself back, keeping my distance, not letting my emotions and desires rule me. Then last night, I did. I let my guard down, and here you are. Sitting right in the middle of it. Dammit!"

Scotty reached out, but Drake batted him away.

"It's okay! I won't tell anyone anything, and I don't care!" Scotty said, his voice taking on a frantic edge.

Drake stopped dead in his tracks and faced Scotty, incredulous. "You don't care?" He took a menacing step forward, feeling guilty but a little relieved when Scotty seemed to finally see that he might very well be in danger and took a step back. Information was power, and Drake had to have as much power as possible to get Scotty out of this mess. "You attracted to the murderous type? You think it's a turn-on beating people up because they haven't paid back money they owe? You think it's okay to go around and fuck people up, just because you can? You know about this stuff and you don't fucking care?"

"Just the fact that you are so upset about it, that I would be any or all those things, tells me that you aren't the bad guy here. You said it yourself—you have tried to keep me out of it. If you were as bad as you're trying to claim to be, you wouldn't have cared if I got involved."

Drake let his anger continue to motivate his body language. He let the past and the present collide so he could continue to intimidate, even though Scotty obviously could see through him, at least to an extent. Enough to know that he wasn't the bad guy. But Drake had done those things. He had used violence to get information and to punish. He had threatened lives. He might not have killed anyone with his own hands, but deaths had resulted due to his actions. He wasn't a good guy. And he didn't deserve someone like Scotty. The man was beautiful inside and out. He shouldn't be involved with someone like Drake. Drake never should have let him continue to work at the club, especially after he started to feel things for him.

Ugh! How did he get himself into this? Thinking with his dick! Isn't that what brought most men down?

Drake stomped up to Scotty, who held his ground, and stabbed a finger in the man's chest. "You have no idea who I am or what I am capable of. If you want to make it out of this alive, I suggest you keep your mouth shut."

Scotty opened his mouth to protest, but Drake cut him off. "No, we aren't talking about this." Drake grabbed Scotty by his thick arm, his fingers digging in enough to leave marks. "You, me, us, this—" Drake gestured between them, pushing Scotty away. "—none of this happened. I can't tell you to stay away from the club because it will draw attention to you, but I can say that if you ever open your mouth about any of this, it may just be the last thing you ever talk about. You hear me?" Drake stared Scotty down, boring his toughened dark eyes into Scotty's contrasting ones. He had to swallow against the dying light he saw there. He squared his shoulders. He couldn't let a little hurt rule him; he was trying to keep Scotty alive. He was trying to keep himself alive.

He couldn't give in, no matter how much his body ached to gather Scotty into his arms. No, that world had died and he was back in reality, and in this actuality, he was to be alone.

Indicating the door with his chin, Drake directed Scotty harshly. "Get the fuck out, and stay the hell away from me."

Scotty stepped back from Drake and stared incredulously, and just when Drake thought he would have to stop him from trying to protest again, he shook his head, casting his eyes to the floor, and turned to leave.

The wave of relief that pulsed through Drake as he watched Scotty's retreating figure almost took his legs out from under him, but he locked his knees to keep himself standing. This was not how he had imagined this happening. Scotty was the only good thing to come out of any of this shit, and here he was threatening him and telling him to get lost. Sure, Scotty didn't deserve the trouble that came packaged with Drake, but didn't Drake deserve something good in his life as well?

It was thoughts like that that had gotten him to this mess in the first place. The good that would happen in his life, the good he deserved, was seeing the cartel go down. To see it struggle or the people who killed his family go down. That's what he lived for; that was his purpose. As much as it hurt, he needed to remember that.

CHAPTER 15

MUSIC PULSED loudly around Drake as he sat in the darkened booth near the rear of the club. He twirled his glass, the remaining scotch sloshing at the movement, as he watched the action. The booth he had chosen was one of his favorites because it allowed the best visual. He could see the dance floor, the front door, and at this particular moment, the area he was most interested in: the bar.

It had been an awkward couple of weeks since he had ended it with Scotty. After a couple of failed attempts to get Drake to talk to him, Scotty finally backed down, and they had been avoiding each other as much as possible ever since. Scotty never arrived early nor stayed late. He showed up for his shift, did nothing more and did nothing less. If Drake happened to be near the bar, which he did his best not to while Scotty was working, Scotty would set down a scotch without a word.

Drake thought he missed that the most. Sure, he missed the bantering and the flirting, the having Scotty look at him with lust-filled eyes, but what he missed the most was the fact that Scotty had cared that he was drinking too much. He had cared that Drake would drink and then drive. Someone had cared about him, and Drake couldn't help but mourn that loss.

To try to keep his head clear, he decided to distract himself. He had delved into his work at the club. He had hired new talent, set up new event nights, added new special drinks to the menu, priced out new dance floors, and he had researched new earpieces for him and the crew because he hated the ones they currently used.

Frankie had also helped to serve as a distraction, giving him interrogation duty for a couple of junkies who had somehow "misplaced" the money that rightfully belonged to Boredega. It had been a cathartic task for Drake. Not only was he able to release some of his anger, but he also confirmed what he knew about himself. Even if he wasn't the bad guy, he definitely wasn't the good guy.

He kept his head low and his mind full. He did everything he could to keep himself away from Scotty, but he could feel the man's absence in his bones. They may have only had one night together, but Drake hadn't realized just how much he had come to appreciate Scotty in his everyday life until Scotty wasn't there. Not in the same way.

He ached, and not even the scotch was able to dull the pain.

So he sat, and he watched as Scotty worked the bar, fulfilling the busy weekend crowd's drink orders. He moved with fluidity and grace, but Drake could tell he wasn't as relaxed as he appeared. He could see the tension in his shoulders, the tightness around his mouth and eyes. He put on a good show, flirting with the patrons and working the crowd, but Drake saw the burst of hope that invaded Scotty's eyes anytime their gazes would meet.

After downing the remainder of his drink, Drake pushed his glass away and stood. He wasn't getting anywhere pining for the dream he couldn't have. If he was going to stay at the club, he might as well go to his office and get some work done.

"Boss Man." The earpiece came alive with a cackle.

Drake reached to unmute his mic. "Yeah, Frankie?"

"Some more money is missing. I'm gonna take Jacob to go figure it out. You cool?"

Sighing, Drake nodded even though Frankie couldn't see him. "Yeah, we're cool. You bringing them back here?"

The mic crackled. "Doubt it. Too much money has gone missing. Tony wants some examples made."

Drake grimaced. "I hear ya. I've got the club covered."

Frankie signed off, and Drake muted his mic before pulling the piece out of his ear. He scowled at the plastic before stashing it in his pocket.

It was the fourth time in two weeks that they'd been called out due to missing funds. Drake didn't know what was going on, but whoever Frankie was after was going to be in a world of hurt.

Drake walked to his office. His path took him past the bar, and he tried to keep his head down, eyes averted, but he failed miserably and before he knew it, he was stumbling over his own feet as Scotty's eyes met his. His stomach clenched at the mix of hope, sadness, and disappointment he saw in them. He tore himself away, clenching his teeth, and trudged past to scurry into his small sanctuary.

However, hiding apparently wasn't an option with Scotty because it hadn't been ten minutes while he had sat and looked blankly at his computer screen, before Scotty barged into his office.

"Knocking is usually the appropriate gesture," Drake said, trying desperately not to look like having Scotty in his presence was in any way twisting his guts into a thousand pieces.

Scotty didn't say anything. Instead, he turned and closed the door with a soft snick, tapping the handle a couple of times before he seemed to come to a decision. Drake's breath caught in his chest as Scotty twisted the lock. His breath came out in a ragged pattern as Scotty, head still tilted down toward the lock, flashed wild eyes at him.

Swallowing, Drake stood on shaky legs. He had never once seen anything as sexy as Scotty standing in front of a locked door, the only exit, barring any escape, with his rumpled work uniform and a determined look in his eyes.

Jesus. There was no way he was going to be able to sleep tonight with this image in his head.

"What—" Drake was cut off as Scotty banged his fist against the door.

"Shut up," Scotty said through clenched teeth. He turned to face Drake square on, his determination clear in his stance. He pointed a finger at Drake. "This time *you* don't get to say anything. Okay? Just shut the hell up, because you aren't the only one with shit going on, and even though you seem to think so, you are not the one who gets to tell me what is or what is not too dangerous for *me*." He took two large steps forward, crossing half the distance between them before stopping again. "You said that I didn't know anything about you. Yeah, well, turnabout is fair play and you don't know anything about me either!"

The raw emotion radiating from Scotty filled the room. His anger was thick, but even more than that was the underlying... hurt? Was that what Drake was seeing? The anger was palpable, but there was more to it than that; that much was obvious. It was rare that Drake had ever seen Scotty upset or angry, and now he was getting it up close and personal.

But it didn't make sense to Drake. He didn't do anything to hurt Scotty. He just needed to keep him safe. Keep him out of the line of fire. The man wasn't cut out for the darkness involved in Drake's life. He wasn't hard and broken, but light and optimistic. He was everything Drake could have been if his family hadn't been taken from him.

He was the epitome of what Drake wished he could be. But it was too late for Drake now. He was in too deep. It didn't mean that he had to take Scotty down with him.

Steeling himself, Drake walked around his desk. "I told you we weren't going to talk about this."

"And I told you to shut up," Scotty said, his voice low.

Drake raised an eyebrow. Shit, Scotty was hot like this, angry and exacting control. He had to look away from him, avert his eyes to regather himself. He couldn't let the arousal get to him. He was stronger than that.

Drake opened his mouth to speak again but stopped when Scotty arched a brow, then spoke over him.

"I don't know what it is exactly that made you so upset, but I want to get one thing clear, okay?" Scotty's voice took on a hiss in anger.

Drake licked his suddenly dry lips. A fine tremor had begun in his knees and was slowly working its way up his body.

"You aren't a bad guy, Drake. You might be in a bad way right now, you might be mixed up in something bigger than you, but what I see is not the workings of a criminal."

"How would you know that?" Drake's voice didn't come out much louder than a whisper.

Scotty took a couple of steps closer so he was now standing toe-to-toe with Drake. He didn't touch him, just stood a breath's width apart never looking away from Drake's eyes.

"Because I know you. I've been watching you since the moment I started working here. Hell, I even considered you a friend before anything happened. Outside of the last couple of weeks, you only drink when you have to do something you don't want to do, and that's generally only after you do something with Frankie. If you were really as bad as you claim to be, you wouldn't be drinking away the guilt. You wouldn't be trying to protect me!"

Drake let his eyes drop. He couldn't look at him any longer. If he did, he would give in, and that would be bad. He had worked too hard to get this far to let it all go crashing around his feet. Or worse.

"Scotty, please." Drake tried to turn away, but Scotty's hand on his shoulder stopped him.

"No, I told you it was my turn." Scotty's voice was no longer as thick with anger as it had been. Now, it was softer, endearing. "Look me in the eye and tell me you are a bad guy. Do it."

Drake shuddered out a breath. He could do this, because it would be the truth. Lifting his chin to look Scotty directly in the eye, he spoke without any inflection. "I'm a bad guy."

He may not be the worst guy, he might not be the baddest guy, but in the grand scheme of things, he definitely wasn't a good guy. He had blood on his hands.

Scotty searched his eyes. "You don't believe that."

Drake worked hard to keep his voice even and his face blank. "I don't have to believe it because it's the truth."

Reaching up, Scotty placed a hand on Drake's cheek, and Drake, for the life of him, tried to ignore the scorching heat that blazed through those fingers and straight into his gut. It took all the willpower he had not to nuzzle against the warm flesh. But he had to stand firm.

"I don't know what you think you know, but I can tell you for certain that if anyone ever hears anything you just said, you won't live long enough to regret it."

Scotty let his hand fall back to his side. "You know, you can threaten me all you want, but it's hard to be frightened of someone who is doing everything in their power to keep me out of danger. You can push me away all you want, but it's not going to stop me from caring about you. I think I'm falling for you, Drake, and...." Scotty trailed off, his eyes wide with surprise at his own words. And that was it; that was the turning point.

His gaze still locked on Scotty, Drake felt his tenacity diminish. In fact, those words threw him into a vortex of happy stupefaction. Because as much as he wanted to ignore it, as much as he wanted to just push Scotty away, he couldn't, because he was falling for him too. Drake was positive that the look of bewilderment on Scotty's face at the confession was mirrored in his own expression.

Drake's shoulders slumped as he lost all resolve. Closing his eyes tight, he dragged a hand through his hair. "Goddammit, Scotty."

The words fell out of his mouth without any force behind them. The only thing that kept him from cursing again, from telling off the powers that be for their horrible timing, was Scotty's warm lips pressed hungrily to his own.

The kiss was rough, hard, a test of wills with lips, tongue, and teeth. It started with their mouths but soon encompassed their entire bodies. Drake had his arms wrapped around Scotty's chest, pulling him as tight to him as was possible while allowing them enough use of their lungs. He trailed his hands along Scotty's back, feeling his taut muscles that flexed with each movement of his own arms exploring and devouring Drake.

"This is not a good idea," Drake managed to say when Scotty had pulled back enough to work on the buttons of his work shirt.

"Too late," Scotty said, impatiently struggling with his shirt. Then with a growl of irritation, Scotty pulled and the last few buttons snapped off, flying in different directions.

"Jesus," Drake gasped. "That was incredibly hot."

Scotty shook the last bit of fabric off his arms and reached out to pull Drake's shirt over his head. But instead of removing the shirt from Drake's body, he pushed it over his head and let his settle behind Drake's neck, keeping his arms loosely secured behind him.

"What did I say about talking?" Scotty said, using his hand to push Drake back against his desk.

Feeling the edge press against his thigh, Drake let himself fall back, pushing anything that would encumber him onto the floor. He landed awkwardly, with his bound arms behind him not allowing him to lie flat. But Scotty didn't allow him to shift into a more comfortable position. Instead he followed him down, pressing him even farther into his awkward position, crushing their mouths together.

Drake's shoulder's protested against the rough straining they were enduring, but he ignored their complaint. He might feel the residual effect of it tomorrow, but that would just serve as a reminder of what they were doing today.

He had never been dominated before. Anytime he'd had the opportunity for power play in the bedroom, he had always just assumed the role of dominant, but now, with Scotty taking the lead, immobilizing his arms and taking what he wanted, Drake couldn't think of any reason to object.

Drake's body arched as Scotty's lips moved from his mouth, to his chin, down his neck to his collarbone, and then down to a peaked nipple. The helpless moan that escaped Drake's lips turned to a yelp of surprise when soft wet lips turned to teeth and gently nibbled his hard nub.

"Oh shit, that's good." Drake sighed, shifting his body to press more of himself against Scotty. He tried to touch him, to pull him closer, but tight fabric around his shoulders reminded him of his place. He fought against it tentatively but stopped when Scotty lifted his head and placed an admonishing finger on Drake's lips.

"Uh-uh," he said tracing Drake's lips with the pad of his finger. "You aren't in charge here."

Drake opened his mouth, allowing Scotty entry. He followed his finger with his tongue, sucking him, but he wanted more. He arched his body up, rubbing himself along Scotty's hardened erection.

"Please," Drake whimpered as Scotty moved back. He fought to keep their bodies pressed together but stopped when he realized Scotty wasn't pushing away, instead just moving enough to reach Drake's fly. His breath released in a whoosh as Scotty simultaneously undid his pants and rubbed him through the rough fabric.

Not soon enough, he was free and his pants were tangled around his ankles, caught on his shoes. He whimpered again as Scotty pushed himself back and off the table. He moved to follow him, but Scotty's hand on his shoulder pressed him back down.

"I just want to look at you." Scotty stood back, taking in the view. Drake could imagine what he looked like, draped over his desk, his own clothes used as bonds, helpless and desperate for more. The indisputable look of longing on Scotty's face only added to the image, and Drake struggled to keep himself on the desk where Scotty wanted him.

"You are so beautiful." The words worked their way into Drake's ears and rested in his chest, where he felt them warm him considerably. Jesus, he had never expected to feel anything like this.

Finally, Scotty quickly finished undressing himself and came back to Drake. He crawled up on the desk to straddle him, their cocks knocking together, making Drake jump and crave more.

Leaning down, Scotty trapped their leaking dicks between their bodies, rubbing them along each other and along both their bellies. He captured Drake's lips with his once again. Then in a tangle of movements, Scotty pulled at the fabric holding Drake's arms at bay, maneuvering it down until Drake could fling it away and finally use his arms to pull Scotty closer to him, crushing their bodies together.

They continued to rut against each other, a tangle of limbs and deep moans. But after being held back for so long, Drake couldn't resist any longer. Pushing his hand between them, he grabbed their dancing cocks. Scotty shuddered as he used his fingers to trace along the head to gather some of the leaking fluid. Then he gripped them both together and started jerking them off.

Drake's movements sped up as his body tensed, preparing for release, and Scotty, unable to hold off any longer, convulsed through his own release as Drake followed closely behind.

Scotty collapsed back down across Drake's chest. They lay there, each working to catch their breath and regain their strength.

"Holy shit," Drake said with a laugh. "That was some of the best makeup sex I've ever had."

Scotty grinned, his head still resting on Drake's chest. "I'll say. I don't know if I can move yet."

"Yeah, but—" Drake shifted, reaching behind him, trying to dig something out. He pulled out a spiral-bound notebook and threw it to the floor. "That has been digging into my back."

"I guess I should let you up, huh? Anything else digging into you?"

Drake shifted his weight from side to side. "I think there's a pen there somewhere too."

Snorting out a laugh, Scotty pushed himself up so he could regain his feet. Once he was up, Drake sat up and rubbed at his back where two pens, a sticky-note pad, and a letter opener had all made indents. Miraculously, the tissue box Drake kept on the side of his desk was still there, so he pulled out a couple of tissues to hand to Scotty, then a few more for himself.

"I probably should, um, see if I have an extra shirt in my car," Scotty said, putting his pants back on and then slipping his arms into his shirt.

Drake stood, pulling up his own pants, buttoning them as he approached Scotty. He reached for Scotty's shirt and felt along the placket, smiling at the spots where the buttons should have been. Using the material as a lever, he tugged Scotty, who stumbled into him. Their bare chests bumped together.

"Hi." Drake smiled, their lips a breath width apart.

Scotty flicked his tongue over Drake's lips in a wet nuzzle. "Hi," he replied as their eyes firmly met.

"I think that maybe we should take the rest of the day off," Drake suggested, his voice wavering in a way that completely gave away how totally turned on he was.

The corner of Scotty's lip lifted. "And how exactly would we explain that one?"

Drake shrugged. "Well, I'm the boss and do whatever I want, and you, well, you aren't dressed appropriately for work, so I had to send you home."

Scotty scoffed, almost pushing Drake away, but Drake didn't let him, holding him close. "As if anyone would believe that!"

Laughing, Drake buttoned the few buttons left on Scotty's shirt before brushing their lips together. "Okay, fine, you aren't feeling well."

Scotty pressed their lips together once more. "That's more like it."

Their kiss was slow and explorative. They didn't need to be rough, fast, and passionate. Instead they explored each other and enjoyed the feeling of warm lips and wet tongues.

"Come to my place?" Drake asked, reluctant to create distance between them.

Scotty pressed a hand to Drake's chest, pushing him back, not far, but far enough that he could look at him. Scotty's eyes searched his. "You're sure?"

Drake returned his gaze, not allowing the panic in the pit of his belly to expel into the rest of him. It was too late to turn back now. Scotty couldn't un-know anything he already knew, but maybe if he understood the danger he was in, then he would understand why Drake needed him to keep his distance.

"I want you to," Drake said not breaking eye contact. "I think maybe it's time for you to know what's going on."

The words sounded even and sincere as he said them, but Drake could feel the uncertainty lying underneath. Once the truth was out there, once Scotty saw what was actually going on, he would realize he couldn't be a part of Drake's life, that it was too dangerous for him to be involved. But even though days ago Drake had been able to let Scotty go—it had hurt and he'd felt miserable but he'd been able to do it—now he couldn't imagine Scotty walking away. Their relationship had grown in that short amount of time, and Drake wasn't sure if he had the strength to let it go.

CHAPTER 16

DRAKE MESSED around with the things scattered on his desk. He had been sitting there for the last twenty minutes, which had felt like an eternity, as he watched the clock tick away the seconds. And even though it felt like torture and wasted minutes that he could be spending wrapped around Scotty, he had to do it. They were playing it like a covert meeting, like you used to do in school when you'd meet in the bathroom for a quickie. Scotty left first, pulling on a jacket that Drake had stashed away in the back of the office to cover his gaping placket. He would go out and tell the girls that he had to go home because he wasn't feeling well and he'd cleared it with the boss. Then after he left, Drake would make a point to make some rounds, make sure everything was hunky-dory, then follow Scotty out. They'd meet back at his place, and since Scotty had to take the train, Drake would probably beat him there even though he was leaving later.

He couldn't keep the stupid grin off his face; he felt like such a schoolboy. He was playing hooky with his secret lover. It was such a clichéd and overused concept, and he would have laughed at anyone who had ever dreamed of being in such a situation. But now that he was experiencing it, it wasn't all that bad. In fact, he would even go down as saying it was downright sexy. The anticipation alone was driving Drake up a wall, but add the secrecy to it, sprinkle on a little danger, and it was all Drake could do to keep from running out the door and speeding all the way to his condo.

He could control himself. He just needed to wait another five minutes to be sure Scotty was gone before making his rounds. He passed the time by fiddling with the items on his desk, smiling idiotically at the notebook that had only an hour earlier been digging into his skin hard enough to pull him out of a very nice afterglow. Using his nail, he plucked along the spiral, imagining that he could still feel the heat of their bodies embossed in the metal.

God, he was being such an idiot right now. But didn't he deserve it? Didn't he deserve just a little taste of a normal life? One-night stands had been his only relationships, that and whatever the hell he and Natasha had shared, which still confused him and kind of grossed him out at the same time. He'd thought that was the only type of relationship he would ever have, but somehow, Scotty had drifted past that mark, and even though Drake had tried to keep him away, Scotty remained. It was probably too much to hope for that they could get through this and stay together. Maybe Scotty would have to go away and hide for a while until Drake finished what he had to do, or maybe Drake's life would catch up with him and he would get dragged down along with the cartel and end up in prison. Maybe Scotty would be waiting for him at the end of each of those scenarios. Maybe he would be at his side.

Uh! Drake pushed his chair back and stood. He had to get out of this office. The sex was obviously messing with his brain, making him a romantic when he had no right to be.

He glanced at the clock. Okay, an acceptable amount of time had passed for him to go out and make his rounds. Gathering up a few of his things, he made sure to grab his keys before heading toward the door.

"Drake!" The voice came from behind Drake, surprising him. He jumped and turned toward the back door to see Jacob struggling his way through with a very saggy, very heavy, very bloody Frankie leaning against him. "You aren't wearing your earpiece again!"

Drake ran for the door, pulling one of Frankie's arms over his shoulder to help guide the man into the building. "What the hell happened?" he shouted, and they pushed open his office door and headed into the back room to lay Frankie down on the table that only weeks earlier had supported Hyde.

"Some dumbass junkies, that's what happened," Frankie gasped as he positioned himself on the table more comfortably.

Drake looked around for something to help stop the blood flowing from Frankie's shoulder. He grabbed some paper towels off a rack and pushed the entire roll in the general area, hoping it was enough to at least curtail the blood flow.

"Jacob, go get some of those towels from the storeroom," Drake demanded as he searched for other wounds along Frankie's body.

"On it," Jacob said, jumping to action.

"Did anyone call Doc?" Drake asked, using his hand to put pressure on another wound lower on Frankie's abdomen.

"He's on his way!" Jacob shouted back as he hurried out of the back room.

As soon as they were on their own, Drake met Frankie's gaze. The man was bleeding out, but he still looked like one mean motherfucker. Drake had no doubt Frankie could still beat him down, even with only a portion of his blood intact.

"Jesus, Frankie! We've gone years without this kind of mess and now we've had two in just a little over a month? What the hell?"

Frankie coughed and a speckle of blood landed on his cheek. He winced against some pain, and Drake noted that his teeth were pink from blood in his mouth. Drake frowned; it had to be coming from his gut wound, which meant the bullet had probably nicked something vital. Hopefully Doc wasn't too far away. Drake didn't know much about anatomy, but he figured blood in the mouth wasn't a good sign.

Shit. He was not cut out to do this.

"Listen," Frankie said, trying unsuccessfully to pull Drake down by his shirt. Drake leaned closer. "Something isn't right. We've got a snitch. You gotta tell Tony."

The words were like lightning through Drake's nerve endings. He could feel the blood draining from his face, even as his knees took a small dip from a sudden weakness.

Shit, shit, shit. It was over—they knew, if they were onto him. He was going to be the next person to die in this room. They knew, they…. Wait.

"Every time, Boss Man. Cops are there every time. Not right. Money's missing, cops are there. Not right."

They knew, except they didn't know. Frankie wasn't accusing him; Frankie was warning him, telling him to pass it on. They had a mole, but they didn't know who.

Drake's strength returned to him at that realization. They didn't know it was him. He was still okay. Maybe not for long, but that just moved up his timetable. They might find out soon, but they didn't know yet.

But Drake stopped his inner monologue. He hadn't called in any tips for the cops since the drug house and Willy. He hadn't had anything big enough and worthwhile enough to risk the exposure, so he hadn't made any calls. That meant that someone else was calling in tips. There was someone else working behind the scenes to bring down the cartel.

"Cops everywhere and not the ones on the take," Frankie gasped out. He arched against the pain but then lay back again as if he were just resting.

Drake shook his head. "Who could it be?"

Frankie shrugged with a grimace. "Could be anyone."

"Doc's here!" Jacob called as he came rushing back into the room, followed by Doc and one of his assistants. "You still alive, Frankie?"

Frankie coughed with what Drake suspiciously considered a laugh, and his tense shoulders relaxed. If Frankie was keeping his sense of humor, then maybe he wasn't as far gone as Drake had thought. Maybe now that Doc was here, Drake wouldn't have to witness another death in the back room of his office.

Drake stepped back to give Doc and his assistant space and looked down at the blood on his hands. It still made him light-headed to see his fingers caked in the deep red fluid, but this time he wasn't panicking about it. This time the blood didn't mean death.

CHAPTER 17

WHEN DRAKE'S car lights flashed over Scotty sitting on his steps as he pulled in, he automatically felt his nerves begin to calm. He hadn't been sure if Scotty would still be here waiting. It wasn't until he saw him sitting propped against his vestibule that he realized how much he had been looking forward to him. No, more than that, needed him.

Drake parked, and before he had his doors unlocked, Scotty was there. With shaky hands, Drake opened his door and stood. Scotty had come to meet him, most likely planning on continuing into the next chapter of what they had started at the club, but as he took in Drake's blood-splattered clothing, he stopped.

"What happened? Are you okay?"

Looking down at himself, Drake nodded. "Yeah, I'm fine. I mean, I'm not fine, but I'm okay. Or...." Drake swallowed, then finished. "It's not my blood."

Scotty's face was a mask of concern, his eyes wide and brow raised. He reached like he wanted to touch Drake but pulled back at the last second as if unsure.

This would be the telling point, Drake thought. If Scotty freaked out and ran, then there was no way he would last in this game.

"Maybe we should, uh—" Drake gestured toward his front door. "—finish this conversation inside? If you want, I mean."

Drake swallowed hard. He wasn't sure what he wanted Scotty's answer to be. Of course, he wanted him to come in so they could talk and explore their relationship a little further, but he also wanted him to cut and run. The best thing that could happen for Scotty would be for him to throw his hands up in the air, say "fuck it," and book it out of there as fast as his feet could carry him. But just the thought of him leaving made Drake's guts feel as if they were being twisted.

Scotty took a step back toward the door with a hesitant smile. "Um, yeah, that's probably a good idea."

With a sigh of relief mixed with grief, Drake unlocked his door. As soon as he crossed the threshold, he pulled his shirt off, careful to make sure the blood spatter didn't touch his face. After wrapping the shirt into a ball, he walked into the kitchen and threw it into the trash. Even if he could get the stains out of it, he would never be able to wear the shirt again anyway. The shirt he'd been wearing when Hyde had died had been burned, just in case, but with Frankie on the mend, Drake felt it was safe to just trash this one.

Scotty followed him silently. He didn't say anything as Drake threw his shirt into the garbage, and he didn't say anything as Drake pulled a bottle of scotch from a corner cabinet and filled his tumbler.

Drake pointed at the bottle, asking if Scotty wanted any, but of course Scotty refused. Shrugging, Drake put the glass to his lips and let the liquid burn its way down his throat, warming his entire body as it made its descent. Drake drained the glass, poured just a finger more, and capped the bottle. Then with glass in hand, he turned to Scotty.

"This wasn't how I wanted this evening to pan out."

Scotty nodded with a slight smile. "Yeah, no kidding."

Drake took a sip from his glass. "You don't have to stay. I mean—" Drake cleared his throat. "—I would understand if you wanted to leave."

"No, no, I want to know what happened." Scotty licked his lips, then lifted his eyes to meet Drake's. "If you want to tell me, I would like to know what happened."

Drake swirled the liquid in his glass for a moment. He wanted Scotty to stay. He needed him to stay, but he didn't want to ask him to stay. That made him more liable for any danger that Scotty would be in. But…. "I want to tell you everything."

The words were out before he could stop them, and to be perfectly honest, he wasn't sure if he would have stopped them if he could. He had been on his own for so long, the little man against the giant, that it was a relief to finally have someone to share it with.

"I need to take a shower," Drake said, "I, uh, I shouldn't be long, so go ahead and make yourself at home."

Scotty nodded. "Um, yeah, sure."

Drake pointed to the fridge. "Go ahead and help yourself to anything in the fridge. I don't know what I have in there but, ya know, have at it."

"Okay, thanks." Scotty pulled out a chair from the table in the kitchen and sat down.

Drake didn't leave right away. He couldn't seem to get himself to move. His need to get the feeling of blood off his skin and the longing to not leave Scotty's sight were warring it out, but in the end, the need to be sanitary won. With a small nod, Drake turned and headed for his bedroom.

Jesus, the hot water felt so good that even with Scotty waiting for him in the kitchen, Drake was reluctant to leave. The almost scalding fluid beating down on his taut muscles released some of his pent-up tension and helped to smooth away the anxiety of seeing Frankie's body bleeding on the table.

Even though the stain was long gone, it didn't stop Drake from feeling the dirty remnants of blood on him. He had it on his hands, and there wasn't enough hot water in the world to clean them. And as much as he didn't want to drag Scotty into it, didn't want to dirty his hands with more innocent blood, he couldn't find the strength to push him away any longer.

After pulling on a pair of his most comfortable sweatpants and a long-sleeved tee, he followed his nose back to the kitchen. He didn't know what Scotty had found to make, but whatever it was, it smelled delicious. Drake hadn't been sure if he would be able to eat with all the stress of the day, but the fragrant smell called to him anyway.

Scotty stood at the stove using a spatula to push food around in a frying pan. Drake leaned against the doorframe and watched him work. It was definitely a view he could get used to seeing. Scotty had lost his work shirt altogether and was bare-chested. Drake couldn't help but admire the way the muscles in Scotty's back worked under his skin, rippling his body as he moved.

"I didn't know if you would want to eat, but I found stuff for omelets and figured it was probably a safe bet."

Drake grinned. Scotty hadn't even turned around to see if he was there before talking to him. "Honestly, I wasn't sure I would be able to eat, but it smells delicious."

Scotty pulled a plate from the counter over and dished some egg on it. He tossed on two pieces of toast he had stacked next to the toaster, turned, and set the plate down on the small dining table. "Bon appétit."

Drake sat down in front of his served plate and picked up his fork. The food looked like a normal omelet, but it smelled so much more delicious. He cut off a small piece and took the first bite.

Scotty set his plate down at the seat next to Drake and plopped down. He smiled at Drake's moan of pleasure.

"It's good?" Scotty asked, forking his own bite.

Drake nodded enthusiastically. "That is probably the best omelet I've ever tasted."

Laughing, Scotty took his own bite and chewed with a critical tilt of his head. "Eh, it's not bad. It's hard cooking in someone else's kitchen."

"Not bad?" Drake said, incredulous. "I didn't even know omelets could taste like this! Where in the world did you learn to cook, and why aren't you a chef?"

Scotty stood suddenly. "I forgot to get us drinks. You want anything?"

Drake gestured with his hand, waving for Scotty to sit back down. "It's my house. I am supposed to be the one worried about serving us drinks. I'll get it. I don't know what I have—probably milk, water, and scotch."

Scotty sank back into his chair, tsking as Drake got up. Drake ignored his blatant disapproval and opened the fridge. He clicked his tongue at the sparse shelves. "I could make coffee."

"Water would be fine for me, thanks," Scotty said.

Drake filled two glasses with water and sat back down. "You didn't answer my question."

"Hmm?" Scotty said taking a long drink.

"Why aren't you a chef?"

"I like to cook. It's something I do as a hobby and as a stress relief." He leaned back in his chair as he spoke. "I didn't want to take the fun out of it by making it a job. I watch those shows with the chefs on them acting all crazy in a kitchen, and I didn't want cooking to be like that for me."

"Oh yes, those chefs from hell or whatever," Drake said with a laugh. "I can't imagine you ever being able to pull that domineering bullshit off."

Scotty smirked. "Can't see me taking control, can you?" He waggled his eyebrows.

Drake felt a blush creep up his cheeks at the memory of Scotty from just hours earlier. He cleared his throat. "Not as an overbearing douchebag."

"Yeah, me either, another reason I didn't do it."

Drake used his toast to pick up the last remaining pieces of his eggs. "Well, consider me glad that your path led you to the bartending gig, otherwise I might never have had the opportunity to eat these eggs, and that would have been a crime."

"So, what about you? What hobbies do you have?" Scotty propped both elbows on the table, leaning forward.

Drake shifted uncomfortably in his chair. Hobbies? Like he had time for hobbies or doing anything just for the fun of it?

"You mean, besides finding remedies to get blood out of clothes?" Drake muttered. He kept his eyes on his plate. He didn't want to see what Scotty must think of him.

There was a long silence before Scotty spoke. "Peroxide, I have heard, is a great stain remover," Scotty said softly.

"I will give it a try."

Drake fidgeted in the long silence that followed. He contemplated getting up and walking out of the room in silence; he thought about telling Scotty everything right then and letting the words flow out of him like a waterfall. But instead, he stayed quiet, eyes downcast. He was so lost in his own thoughts that he startled when Scotty touched a finger to Drake's chin, pulling Drake's gaze up to meet his. Scotty didn't say anything as their eyes met. Drake searched for the alarm and disgust he had expected to find but instead found a calm acceptance. Drake let out a relieved breath at that discovery.

Scotty let his hand drop back to the table. "Besides that, what do you do?"

Clearing his throat, pulling himself out of that intense moment, Drake pushed his plate to the side. "I, uh, I don't really have any hobbies."

Scotty raised a questioning brow. "Everyone has to have at least one hobby. What's something that you do for you, just for you?"

Drake licked his lips uncertainly. The only thing he did for him was on the board in the other room. Other than that.... "Drink?"

"That is not a hobby; that's a vice."

"Well, that's the only thing I can think of."

"Reading? Writing? Painting? Drawing? Am I hitting on anything here?" Scotty asked.

"I used to read a lot. When I was younger, I was into comic books. I was a big fan of *The Amazing Spider-Man*. But that didn't really stick for long."

Scotty eyed Drake inquisitively. "How do you get through life without having any hobbies?"

Drake felt his nerves returning quickly. He had been enjoying having the lighthearted conversation but too soon it was already taking a turn down the darker path.

"I guess I do sort of have a hobby, but…." Drake let his voice trail off.

Scotty pursed his lips. "I'm sorry. I didn't mean to—"

"No, it's okay. I mean, it's why we're here anyway, right?"

"You don't have to tell me anything you don't want to." Scotty put his hand on Drake's arm for emphasis. "We don't have to do this tonight."

Drake looked down at Scotty's hand on his arm. Then closing his eyes, he swallowed hard. "No, if this, whatever this is between us, is going to continue, then you need to know what you're getting into."

Standing up, Drake took Scotty's hand in his and pulled him up. They stood facing each other for a couple of silent minutes. Drake was certain that Scotty would be able to hear his racing heart.

Then as if a silent cue was given, they moved out of the kitchen and down the hallway toward the room that Drake was certain he would never share with anyone. Even though there were only a few steps down the hall to the room, it felt like it took forever to get there, and when they stopped in front of the closed door, it felt as if they had suddenly materialized there. Drake's breaths became shallower as they approached the room, and Scotty put a reassuring hand on his shoulder.

"I never imagined that I would show anyone this part of my life." Drake stopped in front of the closed door. He licked dry lips. "Once we do this, once you know what's happening, we can't go back."

Drake turned so his back was to the closed door. His wide eyes met Scotty's in the dim light, and he searched for any sign that Scotty was unwilling to move forward.

"Once I tell you, you're in the thick of it. Do you understand that?"

Scotty never took his eyes from Drake's. Even with the danger hanging over their heads, his gaze never wavered. He put a hand to Drake's cheek, letting his thumb caress Drake's jawline.

"I'm not going anywhere."

Drake closed his eyes in a moment of grief, while simultaneously leaning into the comfort of Scotty's hand. Then with a deep breath, a rolling back of his shoulders, he turned around and pushed the door open.

Scotty followed Drake into his bedroom slowly. He moved cautiously, as if he didn't know what to expect. Drake walked across the room and opened the door to his walk-in closet. Flipping on the light, he glanced in to make sure his clothes were pushed to the side, then turned back to face Scotty, who was watching him uncertainly.

"This," Drake said, indicating the closet with a swing of his hand, "is my life's work, my job, my hobby, my reason for living."

Eyeing the closet warily, Scotty raised a brow. Drake watched him somberly. Looking back and forth between the open closet and Drake, he finally squared his shoulders and walked to the closet. He reached the door and took a last fleeting look at Drake, who stood near the foot of his bed, head down, before entering.

When Scotty disappeared, Drake collapsed onto the bed with a huff, his knees weak. He had never shared this part of himself with anyone, and having a living, breathing person in his most secret of secret places was messing with his lungs. The air felt heavier, as if he were trying to breathe through water. Putting his head down to his knees, he focused on his breathing, *breathe in, one, two, three, breathe out, one, two, three.*

Time passed. Drake had no idea if it had been three minutes, three seconds, or three hours before Scotty reappeared in the closet entryway. Drake sat tense, expecting the face that confronted him to be one of disgust, shock, and fear, but like always, Scotty surprised him.

Unable to meet Scotty's eyes, Drake lowered his chin, eyes on his knees. The silence grew around them, and for the first time Drake felt solace in the quiet. He didn't need to fill the void with rambling words. No, he had just shared the most private part of himself, and finally he felt comfortable enough to face the silence.

The bed next to him dipped as Scotty sat down, his thigh pressed lightly against Drake's. Warm fingers sought his and squeezed, taking Drake's breath away. Mustering courage, Drake looked up and met brilliant eyes.

"Tell me."

Drake let out a breath that hinged on the edge of a sob. Twisting his hand around, he flipped his palm up so they were now palm to palm, fingers entwined. He let the warmth sink into him, comfort him. Then before he could allow himself to think any further, he stood, releasing Scotty's hand reluctantly, and walked into the closet. He ignored the whiteboard, the notes, and the articles, and pushed his clothes to cover them. The smiling family stared back at him without a care in the world, and he caressed the photo before removing it from the nail on the wall.

Drake returned to Scotty, a hitch in his step. This was the last piece of himself he had left to give, and he couldn't think of anyone he wanted to share it with more. He sank down on the bed next to Scotty and held the framed photo out like an offering. Scotty took the photo gently, as if afraid that any sudden movement would frighten Drake, and truth be told, Drake wasn't sure if it wouldn't have. For years after he had roused from his coma, he'd been plagued with what the doctors diagnosed as PTSD and night terrors. The social workers and the staff of the hospital he'd been whisked away to under a new identity had all tried to tread carefully around him. The slightest noise or painful reminder of that horrible night would send him into a blind panic, usually resulting in an injury, most of the time himself, but every so often, it happened to someone who chanced to be near him.

The only thing that had helped him to get his symptoms under control was finding his purpose. Working tirelessly on a plan to exact his revenge had helped quell the panic and fear inside him. Once the blueprint had been embedded in his mind, he'd started to sleep more peacefully, and shadows at the corners of his eyes didn't make him jump out of his skin. He had tamed the fear, but he had not eradicated it. Not by a long shot, and he could feel the tingling grip of trepidation take hold of his deepest thoughts and begin its climb.

Scotty turned the photo in his hand, eyeing the happy, smiling faces with a frown. He ran a finger along the father in the photo and looked up at Drake.

"You look like him."

Drake had expected a lot of words to come out of Scotty's mouth, but those words, those few words that he never got to hear from anyone, choked him. He'd been prepared to tell his story, but instead his throat closed. Drake shot to his feet. He couldn't have this conversation sitting down. In fact, he couldn't have this conversation sober. Why hadn't he thought about grabbing his scotch before he came in?

Running trembling fingers through his hair, Drake paced. He didn't need to drink, and he was in control of his environment. His mind flew in a frenzy, and he hadn't realized that his breathing had quickened until he felt a soothing hand caress up his back. He stilled at the touch, allowing the warmth to spread through him, steady him.

Scotty pressed his body to Drake's back, easing his trembling. His lips found Drake's ear, and he murmured soothing sweet words that settled Drake's chest, giving his lungs room to breathe. After a handful of moments, Scotty coaxed Drake back to the bed and they sat, still touching, Scotty still pressed against him, a soothing tenderness amongst his pain.

Drake took a deep breath in, did his count, let it out.

"That picture was taken when I was nine years old. It was the last vacation I had with my family. Three months after that picture was taken, my father, mother, and sister were killed in a home invasion."

Scotty put a hand to his mouth but didn't say anything.

"Four men, dressed in black, broke in through the back door of our townhouse. My dad was with me in my bedroom because I was scared of some monsters under my bed. My sister was asleep in her room, and my mom was in my parents' room." Drake counted his breathing before continuing.

"My dad was reading a book to me, something about how monsters aren't real, when we heard the noises coming from downstairs. He told me to wait in my room, but I was too scared to be alone. So, as he went to check everything out, I followed behind.

"What happened next is so much a blur now that I can't be sure exactly how it all happened. What I clearly remember is that I saw a shadow move on the stairs, and because I was so worried about monsters, I cried out for my dad. The look he gave me when he turned to see me in the hallway right behind him is engraved in my mind. I will never be able to forget that look."

Stopping abruptly, Drake ran a hand over his face. "I need a drink. You need a drink? I'm going to get a drink."

Without waiting for an answer, Drake left Scotty to find his scotch. The air outside the bedroom was cooler, lighter. Stopping next to the door, he leaned against the wall and let his head fall back. He stared blankly up at the ceiling.

How was he going to get through this? How was telling Scotty any of this going to be okay? Right now, Scotty probably thought he was hooking up with a tough-as-nails drug dealer, but what he was *actually* getting was a screwed-in-the-head, bent-on-revenge, broken man with more baggage than Miss Piggy on a road trip.

Shit. What had he gotten himself into?

Hearing shuffling in the room behind him, Drake pulled himself upright. It was too late now; he couldn't go back from here. They'd passed the point of no return and were heading straight for Fuck Mountain.

He found a bottle of scotch sitting on the small cabinet he used as a mock bar in his living room. After unscrewing the cap, he took a long swig out of the bottle, before opening the cheap plywood door to pull out a glass. As soon as the burning fluid eased down his throat, his tension began to taper off. Taking another long swig, he pulled another glass out, just in case, and headed back into the room.

Scotty was no longer sitting on the bed but instead stood reading some newspaper clippings that Drake had yet to assemble on his wall. He cringed as Scotty flipped through them, lifting up the top article to see the ones below. Willy's smiling face stared back at him, and Drake couldn't get another drink fast enough.

He'd always been a firm believer that the faster you drank, the more the fluid was medicinal rather than a folly. Already he could feel the effect of it on the muscles in his back. They'd been stiff with tension, and now his ribs had loosened.

Scotty looked up from the newspapers, his eyes wide but still not accusatory, and watched as Drake set the glasses down and poured his drink.

Drake started to pour some into the glass for Scotty but stopped after Scotty gave a minute shake of his head. Sighing, he poured more into his glass. Scotty stayed at the desk, still watching him, his fingers lingering on the newspapers.

Drake took a long swallow, breathing out the smooth, burning sensation left on his tongue. *In, one, two, three, out, one, two, three.* Then he continued, voice rough. "So, uh, anyway, my dad didn't get a chance to do anything to help us, because instead of getting his weapon and calling for backup, he came for me."

Drake downed the rest of his glass and set it down with a loud crack on the table. Scotty jumped at the sound but didn't make another move.

"The shadow on the wall, it did turn out to be a monster, but it wasn't like anything I ever could have imagined then. The first man who came up the stairs already had his gun drawn. And while my dad could have been prepared, could have at least tried to get us out of there, he had taken care of me instead. He'd shoved me behind him and put out a hand in surrender. I remember that. I remember he had his hand out telling the man not to shoot, but the man in the mask didn't even give him a second glance. He shot him, three times in the chest."

Drake reached for the bottle and tried to pour some more scotch into his glass, but his hand trembled too much. Liquid sloshed, more hitting the table than the glass. Scotty reached out, laying his hands atop Drake's. Their eyes met and he gently removed Drake's fingers from the bottle. He kept the bottle in one hand while the other stayed on Drake's, offering a comforting touch. He ran his thumb over the back of Drake's hand soothingly.

After pouring a small amount into the glass, Scotty slid the bottle out of Drake's reach. Drake wanted to resent that action—he wanted to reach out and grab the bottle back from Scotty—but the look on Scotty's face wasn't malicious. He wasn't trying to hurt Drake; he was trying to help him. So, Drake put his glass to his lips and took a small sip, savored it, then swallowed.

"I screamed as he fell back on me. And while we laid there in a puddle of his blood, my mother and sister were dragged from their rooms by the other men. When my mom saw my dad, she screamed the worst scream I have ever heard in my life and fought against the men and got loose enough to try and save my sister. But nothing she did stopped them. Instead of just shooting her, they beat her. They beat her to a silence, and when they were done, they shot my sister in front of her and then turned the gun on her." The memory assaulted Drake, and he couldn't stand any longer. Telling the story for the first time in over a decade was taking its toll. His knees slackened and he started to droop, but Scotty rushed forward and put a steadying arm around him before he slipped to the floor. They stumbled together toward the bed, the soft mattress giving way under the weight of their bodies.

Drake crumpled on the bed. Pressing the heels of his hands into his eyes, he tried to obliterate the visual from his past, but no amount of damage to his eyes could erase what his brain had endured.

"Jesus," Scotty whispered. He petted Drake evenly, his hands a soothing rub against his back and along his arm.

Drake fought to pull himself out of his nightmare to look up at Scotty, to be strong. He hadn't wanted to be this weak. He knew he was stronger than this, but his voice cracked when he tried to speak, and he snapped his mouth shut. He hadn't cried about that night in a long time, and he wasn't going to cry now.

"I was still under my dad's cooling body, hiding, hoping they wouldn't notice me. I remember holding my breath so they wouldn't even be able to hear my breathing. I tried to lie completely still, but before they left, one of them spotted me." Drake wrapped his arms around himself. "He kneeled down and waved at me, like you would to a spooked kid lost in the park." Drake looked at Scotty, who stared back at him in horror. "The fucker waved at me! Then pulled his gun and shot me. I lost a kidney, a part of my intestines, eight months of consciousness, and my entire family from that single night."

Drake swallowed hard and looked away from Scotty. He let his chin fall to his chest and stretched the muscles in his back. Scotty's hands continued to move along his body, a beacon of comfort. Time passed and the silence thickened. Finally, Scotty gently claimed Drake's chin between his thumb and forefinger and turned Drake's head toward him. Their eyes met. "You know that it wasn't your fault, right?"

Drake laughed, a deep guttural sound, more a sob than a laugh really. "Trust me, I have been through enough counseling to know that none of it was my fault. That doesn't stop it from feeling like it was my fault. I can know it all I want, but the voice in the back of my head still wonders how things could have been different if I had just listened to my dad and stayed in bed."

"Maybe nothing would have been different."

Drake shrugged, a lifeless lift of shoulders. "Maybe." The word came out barely louder than a whisper.

Scotty slipped from the bed and dropped to his knees. Drake startled at the movement but couldn't go anywhere as Scotty shuffled the small distance to position himself in front of Drake. He cupped Drake's face in his hands. "You are an incredibly remarkable man."

Scotty brushed a hand up Drake's cheek, tracing his thumb under Drake's eye, pulling away a drop of moisture that Drake hadn't even realized he'd released.

"You pulled yourself out of the ashes and created a life for yourself. There are many others who wouldn't have been able to do that."

Drake caught Scotty's hand with his own, stopping the soothing caress. "Don't judge me yet. You haven't heard everything."

Instead of pulling his hand away, Scotty twisted his wrist so their fingers could interlace. He pulled their connected hands to his lips and laid a gentle kiss along their knuckles.

Drake sucked in a deep breath at the feel of Scotty's lips. The aching in his chest no longer originated from pain alone. Now, the ache had shifted and it felt like something else. Like something more.

Hope? Desire? Love?

"The Boredega cartel is the largest drug-running cartel in the Midwest. It's been growing strong since the late '80s and only getting bigger and more powerful. Over the years there have been multiple operations trying to bring the cartel down, but so far no one has been able to figure out where Boredega's headquarters are. As for the man, Boredega himself, it's become a popular theory that he doesn't even really exist.

"Multiple operations, multiple organizations, and no one can get far enough into the damn cartel to make a fucking dent. Every time someone thinks they're getting close, the whole investigation comes crashing in on them, usually taking everyone involved down with it."

Drake took the framed photo from the bed, where Scotty had placed it earlier. He turned it around, undid the back, and pulled out another smaller photo. He handed the picture to Scotty.

"That's my dad and his partner, Rouley. My dad was the lead investigator in a Boredega case. It was the investigation that had delved the deepest into the cartel, and they'd had a man in custody who had, for all intents and purposes, seemed the most likely candidate for Boredega. Before they could go to trial, before too much information could be unearthed, a sniper took out the proposed Boredega, and then slowly, every single person working on the case was killed in some fashion or another."

Scotty was still crouched at Drake's feet, one hand holding the photo while the other moved back and forth along Drake's forearm.

"When I woke up from my coma and my memory came back, I was a mess. It took years for me to be able to function like a human being again and even longer than that to be considered anything resembling normal. I grew up in witness protection and in the system. Basically, once the hospital deemed me sane enough to rejoin society, I was thrown into foster home after foster home and was just another damaged kid in a long line of equally forgotten and broken children."

Mouth dry, Drake eyed his bottle of scotch, but in order to get it he would have to break contact with Scotty, and he wasn't sure if he could take the isolation that would come with that. Distracting himself by running his fingers through Scotty's light hair, he ignored the bottle on the table.

"Since I woke up, the only thing I've been able to think about is Boredega. My entire life has led me to this," Drake said, indicating the closet. "I created contacts, made friends, found ways to change my identity. I got my inheritance when I turned twenty-one, and I invested it all in Semblance. I needed a tool to be useful, to get noticed." Drake huffed a derisive laugh. "It didn't take long for them to approach me."

Drake paused, the silence a heavy weight. "The only thing I have left is revenge. I always wondered why my entire family died and I lived, and the only thing that makes sense, any sense at all, is that I was spared so I could finally take them down."

Scotty sat tall on his knees. "Jesus, Drake!" he said emphatically, taking Drake's head in his hands. "Why haven't you gotten the police involved?"

"The police had their chance. They tried to take them down, and I lost my entire family for it."

Shaking his head, Scotty pulled Drake toward him, forcing him to look him straight in the eye. "You can't take down the entire cartel by yourself, Drake. You're one man infiltrating a trained army!"

Drake swallowed, diverting his eyes from Scotty's worried ones. "That's the point. What better way to take them out than to gain their trust, work my way through the ranks until I'm face-to-face with Boredega himself, and pull the trigger. They aren't expecting a single missile. They're always looking for the mass attack."

Scotty searched Drake's face. Drake wasn't sure what Scotty was looking for, but he was sure he didn't find it. Scotty's eyes dulled a little at the lack of confirmation he found. He tilted their heads so their foreheads were touching.

"You aren't planning on coming out of this alive, are you?"

Releasing a strangled breath, Drake shuddered at the bleakness of Scotty's voice. "I don't know if I would know how to live if I did somehow make it out alive."

Making a whimpering sound in the back of his throat, Scotty pulled Drake tight against him. Their lips met in a flurry of movement, both seeking reassurance and both looking for comfort. Although Drake desperately wanted to fall into the kiss, lose himself and not look back, he couldn't. He held a piece of himself back.

"I can teach you how to live. Let me teach you?" Scotty said, pulling back only far enough to say the words against Drake's lips. "Please, let me teach you."

A piece of Drake that was locked away, a piece of him that had been told that hope and love were not things he had a right to, pushed against its barricade. The sturdy walls felt the force of the wrecking ball at Scotty's words, but no matter how hard that piece of him tried to dislocate itself, it stayed trapped. For Drake had worked hard to weld its cage.

Unable to say anything, unable to do anything, unable to make anything better, Drake pressed his lips back to Scotty's and prayed to any god that would listen that he could keep Scotty safe.

CHAPTER 18

CLOSING THE medicine cabinet door, Drake stared at his reflection. He hardly recognized the man looking back at him. There was something more to him than he ever remembered seeing before. Was it happiness?

That couldn't possibly be it. Happiness was something that he thought lost to him. Would he know it if he did feel it? How could he since happiness had been such a long-ago and distant pleasure?

After Drake's confession, he and Scotty had lain in bed and held each other. Or rather, Scotty had held Drake, offered him comfort that Drake hadn't realized he needed until then. Scotty soothed him while he grieved in a way he hadn't grieved for his family in a long time, tears and heartache replacing his anger and need for vengeance. Somehow that closeness, that ability to be held, had calmed something deep within him. The raging beast deep in his soul, for once, in so long many years, finally felt calm, at rest.

Tinkering from the kitchen made Drake smile. The sounds of a shared home were another one of those things he never thought possible for him, but hearing cabinet doors open and shut and the delightful smell of something waft from the kitchen brought another shred of lightness to his chest.

Taking another long look at the stranger in the mirror, Drake let a hopeful smile touch his lips before turning to follow the delicious scents.

"I don't understand how you can make something smell that good with the food I have in the kitchen."

Scotty turned slightly to look back at Drake with a wide smile before returning to his work of mixing up a batter of some kind.

"What can I say? It's a God-given talent."

Approaching Scotty from behind, Drake snaked his arms around his chest, pulling their bodies tight. "What are you making?"

"Banana nut pancakes."

Drake whistled. "I had no idea I even had the ingredients for that."

Scotty shrugged. "Eh, I may have fudged some parts of it by using a Jiffy mix you had stashed away."

"How dare you? You are a cooking liar and a cheat."

Laughing, Scotty turned his head and pressed a quick kiss to Drake's cheek. "When the national cooking board comes to take me away and throw me into pancake jail, will you visit me?"

Drake rested his chin on Scotty's shoulder. "Hell, if you keep cooking like this, baby, I will bust you outta that place."

Scotty sighed dramatically. "Mama always said the way to a man's heart was through his belly."

Leaving a chaste kiss behind Scotty's ear, Drake moved to set the table. "Your mother sounds like a smart woman."

Setting the table for two made a part of Drake's chest hum. Placing a hand above his heart, he massaged his chest, back and forth, letting the truth of his actions settle in. He wasn't just a "me" any longer. By setting down that second place setting, by allowing the man who was now moving comfortably through his kitchen into his home, into his *life*, he had become an "us."

The thought brought a rush of butterflies into his belly and a lightness to his head. He had to place a hand on the table to keep standing straight.

But along with the giddiness, the joy at having something he never thought was possible, was a black fog of panic. He pushed it down and away before it could fully materialize and take away this moment, this time he had to feel completely and utterly unlike himself.

"Okay, let's eat," Scotty said, putting a plate of heaping pancakes on the table. He paused at Drake's side, looking him up and down, taking in Drake's dramatic position. "Are you okay?"

Letting out a breath with a laugh, Drake leaned forward to kiss Scotty softly on the lips. Smiling, he said, "Yeah, I think I am."

Scotty placed a hand on top of Drake's on the table, his fingers caressing over his skin, once, twice, and then he moved away enough to sit down. He picked up the serving fork and stabbed two pancakes, placing them on Drake's plate.

Taking the cue, Drake sat down and watched as Scotty served them both. Plates loaded, they ate in a peaceful silence that was only broken by the occasional moan of delicious pleasure.

This was the life Drake had missed, the contented life. The share the morning with someone and enjoy breakfast life. Holding someone all night and talking. Trusting someone enough to tell your deepest darkest secrets to and still have them in your arms in the morning.

It was almost too much to believe, almost too good to be true, but maybe, just maybe, his life could be more than anger and rage. Maybe he could find a way to sink into the bottom of the cesspool with the rest of the monsters and see the sunrise. Maybe he could be someone that he could be proud of, that Scotty could be proud of.

"Hello," the voice interrupted Drake's thoughts, snapping him back to reality. "Earth to Drake. You in there?"

Drake shook his head with a smile. "Um, yeah, sorry. What did you say?"

"I said that I had to go home and get new clothes before work, since my shirt was... irreparably damaged yesterday."

"It was, wasn't it?" Drake smirked with a cocky raise of his brow.

"Um-hmm, and once I sew the buttons back on it, I might even damage it again."

"You're going to sew the buttons back onto it?"

Scotty scoffed, "Really? That's what you chose to focus on in that statement?"

"I'm just saying that those shirts really aren't that expensive." Drake dodged Scotty's smack with a grin. "We could just buy a pack of them."

"Just for that, you can stay here and wash dishes while I go take a shower." Scotty pushed away from the table.

Drake bit his lip. "But I need a shower too."

With a smug grin, Scotty leaned down so their noses were practically touching. He nuzzled forward, giving an eskimo kiss. "You should have thought of that before you opened your big mouth."

"But you like it when I open my big mouth."

Scotty pressed forward so their lips were touching and, true to his word, groaned when Drake opened his lips so his tongue could slide through. What had started off as tender and light, quickly grew deeper and hotter. It was a battle of tongues and teeth where there was no winner.

"Wait." Scotty pushed Drake back with his hand, their lips parting roughly. "I... wait."

Drake stopped, and the distance between them, though only inches apart, felt vast. The happy buzz still humming along in his chest stuttered at the distant look in Scotty's eyes.

"What? What is it?" Drake asked. The black fog rose from its depth, threatening to resurface.

Scotty let his chin drop for a moment, his light hair brushing against Drake's face as he hid his face from him. But Drake had seen his expression. He had seen hesitancy, uneasiness, emotions Drake wasn't sure he had ever seen on Scotty's face before. Drake swallowed against a gorge in his throat at the man's sudden retreat.

"I need to…," Scotty said, voice so quiet Drake could hardly hear him. He'd stopped before he could finish his sentence, and Drake took a step back, trying to give him room to gather himself, but Scotty's grip didn't loosen. Instead, he pulled Drake closer. Bringing his head back up, Scotty searched Drake's eyes. Drake didn't know what he found there, but whatever it was made Scotty pull him even closer, and their lips were once again pressed firmly together.

The kiss went on and on, and Drake, back in his happy state with the fog once again repressed, never wanted it to end.

After what was surely only moments but felt like an eternity—also over too soon—Scotty pulled away. This time his eyes found Drake's, and there was no hesitation or reluctance in his expression. Licking his bottom lip, Scotty shivered. "What were we talking about?"

Drake's heart pounded. "You were saying that I couldn't take a shower with you."

"Well," Scotty said, pulling Drake to his feet, "that was a very stupid idea."

CHAPTER 19

"YOU SEEM chipper today," Julie quirked, brushing back her long, wavy locks before pulling out a tray of glasses to stack behind the bar.

Drake tried to hold back his grin but failed miserably. "I'm doing all right."

"Hmm, I wonder how Scotty will be doing...." Julie's voice faded off.

Surprise ignited along Drake's spine, but he smothered it before it could form on his face. He tilted his head questioningly. "Yeah, I hope he's feeling better."

With a roll of her eyes, Julie pulled a list from her apron pocket and handed it to Drake. "This is the inventory list from last night. We should be fine for now, but we're going to need a full restock before the weekend. We had calls about at least two bachelorette parties that will be coming."

"Yeah? That's good. I'll make sure to schedule some extra hands for the weekend, then." Drake took the list and looked it over, nodding. "Everything went okay last night?"

Julie shrugged. "More of the usual. The only weird thing was some big guy came in and asked for you or Jacob. They went and talked in your office for a while. I didn't know what it was about, and I was going to call you, but then they both left."

Drake stilled. "They met in my office?"

"Yeah, I was going to tell Jacob that he couldn't have guests, especially in your office, but he left before I had a chance."

Drake shook off the chill that coursed through his veins. It probably had been someone who had come to see about Frankie. Usually they only did business like that through the back entrance, but if the person hadn't been to the club before, they might not have known. It was fine.

"Nah, it's fine. No biggie." Drake smiled reassuringly. "I'm going to go put in this order and let you finish getting ready."

"Sure thing, Boss." Julie gave him quick salute, ticking a single finger from her forehead before returning to preparing her station.

Walking back to his office, Drake couldn't help but feel a little nervous at the fact that Jacob had met with someone there. Had they brought someone else in while Frankie was out of commission? Frankie had said something about there being a narc in the organization. Maybe he had already passed that information to Tony, and now they were bringing in people to check it out.

The thought was enough to raise the hair on his arms.

Drake never had anything incriminating at the club. He kept everything in his room, and the only person to ever see that was Scotty.

Drake pushed open his office door and stopped. Jacob was sitting at his desk, drawers open, riffling through the folders.

"What are you doing?"

Jacob looked up as Drake pushed through the door, his face pulled into a smug tilt of lips. "Drake, you missed a hell of a meeting yesterday. Too bad you'd already left for the night."

Keeping his shoulders back and head tall, Drake walked to his desk, dropping his paperwork. "That doesn't sound like an answer to me."

Putting both elbows on Drake's desk, Jacob leaned forward, tapping his fingertips together. "Well, with Frankie being out of commission, Tony put me in charge. That's what he came here to do yesterday."

A chill ran down Drake's back, but he tried to school his features. It made sense that Tony would put his nephew in charge with Frankie out, but Drake couldn't help but feel a little offended at the jump in the chain of command.

Meeting Jacob's arrogant gaze with a glare of his own, Drake growled, "Still doesn't explain what you're doing sitting at my desk."

Completely unaffected by Drake's power play, Jacob shrugged. "Chill, man. I just had some stuff to do is all."

"What stuff could you possibly have to do at *my* desk?"

"Don't worry about what stuff. I needed to handle a few things and I did."

Drake didn't let his eyes waver from Jacob's. The kid was trying his hardest to be the alpha dog, but Drake hadn't worked this hard and gotten this far to be usurped by an egotistical ankle biter. The kid was subbing for Frankie, that was fine, but even Frankie didn't act as if he owned the place. Drake crossed his arms over his chest, chest out, shoulders wide, looming the best he could in an intimidating manner. He knew it had nothing on Frankie's menacing posture, but he could sense Jacob's courage shrinking even if the kid didn't show it.

"All right, so you're subbing for Frankie. That's great, kid. Just one question. Do you own the club?"

Jacob's brows jumped like the question surprised him. He shook his head.

Drake pulled the corners of his lips up into a tight smile. Drake shot out a leg to push the chair back enough to make Jacob reach out for a support. When his arm flailed near Drake, searching for a stable surface, Drake grasped his wrist and twisted it, using the momentum to wrench Jacob's hand behind his back. Then with one hard thrust, he bashed Jacob's chest against the top of the desk, following it with his weight. He gave the wrist one more twist, making the kid jerk underneath him, before growling, "Then get the fuck out of my chair."

The words spat with venom vibrated over the desk. Drake let it sink in before releasing Jacob's limb. He backed up just enough to give the kid room to get up, but he wanted to make sure his presence was still known.

"What the hell? What the fuck is wrong with you?"

Drake eyed the kid. "Just because you have family in high places doesn't mean that you get to disrespect the order of things. This is my club, my business, not your fucking playground. You do any shit again to undermine my authority, we will see who will be 'in charge' next time."

Jacob pushed away from the desk, holding his hands up in a placating gesture. Sure, he was "in charge," but he was still just a stuck-up, brat kid. Drake followed Jacob with his eyes as the kid moved around the desk. Once the desk was between them, Jacob dropped his hands back to his side, his fingers twitching, and Drake suddenly realized that he hadn't even thought about the possibility of Jacob having a gun. And while Drake's trust was won with Frankie, Jacob definitely did not have the same feelings.

Jacob lowered his chin just enough that he was looking at Drake through narrowed eyes. The silence around them thickened.

"I warned you about getting in my way," Jacob uttered, his voice dark and quiet. "Frankie isn't around for you to hide behind anymore."

Drake kept his expression blank. At least he hoped it was blank and didn't reek of the anger and fear rising in his chest. "I don't need to hide behind anyone."

Jacob laughed, a loud bark of a sound. "You keep thinking that, *Drakeybo*," Jacob said, turning on his heel.

Before Jacob could disappear, Drake stopped him. He sat down in his chair and, duplicating what Jacob had done earlier by placing both elbows on the desk and pressing his fingertips together, he waited for Jacob to turn around and face him.

"The bar is short-staffed this weekend. So, I expect you to be at your best. We wouldn't want bad service to be a reason why the money coming in doesn't match the money going out, now would we?"

Jacob's smile was unwavering, his eyes dark. "You got it, Boss Man. I'm sure *Scotty* and I will get along just fine." The words were crisp, curt, and cutting, and the last thing Jacob said with a smirk before disappearing, the door slamming shut behind him.

In, one, two, three, out, one two, three. Drake raked in a harsh breath and forced his body to relax. He had hoped to savor his newfound bliss for a little longer before returning to the darkness of his life.

Had he really been foolish enough to think he could partake of both worlds? Had he really thought it was possible for him to be happy, that he could get his revenge and Scotty too?

Shit.

Bile rose in the back of Drake's throat as he thought of Jacob and Scotty working behind the bar together. He thought of all the ways Jacob could hurt Scotty. Not only could he use his inexperience and stupidity behind the bar, but Jacob also had the tools of a cartel at his fingertips. He had drugs and weapons at his disposal, any means necessary to hurt him. Not to mention the means of getting rid of a body. Fuck knew how many bodies they had disposed of this year alone.

Drake slammed his fist on his desk, sending a pen hurtling to the floor. His fist vibrated from the impact, but it wasn't enough to calm him, so he did it again, then again, the harsh noises vanishing into the club's pulsing ambiance. When that wasn't enough, he swiped his arm across his desk, sending notepads, pens, and papers flying.

"Fuck!" he shouted because the airiness and light that had carried him to his office had finally been replaced by the dark fog.

He needed to think. What the hell had Jacob been doing at his desk? Sure, Tony had put him in charge but of this side of town's operations, not the club. Drake raked a hand through his hair, pulling at the roots. What the fuck had the kid been looking for?

Drake had come in earlier than he usually did. After Scotty left he thought he'd come in to get some work done, so most likely the kid hadn't expected to get walked in on. He hadn't been on the computer or looking through any of the paperwork on the desk; it had all still been lying in the piles he had left them in yesterday before he'd displaced them. No, Jacob had been going through the drawers. Either he was looking for something, which would be stupid because Drake didn't keep anything but work documents in the desk, or more likely, he was hiding something.

Drake glanced at the clock. There was still about an hour until Scotty would be coming in. Standing up, Drake crossed the office and quickly twisted the lock on the door.

The search didn't take long. Either the kid wasn't the grand marshal of hiding things or he had wanted the small black flash drive to be found. The device had been stashed loose in the bottom of the top drawer, probably the first place anyone would look if they were going to do a search. Hell, it had been the first place Drake had looked. Just to be safe, he completed a search of his desk, looking for anything out of place. Nothing.

Drake fingered the small black plastic box. He didn't really know why he felt hesitant, but a queasy feeling in his gut kept him from plugging in the device. He didn't know what he was going to find, but whatever it was couldn't be good. Not if Jacob wanted him or someone else to find it.

Dropping his head into his hands, Drake let out a frustrated growl. This was not how he had imagined this playing out. Reaching out, Drake blindly grabbed for a tumbler on the shelf next to his desk and set it down so he could search out his scotch. He poured a couple inches of liquid into the glass and looked at it.

It was the first time he had thought about having a drink today. Usually by now he had at least one under his belt, but as he stared at the warm brown fluid, all he could think about was Scotty. Scotty didn't like him drinking. He wasn't going to stop him, but he didn't like it. And even more importantly than that, Drake didn't feel like he *needed* a drink when he was with Scotty. At least, not as much.

But Scotty wasn't here, and Drake needed that spoonful of liquid courage with a touch of recklessness and a lingering smoky flavor of bitter resentment. He put the glass to his lips and sucked down a few smooth swallows, then let out a breath.

Okay, he was ready.

Without letting his thoughts get in his way, Drake quickly pushed the drive into the USB hub on his computer.

The folder opened to a series of documents. None named with anything but instead numbered. Clicking one at random, Drake eyed the information presented. At first look, he thought that the gibberish was code. The random numbers and letters splayed out meant absolutely nothing at all. But as he stared at them, he realized that, while it was in code, it was not going to be that difficult to decipher. All words were abbreviations and not necessarily abbreviated the same way each time. Any numbers that weren't an address but instead money amounts were in roman numerals. It wasn't necessarily code, more like shorthand for dummies. Probably so any Joe Shmoe who looked over your shoulder couldn't figure it out.

Drake's heart pounded with excitement as he flipped through the documents. Money and accounts. Dealers and amounts. The drive was a fountain of information. Heart beating so quickly that he couldn't hear anything above the cacophony in his ears, Drake flipped through the pages, and then he saw something that made his stomach drop. Where his beating heart had almost overwhelmed him, now the silence was deafening. If felt as if the world had stopped.

Drake saw his name, a series of numbers, and then some roman numerals. He clicked through some pages. More numbers with his name. Times, dates, accounts, monies.

"What the fuck?" he breathed.

According to these files and bank accounts, Drake was one very wealthy man.

Drake could hardly breathe as he quickly scanned the remaining documents. He exited out of the program. He stared at the icon on the desktop. The icon that held the files that showed proof of Drake skimming money. Money Drake had never seen, in accounts Drake had never set up.

Drake's vision blackened around the edges. His breathing came in short, quick puffs that didn't feel like the air was actually making it to his lungs. He clicked on the icon, dragging it across his desktop.

Are you sure you want to permanently delete 12 items? The words flashed before his eyes as he hit Delete.

All air left him in whoosh as the files were deleted from the computer. Drake sat back in his chair, his limbs numb, his mind so jumbled and flighty that it might as well be blank. The moment stretched and finally feeling came back to his limbs. Leaning forward, he grabbed the bottle of scotch. Ignoring the empty glass sitting next to it, he took a long swallow directly from the bottle.

An abrupt knock on his door made him jump, goose bumps rising along his arms. His heart leaped into his throat, and he tried to swallow it back down so he could answer.

"Just a minute," he called, steadying his voice. His limbs moved as if in hyperdrive, pulling the drive loose before dropping it carefully back to the bottom of the drawer. He glanced around the floor at the mess of papers and quickly picked up what he could, grabbing the papers and ignoring the pens and paperclips that had been strewn.

Shaking his hands, he tried to quell the nervous tremor tingling through his limbs. In and out, he counted his breaths before opening the door.

Scotty leaned against the wall across the hall dressed in tight black jeans and a black button-down that didn't belie any of his assets. The man screamed sex, and Drake's body didn't care that he was in the middle of a meltdown. The panic ebbed slightly at the electric pull of Scotty. It was amazing the calming effect Scotty had on him.

Scotty cocked his head at Drake, licking his lips seductively, "Hey, Boss, can I come in for a moment?"

"Um, now, isn't, um," Drake stammered. He cleared his throat. "Now isn't a good time."

"Don't worry. I'll be quick," Scotty said and pushed past Drake.

Drake let him pass with a sigh. Scotty hardly let him finish closing the door before he turned and wrapped his arms around Drake, roughly pulling his head down for a kiss.

Drake was ready to protest, had tensed at the man's touch, but as the warm lips devoured his, he changed his mind, melting into the warmth, the black pushed back again. He wasn't sure how Scotty did it, but his presence alone seemed to make other things less important, and the only thing that mattered was the here and now. This. Warm lips on his, arms wrapped around each other. Drake and Scotty bound together in a tight embrace.

Apart just enough that their lips were barely touching, Drake smiled. "Hi."

"Hi." Scotty laughed, quick tufts of warm air against Drake's lips. "I guess I missed you."

Drake let his own soft laugh meld with Scotty's. "I guess you did." Drake nuzzled Scotty's nose with his own. "You're early."

Scotty shrugged. "I had to make up for leaving early yesterday."

"And you thought coming in and seducing your boss by imitating the opening sequence to a bad porno would be the way to make up for it?"

"Hey, it would be a great porno, thank you very much!" Scotty pushed Drake's shoulder teasingly.

Laughing, Drake pressed his lips back to Scotty's. He hadn't intended for it to be anything but a quick brush of lips, but soon they were lost in each other again. Time passed without notice as they slowly and tenderly kissed. Reluctantly, Drake pulled away, but Scotty's arms tightened around him so he couldn't retreat far. He rested his forehead on Scotty's, enjoying the soft breath of each of his exhales along his cooling lips.

"Julie seems to have it in her head that we were together last night."

"Does she?" Scotty said without emphasis. He lowered his head so he could nuzzle along Drake's neck.

Drake huffed, "Yes, she does."

"Hmm," Scotty breathed, the breath tickling along Drake's nape. "Well, I'm not sharing."

"What?" Drake snorted, pushing Scotty back. Scotty met his eyes with a teasing look.

"She can find her own dark and mysterious man."

Drake tilted his head back, eyes heavenward. "That is not what I meant."

Scotty walked farther into the office and propped a hip on his desk. "I know, but it definitely helped get that dark look out of your eyes you had when I arrived. What's going on?"

All at once the mood in the room changed. Shit, the flash drive. Somehow, Scotty had helped him to forget all about it. He grumbled quietly as he rubbed a hand over his eyes.

The energy had once again drained from Drake. His limbs felt heavy, his conscience dark. He let the dark blank look he wore so often mask his face.

"You should get out of here, Scotty." His voice was void of emotion.

Scotty tilted his head, confusion clearly drawn across his face. "What do you mean?"

Drake crossed his arms. "I mean, you need to get out of here, leave, get as far away from me and this city as you can."

Scotty shook his head. "What? No. Drake, we've been through this. I am not—"

Drake cut him off with a growl. "Do not fight me on this. Go home, pack a bag, and get the fuck out of here!"

After Drake's shout, the silence stretched. Scotty stared at Drake with wide eyes, his head still shaking. He took a step toward Drake, holding out his hands in a calming gesture. "No, Drake, no. I am not going anywhere. Talk to me. Tell me what's going on."

"I'm fucked! That's what's going on!" Drake shouted, throwing his hands up in the air. The words rumbled between them, and Drake couldn't do it anymore. He couldn't be strong anymore. He collapsed to the floor, his ass hitting the ground hard.

Scotty was next to him in minutes, arms wrapping around him. Drake tried to shrug him off, but he wasn't that strong.

"Tell me," Scotty whispered, breath hot against Drake's brow. Drake shuddered at the warmth. He wanted to wrap his own arms around the man. He wanted to push him away and send him running. He wanted to kiss him and love him, and he wanted to shout and scream and make it so Scotty would never want to see him again.

In the end, he couldn't do any of those things. He just sat while Scotty soothed him, arms around him, hands caressing in soothing circles.

"Tell me, Drake."

Drake sighed. "Well, for one, Jacob is taking over Frankie's position while Frankie's gone. I found him going through my desk when I came in. I had to throw the fucker out. I checked to see what he was doing and it turns out he's hiding a flash drive in my desk that looks like its details for drug shipments, buying and selling."

"Why do you look so upset?" Scotty asked.

Drake pushed at Scotty, trying to disengage, but Scotty only tightened his arms. Drake huffed. "A bunch of cash has been going missing lately. That's why Frankie and Jacob have been gone so much. Sending out the big guns because money has been disappearing." Drake, unable to fight it any longer, turned so his face was pressed against Scotty's neck. He nestled into the warmth and breathed in Scotty's unique and calming scent. "The flash drive has detailed accounts of the money and where it's been going."

"Where?" Scotty's voice was calm.

Drake dragged in another deep breath, basking in the warm scent before pushing back to meet Scotty's eyes. He licked his dry lips and swallowed. "Me."

Scotty's eyes widened and his hands stilled from their soothing massage. "What do you mean?"

"There are very detailed reports of how I skimmed the money and put it into offshore accounts."

"You what?"

Drake blinked as Scotty pushed him farther away. "*I* didn't take the money."

Scotty shook his head. "Of course," he said as he pulled Drake a little bit closer but didn't bring him back into the hug. "Of course you didn't. But, shit, why? I mean, how?"

"I don't know. Jacob has had it out for me since he started here."

Scotty shook his head again. "That doesn't make sense. If he had it out for you, why not just kill you? I mean, thank God he didn't, but wouldn't that have been easier?"

Drake let out a small laugh, but there was no humor. "Well, this is an easy way to get rid of me and to end up with millions of dollars."

"Jacob?" Scotty asked incredulously. "That kid cannot be smart enough to pull something like this off."

"Yeah, well, that's one thing about playing in the shadows, you never know what monsters you'll find in the darkness." Drake pushed away from Scotty, detangling himself, and worked his way to his feet. If he was going to think clearly, he needed to get some space, some distance. "I need you to leave, Scotty."

"No," Scotty said, pushing to his own feet. He met Drake toe-to-toe.

Drake let his grief show. "Please, I need to figure this out, and I can't think clearly with you here. I can't do what I need to do if I know you're in danger."

"What do you mean, what you need to do?" Scotty asked, his raised voice belying his worry. "Drake? What are you going to do?"

Drake turned his back on Scotty; he couldn't look at him. "What I have to do. I knew this wasn't going to end well for me, Scotty. I told you. I fucking warned you that I wasn't any good for you."

Drake heard Scotty take a step closer, and he closed his eyes. He fought the urge to turn around, grab Scotty, and run. He fought the thought about the two of them walking out of his office, out the door, getting into his car, and driving. Driving and driving until they were safe.

But that was a hopeless fantasy, because there wasn't anyplace safe. Not when Boredega was after you. Sure, they could run. But they would keep running until they couldn't run anymore and then…. Drake didn't want to think about what would happen after that.

Drake's shoulders drooped. "You need to go, Scotty."

"You don't have to do this, you know," Scotty said. Then he wrapped his arm around Drake from behind. Drake startled at the touch; he hadn't heard him get that close. "Please, Drake, don't do this. Take the information to the police, let them handle it."

Drake let the warmth of Scotty's arms linger for just a moment, basking in the comfort, before breaking out of his grasp to retreat out of his reach. He turned back, stopping Scotty's approach with a dark look.

"I can't do that. I know you don't understand, but I have to do this, Scotty. Everything I am has led me to this moment, and I have to go through with it." His voice cracked.

"Then let me help! I can—"

Drake shook his head. "No."

"But I could—" Drake backed up a step as Scotty moved forward, arms outstretched as if to grab him.

"I don't want you involved. I was trying to keep you out of it, Scotty! I can't let anything happen to you. I care about you too much."

Scotty let his arms fall to his side. "Why can't you see that it's the same for me? That it kills me every time I think of you going off to get yourself killed." He lifted his head to meet Drake's eyes, his own brimming with unshed tears. Drake had to clamp his eyes shut against the pain he saw there. "I love you, Drake."

Drake's eyes flew open. He pressed a hand to his chest as a bursting pain erupted violently, almost driving him to his knees. "You what?"

Scotty lifted his shoulders. "I love you."

"You can't," Drake gasped, his entire body trembling.

Scotty shrugged again, his body deflated. "I'm sorry, but I do."

"You can't do this to me," Drake croaked. "I can't—I don't—shit, I don't know what to say."

"You don't have to say anything, I guess. I just wanted you to know that maybe you could have something to live for besides revenge. I know you want me to leave, but for the same reasons you want me to leave, I can't go, not if you are here. So, just think about it, will you?"

Swallowing against a dry mouth, Drake watched with full eyes as Scotty left his office. As soon as the door closed, leaving him alone, his knees buckled. He collapsed in an ungraceful heap on the floor and stared at the now empty spot where Scotty had been standing. The pain in his chest was unimaginable; the only thing to ever equal it was the memory of his family, and even that had dulled with time. This pain was fresh and deep and completely unexpected. It really could only mean one thing.

"I love you too." The words trembled out of Drake's lips as his first tear fell to the floor.

CHAPTER 20

DRAKE WAS stalking again. He couldn't help himself. The last few days had felt like hell for him, and it hurt to see Scotty behind the bar working almost as if nothing was wrong, but Drake could tell Scotty wasn't quite himself. There were dark circles under his eyes, and there was no spring to his step. He had almost dropped two glasses, and he'd mixed up a couple of orders. Drake hated that he was the reason for Scotty's distress. He hated that he had allowed himself get close enough to hurt them both.

Once he had pulled himself together and picked himself off his office floor, he'd busied himself with paperwork and scotch. He had been hasty when he'd deleted the information from the flash drive, because now he didn't know what was there. He didn't know how to fight back because he had gotten rid of his only copy of any damning evidence.

Now that he could think a little more clearly, it was obvious Jacob would have the information saved in other places, and that by destroying the flash drive he had only hindered himself from being able to do any investigating. But it didn't matter. He had information. It wasn't as much as he had wanted. It wasn't enough to get to Boredega or take down the cartel, but it was going to hurt them. And Jesus, did he ever want to hurt them.

He had information on drug houses, on dealers, on enforcers. Hell, he knew how to get to Tony, and he had Jacob serving drinks in his bar. He had notebooks of information about money laundering, and he had absolutely no reason to keep it all to himself any longer. He planned, he schemed. He gathered as much information as he could, and then when he couldn't bear the thought of never seeing Scotty again, Drake made his way to his corner booth to drink and lurk.

Sure, he was being creepy. Sure, he sort of reminded himself of a miserable stalker in a bad slasher movie, but he didn't care. He could wallow. He was *allowed* to do that. He could grieve for the relationship he almost had and let the world continue around him. The crowd was hopping, Jacob appeared to actually be doing his job, and as far as Drake could tell so far, nothing crazy was happening.

Drake laughed, bringing the glass to his lips, and let another swallow of smooth liquid warm his blood. Right, so far, nothing horrible had happened. He lifted the glass once more, draining it, then set it down next to the other three empty glasses, quickly scanning the crowd for sight of Jenny. He didn't see her, but he knew she was around somewhere. He did another quick scan. She wasn't anywhere in sight. However, he did see a familiar figure sashay her way through the crowd.

Shit. It was Natasha. He was so not in the mood to see her right now. He tried to duck down in his seat, but it was in vain. Her eyes lit up as she saw him.

Letting out an angry groan, Drake picked up his empty glass, wishing for at least a small amount to be left on the bottom. No such luck. Drake pushed the glass away and, in a futile attempt at escape, slowly stood. But as he did the world took a little turn and he stumbled back.

What the hell? He could hold his liquor better than this. He should know; he had a lot of practice. But he couldn't seem to make the room stop spinning. Maybe he'd had more than he thought.

Soft hands caught him from behind. "Oh my," Natasha said, her voice flowing in a teasing lilt. "Drunk already, are we? It's not even eleven o'clock yet."

Drake straightened himself, trying to stand without swaying. "None of your business," he murmured, pushing away from the table. "I've got a club to run," he slurred, trying to back away, but Natasha's hands pulled at his arm, keeping him from retreating.

"I don't think you will be doing much in your current condition. Probably wouldn't hurt you to sit and chat with little ole me for a while, now would it? Why don't we go back to your office?"

Drake shook his head. "Nope, I don't want to do that."

Natasha put a hand to her chest in a mock affronted gesture. "Well, if I didn't know any better, I would think that you didn't like me."

With a snort, Drake tried again to retreat, but Natasha pulled him close once again. "I think you might want to hear what little bit of gossip a little birdie let slip." Drake tried to wave her away, but her next words stopped him dead. "Word is the Boredega has quite a bit of money missing and a snitch dragging the cops into everything."

Drake swallowed hard, turning back to face Natasha. He tried to push the drunk away, but it kept a firm grasp on him. He needed a clear head for this conversation, but as the room spun, he knew that wasn't going to happen. He tried not to let his concern show, tugging his arm out of Natasha's grasp. "Yeah? What of it? Why should I care about that? There are plenty of junkies out there willing to give up information to keep their asses out of jail."

Natasha swished her hair provocatively, sashaying her way toward Drake again. She linked their arms as if Drake hadn't just spent all that time trying to free himself of her. "I thought it might interest you because I think I know who it is."

Blood rushed into Drake's ears, creating a swirling ocean of sound. "Wha—" His words stopped suddenly as the floor seemed to quake under his feet. Throwing his arms out for balance, Drake caught himself hard on the table, which was much closer than it appeared. Drake let his arm take the brunt of his weight and closed his eyes. The club was not collapsing around him. They were not in the middle of an earthquake, and nothing was happening out of the ordinary except for him.

Drake opened his eyes and met Natasha's, and her face contorted into a smug smirk. Her usual flirtatious manner was completely void, and instead, there stood a predator. A predator with its claws already sunk into its prey. "Wha—what'd you do...?" Drake managed to choke out between dry lips. The already spinning floor started to pull at his legs, making it nearly impossible for him to stand.

"Oh, Drakeybo, didn't anyone ever tell you not to be so predictable?" Natasha reached down to pull him up, shrugging one of his arms over her shoulder. "It's hardly a task to find the bottle of Black Label set aside for you. Such an easy target. It was almost disappointing."

Drake tried to pull himself away from her, but whatever she'd put in his drink took his fight away. "Drugged me?"

Natasha laughed as she guided him down a couple of steps and onto the dance floor. The way they moved, Drake had no question that they looked like a drunken couple stumbling off the floor.

"Well, you know, you have this reputation for imbibing, sometimes just a bit too much. It would stand to reason that you would finally go a little too far."

Drake was at her mercy, so he allowed her to half carry, half drag him across the dance floor. They were headed toward the back hallway, and Drake felt a cold chill trickle down his spine. Nothing good could come from going to the back rooms in this state.

No, the only things that could happen to him back there were pain and death. Neither very appealing choices. There had to be some way for him to get out of this. All his years of training, his martial arts and his weapon handling training, wasted. He was taken out by his most prominent vice, the bottle.

But maybe there was a chance. The only good thing that had happened from him spending so much time at the mercy of the bottle was his relationship with Scotty. Scotty, who knew it took more than four or five drinks to have him stumbling around like an idiot. Instead of fighting against Natasha's hold on him, Drake let his gaze drift to the bar.

He was there, working as diligently as ever. He was doing everything right, except for looking up to see Drake. Drake willed Scotty's eyes to meet his, glance in his direction, anything. But Scotty kept at it, smiling unknowingly as he passed on a drink.

All the hope Drake had been able to muster sank back down to the depths of his stomach. He was on his own.

Natasha lugged him down the hallway and into his office. As soon as they made it to the doorjamb, Drake mustered as much energy as he could and pushed against Natasha, slamming her against the frame, breaking her hold. Drake tried to gain some ground, tried to push himself back out the door toward the crowded club, but strong hands pulled him back.

"Where do you think you're going?" Jacob pulled him off balance and shoved him into the office. Drake, still unable to correctly maneuver his limbs, fell hard into his desk, papers and pens scattering to the floor.

"The lady said she wanted to talk to you." Jacob stood in front of Drake, hands on his hips, a leer smattered across his face.

Drake willed his body to cooperate, and with the last bit of motivation he could muster, he gathered himself enough to lunge at Jacob, a pen he'd been able to grab from the floor brandished as a weapon. He slammed into the kid using all his weight and felt the pen meet resistance before pushing through flesh. Drake couldn't help the satisfied smile that tilted his lips just before something hard and heavy crashed against the back of his head. Then all there was left was darkness.

CHAPTER 21

DRAKE BLINKED, groaning against the pain crashing through his skull. He tried to reach up to clutch at his head, but his wrist caught against something. He pulled the other, but it too was held immobile.

He tried to get his eyes to focus, but the light glared so bright it burned every time he managed to crack his lids. How had he gotten here? Where was here, exactly? Squinting, he tried to make out his surroundings.

A dark shudder ran down his spine as the room started to take shape. The white room, fluorescent lights, and single menacing cabinet brought it all back to him. He remembered how he had gotten here now. Natasha. She had drugged him.

He attempted to move his arms once more only to have them restrained again, and this time he looked down to find his wrists bound with straps that he himself had strapped to plenty. It was no use; he knew the binds could hold even the strongest man against his will. He knew because he had seen it.

Letting out a strangled laugh, Drake winced as the pain in his head increased.

"You're awake. Finally." Jacob came into view from behind Drake, his fingers fiddling with a bandage on his forearm.

Drake followed his movement, letting a smile stretch his face. He had gotten the fucker with the pen. Good. He chuckled. "Well, if you were going to be impatient about it, you shouldn't have hit so hard."

Jacob scowled. "I didn't hit you."

"Oh, that's right." Drake coughed, wincing against the bolt of lightning that flashed through his skull. "You left the heavy lifting for Natasha."

Jacob's scowl deepened and he raised a fist as if he was going to lash out, but before his fist could connect, a voice from behind Drake stopped him.

"Jacob! If you hit him again, we'll just have to wait longer for him to wake up."

Natasha walked around so that Drake could see her as well. She had changed. Not much physically, but literally she had changed. Instead of her usual voluptuous outfit that emphasized her curves and accentuated her sex appeal, she was clad in tight jeans, a black T-shirt, and a formfitting leather jacket. It was different than what Drake was used to seeing too much of her in. Well, it wasn't like that outfit didn't scream sex; it just screamed sex and danger.

Drake cleared his throat. Apparently being knocked out made his mouth dry. "Wow, Natasha, that's a good look on you."

"You like it, Drakeybo? I didn't think you would notice, as you aren't as interested in me as I first thought." She posed, showing off her perfect profile. "It's what I wear when I have to deal with traitorous scum like you."

"Scum?" Drake remarked, with a cocked brow. "Really? Kind of harsh, isn't it?"

Jacob moved forward, smacking his hand across Drake's face harshly. "Shut the hell up!" Drake laughed as the pounding in his head amplified. He tasted blood on his tongue as Jacob snarled at him and went to hit him again. "What are you laughing at?"

The back of his hand almost connected again but was stopped by Natasha. This time she reached out to grab him and pulled his hand back firmly.

"Jacob," she said with a jab of authority. Drake raised a brow as Jacob quickly obeyed her order to stop.

"Why don't you send him to get a sundae while Mom and Dad talk, eh?" Drake quipped, already prepared for the next backhanded hit.

He laughed again as his head lolled to the side from the force of the hit. He let the blood in his mouth well. The whole scene reminded him of the film *Fight Club*, and it only caused him to laugh harder.

"You fucking piece of shit! Why are you laughing?" Jacob yelled.

"At you, I'm laughing—" Drake had to stop as his head flung to the side with another fist to his face. He let the blood pool, and then while Jacob moved for the next strike, he spit. Blood splattered from his lips, landing in an arch on the center of Jacob's face. The surprise of the liquid caused Jacob to pause momentarily before roaring madly. He lunged for Drake.

Natasha was suddenly between them, her arms pushing Jacob back. "Jacob! If you can't stop hitting him, then get out."

Wiping the spit blood from his face, smearing it along his cheek, Jacob growled at Natasha but in the end pulled himself together. He looked down at his red-streaked hand. "I'm going to go clean up." He looked back up at Drake with a wide, evil smile. "Maybe get something that will help him talk." Then without a second glance at Drake, he left.

Drake closed his eyes and breathed deeply as he thought of Jacob going out and grabbing Scotty from behind the bar. Jesus fuck, he wished he had made him leave. He should have forced him to go. He didn't want him to see this; he didn't want him to experience this. Scotty was too good for this.

Drake pulled against his restraints, knowing it was useless. He struggled, the straps digging into the flesh of his wrists. He pulled again, letting out a furious scream, knowing that no sounds would leave the room. It was hopeless, but he had to try.

Natasha turned back toward Drake, her hands on her hips, lip jutted out in disapproval. "Are you quite finished?"

Drake's head lolled to the side, but he looked up at her. He didn't say anything, just watched her. He was having trouble placing her in this new role. This role of power, instead of the manipulative whore he knew her to be.

Drake licked his cracked bleeding lips. "Who the hell are you?"

"I don't think that you have the right to ask any questions, the condition you're in." Natasha tilted her hips, and that was a familiar move. Drake recognized the cocky seduction in that motion.

Wiggling his fingers, Drake arched a pointed brow at Natasha. "I figured you wanted to have a conversation. You have your captive audience. So, go ahead and spill. Who the hell are you?"

Natasha approached slowly and crouched down so her hand rested on the back of Drake's chair and their eyes were level. Her usually pouty lips pulled into a tight grin. She flipped her hair over her shoulder. "You have no idea what you are involved in, do you?" she asked, running a long nail along the defined bone of his chin. "You were playing with matches, and now you are going to get burned."

Drake jerked his head away. "What are you talking about? Of course I knew what I was getting into. It's a drug cartel not a fun day carnival. What the hell is going on?"

"Where is it?" Natasha asked, pushing back up and away from Drake.

That wasn't a question Drake had been expecting. "Where is what?"

"Oh, come on, Drakey. This could go so much easier if you just told me where it was."

Drake snorted in contempt. "Yeah, and I would love to share the secret location of whatever it is you are looking for, but news flash—" He leaned forward as much as he could against his bonds. "—I. Don't. Know. What the hell you are talking about!"

She turned her back on him to walk to the cabinet that held all the fun goodies that Drake never had the guts or the will to use on anyone he had brought into this room. He flexed against the restraints again, knowing full well that there was no give, but trying again anyway because that's what you did. You tried to survive.

"You know, when my father put me on detail to keep an eye on you, I thought he was crazy. I mean, you were a stupid punk kid who bought a club and then thought he could make it big by joining in with the big fish. I thought you were a waste of my time."

Drake blinked. Natasha had been watching him? All this time, he had thought that she was just a run-of-the-mill prostitute with a fucked-up view of the world, and instead she was another tool Boredega used to keep his people in line.

"Your father?"

"It wasn't until strange things started happening, like the cops somehow being at every drop, or some of our better dealers being picked up for questioning, that I started to think that maybe, just maybe, he didn't have me running a fool's errand." Natasha turned back with a syringe, the green liquid standing out against her black attire. Drake swallowed as she took a step toward him holding the syringe in front of her, showing it off. He knew that move. He had used it before to weaken the resolve of his own helpless captives.

"You see, my daddy, well, he doesn't like it when someone messes with his operation. It makes him angry when the people he's paying good money go bad on him. And when he gets angry, people tend to die. Now, we can do this the easy way, or we can do it the hard way," Natasha said, once again at eye level with Drake. She held the syringe up and squirted a touch of the fluid out the top. "Tell me where the money is."

Drake's eyes widened. Natasha was Boredega's daughter? All along, he'd had something that could have been his ticket to revenge right in front of him and he hadn't known?

"Where is it?" Natasha yelled, flecks of spittle hitting Drake right in the face.

The money, right. He had no clue where that was; he had deleted that information practically the second he had seen it.

"I don't know what you are talking about," Drake started, but he backtracked as Natasha started to lower the point of the needle toward his arm. "Look, I know there is money missing, but I have no idea where it is! I didn't take it."

Natasha sighed, looking displeased, and reached a hand up to clasp Drake's chin. "I really don't want to have to kill you this painfully and slowly, Drake, but I will if I have to. Just tell me where it is, and I can end this now. Quickly and painlessly."

"I think it's a bit late for the painlessly," Drake grumbled. "You should ask Jacob where the money is. I bet he has an answer for you."

Natasha's expression morphed into one of rage. Her dark eyes bored into him, and Drake couldn't help but feel some satisfaction in the fact that he was able to pull that reaction from her. He was the one tied to the chair, but he was the one messing with her.

His satisfied smirk was short-lived, however, when a fist cracked against his jaw, wiping the smile right off. Spitting some more pooled blood on the floor, Drake arched a brow at the woman before him. "You can pack a punch."

Natasha's own gratified leer was back in place. "Well, my father taught me well. Now, tell me where the money is."

Drake grunted, "I. Don't. Know. Just kill me and get it over with. You aren't going to get any information from me."

Natasha bent so that they were at eye level once again. Her smile still steadily in place, she used a finger to wipe away some blood from Drake's lip, her touch soft and gentle like a caress. Drake leaned his head away, and Natasha dropped her hand back to her side.

"Simply killing you would be too easy. I prefer to have fun with prey." Drake didn't even have time to respond to that new bout of interesting information before another quick punch swung his head to the side. "Where the hell is the money?"

"I don't know what happened to the money. Last I saw anything about it, it was from a flash drive that Jacob was hiding in my drawer." Natasha's eyes never wavered from Drake's as he spoke.

Pursing her lips into an irritated line, she pushed the needle under Drake's skin. He hissed at the sting of the harsh metal invading his flesh and then sucked in air as suddenly the world tilted around him. Shit, that stuff worked fast.

Blinking, he tried to focus on the room around him, but it was as if he were underwater. Nothing took a firm shape, instead moving and waving with the water flow, distorting everything. Instinctually, Drake's body started swaying with the waves, trying to help straighten the world, but nothing changed.

"Come on, Drake." The words seemed to come from afar. Drake looked around, trying to see who could be talking to him from that far away. "I only gave you a little. Just tell me what I need to know and I can stop now."

Rolling his head forward so his chin rested on his chest, Drake tried to regain his faculties. "I could tell you," he mumbled through loose lips. Something wet dripped from them, and he didn't know if he was bleeding or drooling. "But then, I'd hafta kill ya."

"Really?" Natasha sniffed. "Do you think that I won't do it?"

"Imma pretty confident thatcha will but I can't tell ya somethin' I dunno," Drake sang in a slur.

"Just shoot up the bastard!" Jacob's derisive voice demanded from behind Drake. "I can't believe you haven't just killed him yet."

Drake tried to lift his head. If Jacob was back, then he would have Scotty, but as he forced his head up, he saw that Jacob was alone. The drugs and the relief made his head heavy, so he rolled it to the side. "Jacob! Yer back! Do you know wha' happened t'da money?"

"You fucking...." Drake tuned out the last of the response, too busy trying to make patterns out of the colors shifting in front of his eyes. There were so many different colors out there. He had never really noticed before. Shame that now that he saw them he was about to die.

He wondered if Scotty ever noticed all the colors. Did he appreciate the different things? Drake bet he did. Scotty had a way of looking at things in a positive light. He probably saw more sunshine and rainbows than Drake ever knew existed.

He hoped Scotty was doing okay, that he wouldn't be too sad when he found that Drake was gone. Drake had never wanted to hurt him.

"—bartender was gone—"

"—we have to get that fucking money back—"

"—get your head out of your ass—" Drake tried to follow Natasha's and Jacob's rants, but the words slipped away from him, through him, over him.

"Father...." He managed to moan. That bothered him. He hadn't known who Natasha's father was. He hadn't known who Natasha was! All this time he had spent combing through the people in the cartel, and he had let some whore slip right under his nose. Some whore with an important daddy. What else had he missed? What other secrets were out there twisted so deep into the darkness that no one could see them, even when they were looking?

Maybe Scotty had been right all along. Maybe he should have just given it to the police and let them handle it. He could be off in bed with Scotty right now, instead of chained to his deathbed.

A hard slap on his cheek roused him back from the inside of his mind. Natasha's face was inches from his and had both his cheeks clasped in her hand so they could meet eye to eye.

"Last chance. Tell me where the money is and I won't finish shoving this drug into your veins. Because trust me, after a couple of hours of intense pain, you won't be able to keep your mouth shut anyway. Just tell me."

"I—" Drake tried to speak, but his mouth was dry, which was funny to him because earlier it had been dripping. His jaw worked silently, and Natasha moved her head closer, leaning in to try to hear. "...hafta kill ya," Drake managed, smiling at his wit. He'd known he would go down with a smile on his face. Of course, he had thought the smile would be because he was taking Boredega down with him instead of muttering a last witticism, but it would have to do. As Natasha's fingers roughly released him, he let his head fall back to his chest.

"Do it," she said and walked away. Do what? He couldn't do anything. He was strapped to a chair, and he had no idea where the money was. What was he supposed to do?

Jacob knelt down in front of him with the syringe, a huge satisfied smile twisting his lips. Oh, she hadn't been talking to him. Drake eyed the tool warily. He could have thought of better ways to kick the bucket, but maybe if he was lucky, they would give him too much Selecure and he could just go out on one solid overdose. He could hope anyway.

"I am going to enjoy watching this," Jacob said with smile, pressing the hypodermic along Drake's skin. "And after you're dead, I am going to go out and find your boyfriend, and do the same to him."

Drake snarled at Jacob's words as the needle slid in. Drake didn't have a chance to fight back, to do anything because all he could do was tense against the hot liquid that coursed through his system. His reaction was almost instantaneous. His back arched as the fluid hit his blood stream and in one fell swoop encased his entire body with inexplicable pain. Every nerve ending jarred awake with battery acid and electric shocks.

Jerking uncontrollably from side to side. Fighting his restraints.

Fighting to free his arms to do anything to help hold himself together.

His body was being ripped apart.

Each nerve ending in his body felt as if it were tearing into a million pieces. His skin felt as if it were ripping as each limb was pulled in a different direction. Even his ears throbbed as a loud and terrible sound assaulted them, crashing into his eardrums, blaring holes into the fragile fabric.

He tried to make it stop.

He tried to cover his ears.

He tried to hold his arms on.

Tried to keep his body from being torn to shreds.

It was no use. There was no escaping the pain.

His lungs burst into flame. He realized for the first time that the loud sound beating at his eardrums was nothing but his own screaming. His own screams, which were so strong, so filled with agony and suffering that the only thing that could make him stop was the suffocating sensation of complete lack of oxygen.

He struggled to pull air into his lungs, but the rise of his chest only ignited new aches and torments.

Hurt.

Jesus Fucking Christ. Hurt. It fucking hurt!

He had no idea how much time passed. It had felt as if it had only been seconds, but it felt like an eternity.

This was hell.

Pain. Agony.

Nothing but red-hot pain.

His entire body focused only on the pain. Nothing else mattered; nothing else existed besides its torture. All he could do was struggle against it and wish for death.

Suddenly the world erupted into a battlefield of lights and sounds, each crash of thunder deafening to his ultrasensitive ears and each flash blinding even behind closed eyes. All he could do was cringe away from the storm, hope it passed or was merciful and engulfed him, sending him away into welcome oblivion, but none of that happened.

Instead, a sharp searing pain pierced his gut, proof that even the most horrid pain could still get worse.

Nothing could stop his screaming now. Pain, fucking pain.

God, he hurt. His burning lungs held nothing compared to the excruciating agony in his abdomen. He fought and struggled against his bonds, and then suddenly one arm was free, and then another, and he was falling to the ground in a mutilated heap.

Hands were on him, moving along him, making him writhe and instinctually recoil, but he couldn't get away.

He couldn't escape. His bindings were gone, but he was still captured in the torment.

Searing pain. Agony.

Red. Red. Red.

Shouting around the room filled his ears, but he couldn't make any sense of it. He screamed as a new torment exploded in overstimulated nerve endings as a hand pressed firmly onto the fire burning a hole through his stomach.

Too much.

It was all too much.

Pain. Hurt. So much pain.

Death. The only thing that could help was death.

His brain in sensory overload did the only thing it could do to ease its burden. He slowly fell into a welcome darkness. But even as the black enveloped him, a small morsel of light vied for his attention. As he sank deeper into the abyss, he could have sworn he heard Scotty's voice above him, begging him to open his eyes, pleading for him not to leave. Drake tried to listen, tried to grab on to that light but in the end, the darkness won.

CHAPTER 22

AN ANNOYING beep drifted into his consciousness, each small sound triggering a sharp throb through his head. Drake tried to shift away from it, but the slight movement left him gasping as pain wracked through him. He tried to draw his arm in to his chest, tried to wrap into a comforting fetal position, but something held him back.

Drake blinked, letting the room come into focus. White, everything was white. He would have thought he had died and was now in a blissful heaven, except for the pain. He refused to believe that pain would follow you into death, and he doubted he would ever be able to witness the purity of heaven.

Using his eyes to look around the room, keeping his head as still as possible, Drake took in his surroundings. A machine directly to the side of him showed a series of graphs and numbers, keeping track of his heart rate and blood pressure.

A hospital. That answered one question anyway. Now he knew where he was, but how had he gotten here? And why couldn't he move?

Shifting his eyes down, he eyed the restraints around his wrists. They weren't incredibly tight, and they were the hospital cuffs lined in fabric, but it was enough to keep him from moving.

Great. So he had gone from one hostage situation to another.

A small cough startled him, and without thinking, Drake turned his head toward the sound. He bit back a groan, regretting the thoughtless motion as severe agony cascaded through his limbs. Once he was able to even think about opening his eyes again, he blinked into focus a very concerned, very tired-looking Scotty.

Standing at his bedside, Scotty put his hands on the rail and gripped it tight. Drake eyed his knuckles as they whitened, and he also eyed the gun strapped to Scotty's waist.

That was new.

Drake licked his dry lips, his eyes darting up to meet Scotty's, "You trying to kill me too?" His voice sounded like gravel, his larynx overused from what he could only assume was his screaming.

Scotty smiled, but it didn't reach his eyes. He put a hand on Drake's forehead, brushing back his hair.

"I'm not trying to kill you." The corner of his mouth tilted to a smirk. "You've been through a lot. Go back to sleep. We can talk later."

"I'm cuffed to the bed."

"Shh, I know. It's okay. No one wanted you to hurt yourself."

"What happened?"

Scotty shushed him, putting a straw between his lips. "We can talk all about it later."

Sipping slowly, Drake winced as the first drops slid down his raw throat, the cool wetness being both a blessing and a torture. His dry tongue and mouth quickly absorbed the liquid, but the pain of swallowing it almost made it not worth it.

Turning his head slowly and carefully to the side, Drake released the straw. Scotty put the cup on the table by the bedside.

"Scotty?"

Using his thumb to brush his fingers back and forth over Drake's forehead, Scotty gave another sad smile. "It's okay. I'm here."

"Don't leave." Drake's eyes started to drift closed and he snapped them open, scared that if he closed them Scotty would disappear and he would be back in that room, tied to the chair.

"Shh, it's okay. Go back to sleep. I'm not going anywhere."

Drake kept his eyes on Scotty's for another series of moments. He didn't understand what was going on, and truthfully, he was too exhausted to try to figure it out now. Blinking once as a sign of agreement, Drake let his eyes close. The darkness consumed him again.

Drifting back to consciousness, Drake eyed the plain white ceiling, uncertain of how much time had passed. What was it with hospitals and everything being stark white? Didn't they think people would want to see something a little more soothing when they woke up? Instead, it was all sanitary white and maddening noises. The heart monitor sound had been turned off in his room at least, so that helped.

Biting back a moan, Drake slowly, very carefully, attempted to move his limbs. Flexing and unflexing his fingers, he let out a breath of relief when there was only an echo of pain remaining. He took a deep breath and lifted his arm off the bed as far as it could go attached to the cuff. His arm successfully in the air, he curled his fingers into a fist, then let it drop back down to the side of the bed.

Feeling more confident, Drake did the same with the other hand and snorted when he saw that his other wrist was wrapped in a cuff as well. He had a way of jumping from the frying pan and into the fire. Sure, he wasn't in serious agony anymore, but technically he was still a prisoner.

A prisoner with both hands restrained and an itchy nose. Great.

"Feeling better?" The voice startled Drake and he jumped, gasping as a burning pain seared through his lower abdomen.

"Aw, shit, sorry," Scotty said, moving to the side of the bed so Drake didn't have to twist to see him. "I didn't mean to scare you."

Drake swallowed against his pain but didn't say anything. He looked Scotty up and down, and his already dry mouth miraculously went more dry. The man didn't look anything like he usually did. He was changed somehow, and Drake couldn't exactly put his finger on it.

Drake wasn't sure if he had seen Scotty in anything but what he had worn to work behind the bar. It had always been the tight button-down and the tight slacks or dark jeans. Now, he was dressed in a suit. But what really was eye-catching was the gun in a holster at his hip. His suit jacket mostly covered it, but Drake could see it.

Working his mouth to try and get some moisture, Drake let his head fall back so Scotty could see his shocked expression.

"No," Drake said with a slight shake of his head. "No way. It's not possible." Frustrated tears gathered in his eyes, and he was too exhausted to try to hold them in or hide them, the wet trails on his cheeks evidence of his sense of betrayal.

Closing his eyes, Scotty let his body collapse into the chair at Drake's bedside. He rubbed his face with his palms, then dropped his hands between his knees and looked back up at Drake.

Their eyes met and Drake didn't allow his own gaze to falter. The wet streams were still there, but he refused to look away. Scotty hitched in a breath and leaned forward, his elbows on his knees. He opened his mouth to speak but then closed it and looked away.

"So, what do I call you?" Drake rasped. "Officer Scotty?"

Scotty closed his eyes again, his Adam's apple bobbing as he swallowed. Opening his eyes, he met Drake's straight on. "Agent, Special Agent Graft." He paused before adding, "Adam."

Drake let out a choked laugh, diverting his eyes. "Adam." The name felt heavy on his lips.

"I'm sor—" Scotty/Adam began but stopped abruptly when Drake made a guttural sound in the back of his throat and turned his head away.

He didn't want to hear it. He didn't want to hear anything Scotty… er… Adam had to say. There was nothing that could be said that would make anything better right now. Nothing that could fix the damage that had been done.

So, the silence grew between them, becoming palpable. Scot-Adam cleared his throat, but Drake couldn't bring himself to look at him. He didn't know what Scot-Adam could look at. He hoped he was having as much trouble as he was.

"I'm going to get the doctor," Adam finally said, breaking the silence. He stepped away from the bed, and Drake automatically felt his absence.

As much as he didn't want to, and as much as he needed to be angry and needed to feel rage at the blatant betrayal, Drake felt panic at Scotty's retreating back. An internal struggle broke out in his mind, but as angry and confused as he was, Drake couldn't let him go.

"Wait!" Adam turned around hesitantly, as if afraid of what he might find when he looked. "Don't… don't go yet." Drake hated the way his voice trembled, just like he had hated his tears earlier, but he didn't have the strength to control himself yet. So he let it all show. He let his anger and confusion, his hurt and his betrayal, and his need and his fear clearly broadcast across his face.

Adam searched his face, taking in each reeling emotion before returning to his bedside, his own face a twisting mask of emotions. He reached down and took Drake's hand into his own. He squeezed his fingers.

"I'm not going anywhere."

Drake looked at their joined hands and then back up at Adam. "I don't understand," he whispered.

Adam's breath hitched. "I know. I'm sorry. I wanted to tell you, I really did, but…."

"You didn't."

"I didn't."

Drake felt new tears in his eyes, and he sniffed, trying to stop himself from becoming a blubbering mess. Jesus, he was better than this. He had infiltrated a dangerous drug cartel! He shouldn't be crying because Scotty lied to him. Drake had lied to everyone. He should be used to lies. Except...

Drake had lied to everyone except for Scotty. Scotty was the only one who Drake had ever told the truth. He was the only person Drake had trusted enough to tell his secret. He had told Scotty everything and Scotty hadn't run, he hadn't judged him, he had stayed and told him he loved him. Scotty had said he loved him! But that couldn't possibly be the truth because Scotty wasn't even his real fucking name. Scotty couldn't love anyone because Scotty didn't fucking exist!

He had been using him. He had been using him, and all the while Drake had foolishly trusted him.

"I trusted you!" Drake couldn't control his anger and hurt any longer. He wrenched his hand away from Adam's, unable to move too far because of the cuffs, but Adam backed off as Drake thrashed. Drake fought at his restraints, words flying out of his mouth. "I trusted you. I told you everything, everything! I let you in, when I couldn't let anyone in. I let you see me, not Drake Clane, not the dumbass club owner who was in too deep with a cartel, but me! But you were just using me. Using me! No wonder you didn't run away when you realized what a train wreck my life was. You needed to get closer to me! You fucking asshole! You fucked me!"

Adam tried to calm him down, tried to keep him from thrashing on the bed, from opening his wound, which he could feel tearing on his abdomen. He used his hands to restrain Drake's shoulders, but he bucked, trying desperately to get Adam off.

"I'm sorry, Drake. Stop! You're going to hurt yourself! Stop! I'm sorry. I am so sorry! Please stop!"

Suddenly the room was full of shouting people. Hands were holding him down, trying to shush him, but Drake couldn't stop. His whole body pumped with adrenaline and he had no way to release it, so he did what he could and struggled against the hands.

"Administer midazolam, one milligram," a voice called, and more hands came to hold him down. Drake fought with all his might, ignoring the pain.

"You fucked me, and then you *fucked* me! I trusted you! I fucking loved you."

The room spun, catching Drake off guard, and he had to close his eyes, but as soon as his lids closed he had to struggle to open them again. His thrashing limbs slowed, too heavy to lift.

"Trusted you. I… loved you."

He felt as if he were sinking into the mattress, as if it were swallowing him up. Darkness swarmed around the edges of his vision, pushing farther in until there was hardly any light left. All he could see was Scotty's face, wet from tears, and then that too was cloaked by the darkness. Then all that was left was despondent whispering: "I'm sorry. I am so fucking sorry. I'm sorry." And then nothing.

CHAPTER 23

THE FUCKING ceiling. If Drake never saw a plain white ceiling again, he could die fucking happy. Who was he kidding? No he wouldn't. He would die miserable and alone. He had always known that he would, except now he felt the loneliness. Never knew what you had until you lost it, isn't that what the people said? Well, he wasn't sure if he'd had it or not; he didn't know what you classify something as "had" when everything about it was fiction. But after having it, real or not, the ache of losing it still hurt.

Deep breathing from the chair beside the bed garnered his attention, but he couldn't bring himself to look over. If it was Scotty, or Adam, or whoever the fuck he was, Drake wasn't sure if he could handle it. Their last interaction hadn't ended well. He still had fuzzy brain to back up that claim. But he could still hear Adam's anguished whispers, could still feel his fingers caressing along his face as he fell into darkness.

Whatever the hell any of that meant.

Drake shifted, trying to get more comfortable on the bed. His body felt as if it had been stuck in a single position for far too long. He needed to fucking move. He tried to pull his body up so he could get into a sitting position but stopped when pain in his lower abdomen screamed. He went to put his hand on it, try to stop whatever was making it hurt, but his arm snagged on the cuff.

He eyed the cuff angrily. Glaring at the unyielding fabric, Drake jerked his wrists back and forth roughly. He knew it would only hurt him and do absolutely nothing else but, dammit, he was pissed! He had been drugged, tied up, tortured, shot, tied up, lied to, and drugged again, and he was sick and tired of being held captive.

"You're awake." The deep voice surprised Drake. Even though he didn't want to see Scotty or Adam or whomever, he had thought it *was* him waiting at his bedside.

Drake turned to face the strange voice, and his eyes widened in recognition. "Well, hello there. Isn't this a fun reunion?"

The man sat up in the chair with a smirk. "Yeah, something like that." Drake snorted. "Something like that. Yeah, sure. Craig, wasn't it? I mean, if that is your real name."

"Special Agent Craig Donnelly," Craig said, rubbing tired eyes.

Drake snickered. "Oh, so it really is Craig. How nice to have a little bit of truth. I would say sorry about before in the parking lot, but ya know, I'm kinda glad I did it."

"Yeah, well, now I know what you can do, you won't get the drop on me again."

Drake lifted both his wrists and jiggled his arms, straining against the bonds. "Well, at this point, it's kind of impossible." He dropped his wrists back down at his sides. "Am I under arrest?"

Special Agent Craig Donnelly shifted and stood. Drake took in his domineering form as it approached. He had forgotten how big the man was. He silently congratulated himself on the takedown in the parking lot. The man was huge.

"As of right now, no, you aren't under arrest, but you are in protective custody. The local PD has a warrant for you, but as of right now you aren't under their jurisdiction."

"Protective custody, right," Drake mumbled. "Isn't that just like glorified imprisonment?"

Craig shrugged. "Depends on how you look at it, I guess. It can be like imprisonment, or it could be the only thing standing between you and an angry cartel eager to string you up."

Drake shook his head with a cynical sniff. "Obviously, you don't know what you are up against because men like Boredega don't let simple things like 'protective custody' stop them from taking out their targets. Seriously, I would probably be better off not in custody, where I am just waiting for them like a sitting duck."

"We've kept you alive so far."

Drake just closed his eyes and laid his head back on his pillow. "I don't even know who you people are. What agency are you from?"

"DEA," Craig said, and Drake opened his eyes to watch him as he took Drake's wrist into his hand. His large fingers fumbled with the buckle on the cuff, but finally the restraint loosened and slid off. "We had to cuff you to keep you from hurting yourself and the hospital staff, even before your little outburst."

As soon as the cuff left his skin, Drake stretched and then flexed his arm, letting the blood flow freely once again. Then as soon as the stretch relaxed his muscles, he scratched his nose with a relieved sigh. "You have no idea how bad I wanted to do that."

The snort Craig exhaled belied his stern expression. "I can only undo one for now. I want the nurses to do the other. Don't make me regret taking it off."

Enjoying the freedom of his limb more than he thought could be possible, Drake itched along his body, then found his bandaged stomach and used his fingers to inspect the damage. He cringed at the pain just a small amount of pressure caused and decided it was probably best not to mess with it. He wondered who shot him. It probably was one of the agents. It would just be like him to get stuck in the crossfire.

"Sorry 'bout that. We hadn't intended to have a shootout in that small room. It probably hurts like a son of a bitch, but luckily it didn't hit anything the doctors couldn't fix."

Drake shook his head. "I figured it was you guys who shot me."

"When you went missing, we decided to raid the place and got into a gunfight with a stupid prick who didn't know when to quit."

"Did you kill him?"

Craig waved a hand dismissively. "The kid? No, we got him in the leg, and he's in custody with the local PD."

"You got the bad guy in the leg and shot me in the gut. My faith in law enforcement is restored."

"Well, we *did* get you out of there instead of letting you slowly, painfully waste away from a Selecure overdose. Instead, you essentially have a flesh wound. Does that help *restore your faith* in law enforcement?"

"I am sure your higher-ups would have frowned on leaving me there."

"I was less worried about my 'higher-ups' than I was about Adam. If we hadn't breached as a unit, he would have gone in himself and gotten you both killed."

Drake huffed. "He that concerned over losing an asset?"

"You're a stupid fuck, you know that," Craig growled, his voice low. "Adam has been working his cover for over three years, moving from bar to bar and club to club to get to a place where the intel was good. This has been a five-year operation, and as soon as he realized that you were gone, he didn't even think twice about breaking his cover."

In his anger, Craig had clenched the sidebar on the bed, and his knuckles were white from his unrelenting grip. "I don't know what all went on between you two, and I don't want to know, but I do know that this damn investigation hit a major pothole as soon as you got involved."

Drake eyed the man warily, blinking up at the domineering figure. He didn't know what to believe because all he knew was that he had spilled his guts out and he hadn't even gotten a real name in return. Scotty knew everything about him, everything about his past, about his role in the cartel. What did Drake know about him? Absolutely nothing.

Drake nibbled on his dry bottom lip. "Where is he?"

Craig stood back, his grip lessening on the bed. "After your little outburst last night, the doctors decided it would be best if he stayed away for now. And I agree with them, due to the nature of your relationship."

"Relationship," Drake mumbled. Could it be called a relationship if it only went one way? But he kept thinking back to when he first woke up and how much better he felt knowing that Scotty was there. Even later, when Adam had been about to walk out the door, Drake hadn't been able to stomach the thought of his leaving, let alone the crushed look on the man's face.

"I don't want to know about it. I already know too much and we don't need anything else to happen that could be damaging to our case. Especially damaging to Adam. He's already taking a lot of flak for breaking cover, but hopefully with the extra information you'll give us it will help smooth the waters."

Drake's brows rose. "You want me to give you information? Testify in court?"

"I figured that would be obvious, what, with your... extracurricular activities, you have a fair knowledge of the inner workings of the Boredega cartel. You've made it in farther than we have ever been able to."

Drake's mouth dropped open. Was he serious? "Really? You want me to testify? Against Boredega? You remember that the last time anyone got close enough to take him to court everyone on the operation was killed, right?"

"Times have changed. We have better intelligence now; we have better knowledge about how the cartel operates."

"Except you still don't have the guy! He's a ghost. No one knows who or where he is, and he's still out there selling drugs and killing people, while you and every other agency chases their tails!"

"Well, actually, thanks to you, we have a pretty good idea where to start looking. That flash drive we picked up has quite a bit of good information on it. Now, we need someone to back up the claims with some cold hard facts, which you should be able to do for a good portion of the evidence...." Craig let his words trail off as Drake gaped at him. "What?"

Drake blinked a couple of times trying to put everything together in his head. "Flash drive? What flash drive?"

Craig gave him a derisive look. "The one that shows all the offshore accounts. The one you told Adam about. When Adam reported it in, we felt it was too important to let sit."

"But I deleted it," Drake said. "And none of the information on that is real. It has the money going into accounts with *my* name on them! *I* didn't take the money!" As Drake spoke, his voice became louder. "What could that flash drive do but put me behind bars? Boredega wouldn't have any trouble getting to me then!"

Waving off a nurse who stuck her head in the room, Craig frowned. "What are you talking about? Of course we took the flash drive. We had the information restored, and we have analysts looking it over. Agent Graft already put in his report that it was a falsified document. Doesn't mean that there aren't facts on there or areas to pursue. Besides, to be authentic the money would have to sit in those accounts for a while until the kid or whoever is behind the money skimming moved it. We at least have a place to start looking now."

"But why me? You said Jacob is in local PD custody, and Natasha would have more information than me." Drake didn't like the silence that met that question. "I'm assuming that you picked up both Jacob and Natasha.... You did get them, right? I mean, they were both right there."

Craig nodded. "We got the kid, but the girl had already left by the time we breached. We have an APB out on her, but right now she is in the wind."

Drake laughed, the sound coming from deep in his throat. "Yeah, well, good luck finding her. I'm sure she's long gone by now."

Craig looked down at Drake curiously. "She wasn't in any of the reports as anything more than a possible user and occasional dealer. She wasn't a main priority. What do you know?"

Drake laughed again closing his eyes to lean back into his soft pillow. "She's not just some stupid hooker. She's Boredega's daughter."

Craig cursed, reaching into his pocket to pull out a phone. "You're sure about this?"

Drake huffed, "Straight from her lips."

"You didn't think it was important to lead with that information?"

Drake smirked, eyes still shut. "I didn't realize it was my responsibility to tell you how to do your job."

Cursing again, Craig used wide fingers to navigate on his phone. "Agent Donnelly here," Craig said as he walked toward the door. Before he could leave, Drake called his name.

Craig asked the person who answered to hold and waited, brows arched.

"Could you, uh, ask Special Agent Graft to, uh…." Drake let his voice trail off.

After a moment of hesitant deliberation, Craig dropped his chin in a firm nod, then walked out of the room, issuing the new information over the phone.

Another suit stood in the doorway as soon as Craig exited. The man peeked in, giving Drake a quick once-over, then with a subtle nod closed the door, blocking out the hospital ambiance with a severe snick. Drake let the silence glide over him, let the new information and situation sink in. Exhaling a tight breath, he let his head fall back on his pillow. With heavy thoughts whirling through his head, he blinked up at the white ceiling, the simplicity of it soothing some of his frenzied anxiety. Huh, maybe there was a point to the white after all.

CHAPTER 24

TIME PASSED in a haze. The drugs they had him on kept Drake in a sort of stupor. All he knew was that there was a flurry of nurses and doctors that he saw through each bout of consciousness, but he couldn't be sure how long he'd been in the hospital bed or how long each fall into unconsciousness lasted. He had checked the chair next to his bed each time he was able to pull himself out of the black, but he had yet to see the man he desperately, although reluctantly needed to see. More times than not, there was a suit sitting in the chair, but it was never the one he thought (hoped?) would be there.

Drake couldn't help but find the humor in personal guard. If having a man with a gun was enough to stop Boredega or his men, they would have stopped the cartel by now. In fact, Drake couldn't be sure that one of the men sitting at his bedside wasn't on Boredega's payroll. It was one of the factors that had brought his father's case to the ground—inside men—and Drake knew all too well how resourceful they could be. It wasn't a question of *if* Boredega would get to him, but when.

However, before he succumbed to that particular dark fate, he needed to see Adam at least one more time. No matter how much the betrayal hurt, how much it pulled at his chest to think that nothing Scotty had done or said was real, he needed to see Adam. He couldn't leave it how it was. He didn't want the last memory Adam had of him to be one of rage. He didn't want the last words he heard from Adam to be begging for forgiveness.

Drake was counting on Special Agent Donnelly keeping his word and telling Adam about his request. As much as it was probably a bad idea for both of them emotionally and especially for Adam professionally, Drake thought the agent understood. Craig may have been big and brawny, but he wasn't stupid, as much as he did deny knowing anything about what had happened between Drake and his partner.

"You know," Drake said, shifting to pull himself into a straighter position, "if you're going to just be sitting there, you could at least make yourself useful."

The suit arched a brow, watching Drake struggle with his bandaged abdomen. Finally getting himself into a more comfortable position, Drake picked up his glass of water and sucked a large gulp out of the straw. He set the cup down with a sigh of satisfaction and eyed the seated suit once again.

"Did you bring cards? Please tell me that at least one of you *Men in Black* guys thought to bring some cards." At the unamused look from the suit, Drake quipped, "Dice? Crosswords? Sudoku? Anything? Scotch?" he ended with a hopeful lilt.

"Not my job to entertain you," the suit remarked.

"Um, yeah, it's to keep me alive, but right now you are killing me with boredom. At least with scotch I could enjoy the boredom."

"Don't they have you on the good stuff?" The tentative voice came from the doorway, and Drake's heart leapt as, finally, golden eyes met his.

Adam entered the room cautiously, probably expecting Drake to throw him out or possibly to rampage again, but as much as Drake wanted to be angry, wanted to yell and scream, it was nothing compared to the relief he felt at being in the same room with him again.

"May I come in?" Adam asked tentatively.

Drake swallowed hard past the lump in his throat and nodded. The suit stood as Adam entered, passing him with a nod as he walked out the door, closing it behind him, sealing the two of them in alone together.

"How, uh—" Adam started, then paused, fidgeting, and tried again. "How are you feeling?"

"I've been better," Drake answered with a slight lift of his shoulders.

"I'm sorry. Stupid question." Adam coughed awkwardly. "But.... you, uh, you seem better. Than before, I mean," Adam said. His mouth opened like he was going to continue, but nothing came out.

Silence stretched around them, the awkward quiet heavy in the air.

How did they go from here? What did you say to someone who you thought you knew, only to find out that their entire being was a lie? How did Drake tell Adam how angry he was, how incredibly betrayed he felt? How did he tell him that none of it mattered and that what they had transcended physical limitations? In the end, what did it matter what either one of them said, because Adam was a cop and Drake was a criminal, no matter his intentions. The path to hell and all that jazz.

Drake cleared his throat, breaking the silence. Adam, who still stood just in front of the closed door as if ready for a quick exit, looked up. Hope-ridden eyes met his. Drake had to lick his lips before he could speak. "Agent, er, uh, Craig, he uh, filled me in on some things."

Adam swallowed visibly, nodding. "Good. That's... good."

"I'm sorry about before—"

Stepping forward, Adam held out a placating hand. "No, no, don't apologize. You have nothing to be sorry for. You were right. I was the one who lied. Who kept lying. Even after you told me everything, even after I told you...." Any power Adam had to hold himself straight seemed to leave him at that moment. His body buckled and he landed in the chair next to Drake's bed.

"I hurt you. I hurt you, and that was the last thing I wanted. I know you probably don't believe anything I say anymore, but please believe that. I didn't want to hurt you. I was trying my best to protect you."

Watching the man who had the ability to light up the atmosphere with a smile, and flirt his way into a 40 percent tip with just a wink, slump in the overstuffed hospital chair with his brows knit and his hands wringing made heat sear behind Drake's eyelids.

"Did you—" Drake had to stop to gain control of his voice. Fighting the lingering waver, he continued, "Was it all an act? To get information from me?"

Adam's head shot up. He shook it vehemently. "What? No."

"You didn't sleep with me to get close to me?"

Adam continued to shake his head. "No, I didn't sleep with you because of any of this!" He gestured wildly around the room. "I slept with you *despite* all of this."

"So, what was that thing with Craig in the parking lot, hmm? You do that for shits and giggles?"

Adam had the good sense to look bashful. He averted his eyes momentarily. "Yes, I was supposed to get to close to you. You were my target. I was supposed to become a confidant for you, someone you would feel comfortable sharing information with. And I had to do that any way possible, and let's face it, damsel in distress works for you. But.... Maybe it started out that way. And if I could, I would go back and tell you the truth before everything happened, but please believe me when I tell you that I didn't sleep with you because I had to. I did it because I wanted to. Because I found myself thinking about you when I shouldn't have been, and the image of you in my head was enough to... to...." Adam swallowed, closing his lips tight, then let his shoulders hang.

Nodding, Drake let his head fall back. He stared up at the white ceiling, the simplicity of it calming him.

"I never meant to hurt you, Drake. After you told me about your past and about your family, I wanted to protect you even more, and I thought that the only way I could do that was to keep my identity secret."

"Were you ever going to tell me?" Drake's voice was hoarser than he liked.

Silence filled the air as Adam contemplated the question. "I wanted to. I really wanted to." Adam left it at that.

Drake got it. It wasn't like he had hidden his feelings about the authorities or their abilities. Scotty had begged him to go to the police, and every time, Drake had shot him down without hesitation. So he did get it. He did. He just hadn't expected it to hurt so fucking much.

They both had regrets about their past, but in the end what did any of it matter when Drake was living on borrowed time? No one ever testified against the cartel. No one ever made it that close to a courthouse; usually they didn't even make it that close to the police station. As much as Drake wanted to latch on to the words that Adam was giving him, wanted to engorge himself on the knowledge that Scotty hadn't all been a lie, that if things had been different maybe they could have had a life together, it wasn't the reality and they both knew it.

With each breath, he felt his resolve strengthen. Dropping his chin back down to once again meet Adam's eyes, Drake couldn't help but notice how young Adam looked in his dark suit. Sure, it looked good on him, the dark color bringing out the yellow hues in his eyes, but more than anything he looked like a kid playing dress-up with his daddy's clothes. His face was too young, too innocent to be encased in something with so much responsibility.

"Look, I—" Drake began, but just as he was about speak, the door pushed open.

Special Agent Craig Donnelly strode in, and in an instant Adam lost all of his uncertainty. His little-kid-in-a-big-suit look melted away, and suddenly he was an agent. Seeing the transformation before his eyes, Drake swallowed. That was more like the Scotty he remembered, confident and ready for anything.

"What is it?" Adam said, and Drake's eyes widened. Even his voice had hardened. It was as if the timid man from just a few moments ago didn't exist.

Drake needed to remember that. The man was a chameleon. He had been working undercover convincingly enough for over three years; his identity might be as unknown to Adam as it was to Drake.

"There was an attempt on the kid in holding," Craig said, pulling some clothes out of a bag he'd brought into the room. He threw them on the bed at Drake's feet. "Get dressed. We're going to move you to a more secure facility."

Drake moved gingerly as Adam pressed for more information. "Attempt?"

"A drunk and disorderly made it into holding with a shiv. Jacob lost a lot of blood, but they got it under control. They're putting him in solitary for the time being."

Adam cursed. "I thought he would get a little leeway being family."

"Solitary won't help if it's a guard or a cop, hell, even a lawyer, on the Boredega payroll." Drake coughed, holding his side. He hadn't realized how much he still hurt until he tried to dress himself. "I'm surprised I'm still kicking with the amount of doctors and nurses in and out of here."

Craig shrugged. "You're here under an alias." Craig ignored Drake's snort of contempt. "Anyway, word on the street is that Tony is the one who put the hit on him and Drake both. The local PD is doing everything they can to make as little interaction as possible."

Adam reached forward to help Drake slip his shirt on. He moved cautiously, careful not to make any skin-to-skin contact.

As much as they were in a hurry, and no matter how much Drake was aware that now was not the best time to be worrying about something as small as lust, he couldn't help but shiver at the heat of Adam's fingers as they smoothed the cotton over his shoulders and down his sensitive torso. Closing his eyes, he dragged in a ragged breath, before meeting Adam's gaze. Mere seconds passed, but it felt like an eternity of time as Drake swam in fields of goldenrods teeming with the same longing that gripped him.

In, one, two, three and out, one, two, three. Pulling away, Drake cleared his throat. "You couldn't have grabbed me some sweatpants and a loose tee, could you?"

Craig smirked. "Just quit your bitchin' and let's get the hell out of here."

Slipping on his shoes, Drake clutched his abdomen and shrugged at both men. "I'm ready. Where are we headed?"

"If I told you, it wouldn't be secure, now would it?"

Drake tried to laugh but thought better of it, as it pulled the muscles in his side. With a small groan, he followed the two agents as they led the way out of the room. "Has anyone ever told you that you're a bastard?"

It was Adam's time to smirk. "Every day."

CHAPTER 25

THE TREK to the black SUV parked on the second floor of the hospital parking garage had been slow but better than Drake had anticipated. Having been in bed since he was injured, any slight movement had generated a shooting pain to radiate from his stomach through to his lower back, but now that he was mobile, his body was gaining a tolerance to the pain. It wasn't fun, by any means, but he could walk briskly down the never-ending flights of stairs without wanting to kill someone or himself. So, he took that as a positive.

They took the most roundabout way out of the hospital. If Drake hadn't been ready to collapse into the fetal position and cry himself to sleep, he would have probably found it humorous. They went down two floors on the elevator, took the stairs up a floor, then the elevator down again another two floors, and then the stairs the rest of the way. Any other time, Drake would have really enjoyed the cloak-and-dagger routine. Hell, for someone who had lived in a perpetual shadow of lies and deception, he found their little procedure adorable, but he'd much rather have done it without a hole in his abdomen.

Finally, they made it to the parking garage. Drake took a moment, leaning his shoulder against the chilled concrete wall, to catch his breath. Adam stopped with him, running a hand up Drake's back, then grasping his shoulder.

"You doing okay?"

Drake shrugged, pushing off the wall. "Peachy."

"Yeah, you look like it," Adam teased. As Drake started to move, Adam's hand slid down Drake's arm, and he shifted so he could support Drake as they walked. "It's not that much farther. The car is right up there."

Looking where Adam was indicating, Drake let out a tired laugh. "Are you kidding me?"

Craig reached the black SUV, pulling open the passenger door. He glanced back at Drake's comment with a frown.

"What?"

Adam moved away to open the back door for Drake. Still caught in his incredulous chuckle, Drake shuffled his way into the vehicle.

"Did you make me walk all those stairs, some of them multiple times for shits and giggles? Because you can't be seriously taking us to a secure location in the most obvious government vehicle to ever exist after that ridiculous jaunt around the hospital."

Once Drake was situated in his seat, Adam closed the door and rushed to the other side of the car to jump in. He barely had his door closed before the SUV began its twisting way out of the garage.

The driver was another suit. This one a dark suit and matching black sunglasses, just perpetuating the whole law enforcement, *Men in Black* image.

"I mean, come on! Look at this guy." Drake waved a hand at the suit. "There is no way that someone watching the hospital didn't see him sitting in this car and say, 'That's it. That's the one, follow that one.'"

Craig twisted around in his seat to eye Drake, one side of his lips tugged up in a half smile. "Haven't you heard? The best way to hide is in plain sight." Giving a wink, he twisted back to face front.

Drake laughed. "So that's your strategy. Hide in plain sight. They can write that on my tombstone."

Adam buckled himself in, gesturing for Drake to do the same. "You're going to be fine. Don't worry. We'll get you to a secure location."

"Like where?" Drake asked, his voice louder than he intended. "Where can you put me where you can be sure that someone on Boredega's payroll can't find me?"

Adam shifted in his seat so he was facing Drake. "We can get you to a safe house where only a select few will know where you are. Those, only people we can trust."

"You can't trust anyone! Don't you get it? Hasn't anything that happened over the last few years sunk in?" Drake realized he was shouting and made a point to lower his voice. "Everyone has a price. Somebody you trust today could be bought or bribed tomorrow."

Craig's hard voice carried to the back seat. "What would you have us do? We can't just leave you in the wind. You are a known member of Tony's crew. Semblance is used as a money-laundering site for a cartel. It's only because we were the first agency on the scene that you aren't locked up in local PD custody, where you would be in the same cell as Jacob."

"Or dead already," Adam whispered, and it was only because Drake had been watching him while Craig ranted in the front seat that he saw the shiver accompanying the comment.

He wanted to continue the argument, wanted to make them see sense. None of them were safe. Not now, not while Boredega was still out there somewhere offering money for their heads and threatening harm on anyone who would have any information. But he bit his tongue.

If he was going to go underground, he would have to do it on his own, on his own terms and alone. He couldn't have someone looking over his shoulder, checking in. He had to disappear.

Or he could do what he had planned on doing all along. He could take them out. As it was he was a dead man either way. He had no reason to hide any longer. Now he could just go in guns blazing, Punisher-style.

First, he had to get rid of the feds. They wouldn't let him walk away, but Drake could be pretty resourceful when he needed to be. He was sure he would find his chance.

As much as he hated to think about it, Adam trusted him. What they'd had was strained to the point of practically nonexistence, but Drake knew the hope was still there. A useless hope that he knew he could use to his advantage. Just the thought raised a flurry of unease to clench in his gut, and he had to swallow around the bile buildup stuck in his throat.

"She didn't have motive to falsify the drive," Adam was saying as Drake faded back into the conversation. Craig was shaking his head in the front seat. Now he had a laptop on his lap and he was punching the keyboard.

"Yes, she did. She's the guard dog Boredega sends out to find traitors, right? Maybe that's what she was doing, only she got Jacob to do the dirty work. Two birds, one stone," Craig said, and Drake turned his head to look out the window. The unfamiliar scenery indicated they were officially out of the city.

"But Jacob is Tony's nephew—"

Drake broke in, "I don't think that Boredega would hesitate to take out his own daughter if it would mean keeping his cover concealed."

He turned back to face Adam. "It's what makes him so dangerous. He doesn't hesitate to wipe out an entire task force just for revenge. He killed my entire family. My sister! She was thirteen years old and they killed her because my dad had gotten too close. My sister was just a kid. She didn't know anything. How could she?"

Adam's breath hitched as Drake spoke. He fidgeted in his seat as if he didn't know what to do with himself. He reached out—to pull Drake into a hug? To comfort and sooth Drake's furious pain? Drake would never know, because his hands dropped before they could complete their mission, and Drake wasn't quite sure if the ache in his chest was disappointment or relief.

"I'm sorry," Adam whispered so low that only Drake could hear him.

He tried to smile. Tried to reassure Adam, but the act of smiling took more strength than he was willing to give.

"That's why we are getting you to a se—" Craig's words were cut short by a cracking sound that sent chills down Drake's spine.

Before anyone could react, before the situation could be assessed, the driver, who had remained silent for the entirety of the ride, slumped forward in his seat, head resting against the steering wheel, arms slack at his sides.

The car jerked left in a hard turn, and Drake barely had time to brace himself before the SUV hit the guardrail, careening back to the right.

"Shit!" Drake heard Adam curse as suddenly they were on two wheels, traveling a small distance in a horizontal wheelie. Then everything turned to chaos. The SUV spun and flipped, shattering glass and crunching metal deafening in the madness. Unable to tell what was up and what was down and wedged in a tight embrace from the seat belt digging into his shoulder and hip, Drake dropped off into darkness.

"Drake." The voice came from far away, but its frantic tone demanded attention. "Drake!" It said again with more force.

Drake blinked. He tried to focus, but his vision swam. Trying to sit up, he gasped as he became aware of blinding pain searing through him. His head, his abdomen, his arms, his legs, all of it ached and burned. He pressed a trembling hand against the wound in his abdomen, expecting to feel a hole the size of a baseball for the amount of pain, but his hand met bandages. He lifted his hand up to see if there was blood on his fingertips, but his eyes continued to swim behind a red haze.

He was bleeding, he realized. Blinking enough that his eyes watered. He was bleeding enough that it was pooling into his eyes. Drake swallowed around a bout of panic and tried to wipe at his eyes, shaking away some of the broken glass.

"Drake!" the voice shouted again, and Drake blinked around the red, looking for Adam. Blood coursed down Adam's pale face, following the paths, the natural crevasses, mimicking tears. Drake felt spellbound by the sight. He wanted to touch it. He needed to feel it, press the blood between his fingers, smell the coppery odor. Because that blood was what made the man real. Not his name, whether it be Adam or Scotty, or if he was a bartender or a federal agent—that blood was what made the man real.

"What the fucking hell?" Another voice groaned from the front seat. More shattering glass sounded as Craig pulled his weapon from his shoulder holster.

The soft tinkling of glass shattering was overcome by the loud cracking echo of the car cushion as a bullet jarred the bucket seat Drake was still recuperating in. A poof of disintegrated cloth rose from where the bullet made impact.

"Sniper!" Adam shouted, finally escaping the belts once meant to protect their occupants, now holding them prisoner. After sliding down to the floor, he crawled toward Drake, who was still slowly returning to his senses. Adam pushed Drake's vibrating hands away from the seat belt clasp and undid it himself, pulling Drake close.

"You okay?" Adam asked. His hands roamed up and down Drake's body, probing for any sign of unknown injury. "You hit your head pretty solidly."

"You're not much better." Drake's voice slurred, much to his surprise.

Cursing, Craig unsuccessfully pulled at his door handle. When the handle clicked like the door should open but it didn't move, the big man let out a shout and shouldered it open. He fell out of the car, rolling to a crouch, using the door as a cover. His gun held at the ready, Craig shouted into his cell phone, requesting immediate backup and reporting an officer down. He barked commands while simultaneously scouting the area. The world came slamming back into focus, and Drake pushed Adam's searching hands away.

Another bullet whizzed past, embedding itself in a twist of metal and plastic in the seat next to Drake, and Adam dodged in the small area, ending up against Drake's chest.

"Jesus Christ!" Adam's breath was hot against Drake's neck. "We need to get out of here!"

"We need backup, now!" Craig yelled into his phone before tossing it back onto the seat. "We have incoming!"

Adam lifted his head enough to peer out at Craig's shout. Over his shoulder, Drake could see the approaching vehicle coming in fast. The car was still a distance away, but as it approached, it gained more speed. As torn up as their current vehicle was, there was no way it could take another solid impact.

"Shit," Drake breathed as it dawned on him that the car definitely was not going to stop. He twisted, pushing hard against the door. It didn't budge. He hit along it, trying to find the lock or any reason that it wouldn't open.

Realizing that the cause of the jam had nothing to do with the locking mechanism, Drake turned back to Adam, who now had his own gun drawn. And even though they didn't have time, even though they were going to get crushed if they didn't get out of the car, Drake couldn't help but notice that the look suited Adam just fine. But the thought passed as he eyed the car that had seemed to double its speed.

He continued his struggle with the door. "It's stuck!"

"Go out the window. I'll cover you!" Craig shouted.

Drake eyed the speeding car, and although he wasn't the best at math, there was one thing he could tell for certain.

"We can't both make it." He turned, wide-eyed, to Adam. "We can't both make it out!"

Adam pushed Drake toward the window. "Go!" he shouted. "When you get out, go for cover and get as far away as you can!"

Drake shook his head frantically, and he bunched his fist in Adam's suit, unwilling to let go.

Adam pulled Drake harshly to him and mashed their lips together in a bruising kiss. Violently pushing Drake away, Adam tried to shove him through the window.

"Neither of us are going to make it if you don't go! If you go now, I can try to make it out the front! Go! Now!"

Four hard gunshots rang loud in Drake's ears as Craig laid down cover, shooting at the car that was alarmingly close. Drake pushed himself up to the window as another few shots were fired. The last shot answered in a thundering boom as the approaching car lurched as its front tire blew. It swerved left and right as the driver tried to get the fishtail under control. Oversteering one too many times made the car spin. It traveled toward them, the metal grating along the pavement, sending sparks flying. The car slid toward them now horizontally.

In one, two, three. No time!

Drake closed his eyes and clenched his teeth, trying to ignore the smell of burnt rubber in the air. Not giving himself time to think, he dropped out the window, falling heavily onto his back, just as the approaching car made impact. Pushing away from the metal monstrosity with his foot, Drake ignored the searing pain of skin tearing against glass and pavement, then pulled his limbs into the fetal position, protecting himself as much as he could from a metal beast skidding toward him. Metal ground and groaned as they twisted around each other. Glass and rocks flew, pelting Drake, but he held his position. Even though the crash was greatly simplified due to the other car's loss of control, it was still enough to send both vehicles back a couple of feet.

Eyes clenched, Drake waited for the impact to hit him, because there was no way he was going to make it out of this alive. But as he gritted his teeth, braced for the pain he knew was to come, the screeching metal stopped. Letting out the breath he had been holding, Drake eyed the cars warily.

Two men were inside the car that rammed them. From what he could see, the passenger's head hung loosely with blood running thickly down his head onto his neck and shoulders. Drake couldn't see the driver side of the vehicle, but the cursing coming from inside indicated that he was far more conscious than his buddy.

Rolling to his stomach, Drake pushed himself to his hands and knees and quickly regained his feet. Shooting a hasty look around, he tried to spot a place for cover. They were in the middle of a service drive. No houses or business could be seen in either direction. They were well out of the city and seriously lacking coverage.

Drake cursed, then breathed a sigh of relief as he spotted a gray metal power box fifty yards down the road. Smiling, he started toward the box, but gunfire behind him pulled him short. He turned, searching frantically for the source of the gunfire.

Craig was on his feet, using their ruined SUV door as a shield, gun drawn. He aimed at the now demolished vehicle that had collided into them, shouting for the man to exit the vehicle with his hands up.

Drake's heart raced. He didn't see the man he was looking for. Had Adam made it out of the car before the collision? Was he still inside? Jesus, was he bleeding and broken?

The pounding of his heartbeat drummed through his ears, eliminating all other sound. Deaf and blind to the world, Drake started back toward the mangle of metal with a limp. His body ached, but he pressed forward.

Adam had to be okay. He had to be.

A breath away from running back to the wreckage to search for any sign of Adam, Drake watched as Craig staggered back from the force of a bullet to his chest. He couldn't stop the inhale of panicked breath as the large man toppled back, lying flat.

Drake's hobble turned into more of a gallop as he became even more determined to get back to the chaos and the rubble. Dropping low so the SUV mostly covered him, he was almost to the fallen man when Adam crawled out of the heap of metal and knelt beside his sprawled partner.

Blood rushed in his ears, as Drake felt a tidal wave of relief crash around him. His knees collapsed beneath him, and he knelt on the ground watching as Adam checked over his partner, who grabbed his wrist and then pushed him away.

Drake watched. His body ached to go to Adam, to sweep him away from all of this disaster and carry him to safety. But the rest of him, no matter how reluctantly, couldn't move, couldn't take those few steps. So, he stayed and watched as Adam took Craig's gun and wound around the door to return fire.

As if sensing his inaction, Adam twisted, and even from that far distance, the world stopped as their eyes met.

Go, Adam mouthed, gesturing with his gun for him to run, but Drake shook his head, taking a step closer.

"Get out of here!" Adam yelled. "Find cover!"

Drake bit his lip, hesitating. He almost didn't listen, his entire being now fully yearning to run back, to do anything it took to keep the only man who had ever gotten to know him, the real him, out of danger.

A bullet struck the ground at his feet, flinging up bits of debris, triggering him into action. In a single dive, he flung himself off the road and into the shallow ditch. It wasn't much cover, but he would take what he could get. In a low crouch, he ran until he was behind the power box.

More gunshots were fired as another black SUV careened down the service drive, an arm stretched out the window shooting blindly. Drake watched as Adam hugged the car door to him and Craig pulled himself up from the pavement to crouch next to him, and Drake was surprised about the relief he felt for that man.

But the relief was short-lived as the injured man from the damaged car jumped out of the wreckage and opened fired on the agents. As they kept their heads down, the SUV slid to a stop, doors opening with more men with guns coming out.

Drake's breathing faltered as he watched the swarm of men descend on the crouching, outnumbered agents. Banging his head against the metal box, he cursed his helplessness. He didn't have a weapon, and he didn't have cover outside of the stupid metal box that would do him absolutely no good once those men finished the agents, then came after him. He couldn't do anything. He was going to have to watch.

He was going to have to watch while Adam was shot right in front of him, and he couldn't do a damn thing to stop it.

Rage engulfed him even as his throat closed and tears filled his eyes.

He couldn't do it. He couldn't let this happen. He had to do *something*.

Just as he was about to scream "fuck it!" at the world and run to Adam and hold him until they were both shot down in a blaze of glory, he heard the sound of salvation.

Sirens blared in the near distance. Help was on the way. Finally, they were getting that backup they desperately needed.

The men who had just exited their car glanced around, searching for the direction of the sirens. The spinning reds, whites, and blues sped toward them. The men, seeing the cavalry, hopped back into their SUV and peeled out, tearing down the road in a flurry of burnt rubber and thrown pebbles.

Drake collapsed against the cool metal, letting the box hold him for moment. He let the entire situation sink in and come together. The new "Scotty," Adam with a gun, continued to check over his partner now that the immediate danger was gone. Drake watched him and swallowed the bile in his throat. The man could handle himself, he was good under pressure, and he did not need Drake to protect him. Unfortunately, Drake couldn't protect anyone anymore. At least, he couldn't protect them by being around them.

Drake watched the agents until he couldn't watch anymore. It was now or never. The police vehicles were almost upon them, and Drake knew that once they arrived, his chance was gone. If he was going to leave, he needed to do it now. Drake hoped Adam would understand. Hoped the man would let him do what he needed to do so it could be over. At least over for Drake. He had spent his life working toward this, and he couldn't allow himself to be taken down before he could at least put a dent in the cartel.

Setting his jaw, Drake pushed away from the metal box. Shoving the threatening guilt aside, he took two steps back, then with one last parting glance, he turned and ran as fast as he could, heading toward the trees, making his grand getaway.

CHAPTER 26

THE JOURNEY back to his condo was a long one. By the time he reached the parking lot of his small community, it was dark. He pulled his stolen car into a spot a building over and watched the shadows play across the sitting vehicles.

It was stupid to return to his condo. It was a bad move; he should have taken the car as far as he dared before ditching it, then disappeared. But he never claimed to be a smart man. Shady as fuck, but smart? No, he'd never claimed that.

If he was being honest with himself, he knew that leaving had never really even been a possibility. Leaving at this point would only consist of him running from the cartel and from the law, and Drake knew he wasn't strong enough to live through both of those encounters. Even if the cartel didn't kill him, his resolve would crumble when met with Adam. If Adam asked him to testify, he would do it. He would do anything for him. Against every fiber of his being, he would do anything for him, even if it meant dying for him. That's why he had to do this, because Adam was his weakness, his Achilles' heel. If he stayed, they would both be in danger, and he wouldn't be any closer to taking down the cartel than he was at the moment.

No, he wasn't in the business of making smart moves any longer. No more undercover stealth, no more faking it. It was time to give that last sudden burst of speed because he could finally see the finish line.

After exiting the vehicle, Drake closed the door softly and hunkered down. Sticking to the shadows, he moved as quietly as possible. Ducking from car to car, he crouched low, scuttling through the grass, and pulled himself to his feet behind a tree.

From his new vantage point, he eyed the parking lot, searching for anything out of the ordinary. Not that he had been home that often—he worked long and unusual hours—but he had some idea of what was normal. Even though nothing stood out as an obvious tip-off, it didn't mean they weren't out there.

They would be waiting for him. The cops and Boredega's crew both would be looking for him. It was simply a matter of who found him first.

Not seeing any unusual movement or blatant surveillance vehicles, Drake made his move, creeping along the building and reaching a small decorative garden that ran along the edge, supposedly giving the condo a homier aesthetic. He ducked under windows, keeping his body tight to the wall. He followed the path until he came underneath the fourth window. Stopping, he cautiously peeked up over the sill, keeping his head down and to the side, not wanting to become an easy target if someone was inside waiting for him.

It was dark, the outside lighting reflecting in the glass and making it hard to see. Squinting, he tried to decipher any movement from inside. He moved his head from side to side, trying to look through the dim glare. No movement that he could tell. Definitely no lights on inside to help him see. Confident that the room was clear, he hefted a rock and took another watchful peek through his window.

Still nothing.

Using his shirt as protection and as a tool to help buffer the sound, he gripped the cloth-clad rock and then thrust it hard and quick against the windowpane. The glass splintered with a sharp crack. He hit the rock against the glass again, harder this time. Success. A few pieces of glass fell away into the room. Carefully, Drake used his shirtsleeve to dislodge a few more pieces, and then, mindful of the sharp edges, he reached inside and pulled the latch to unlock the window. Quietly and efficiently, he pushed the window up and hauled himself onto the ledge and through the opening. He twisted, landing lightly on his feet next to his bed. Dropping into a crouch, he listened in the darkness for any signs that he wasn't alone.

Keeping low and alert, he surveyed the room. He wasn't a cleanly man when it came to household chores, but even he hadn't left his room as trashed as it currently was. The floor was littered with clothes, books, papers.... Anything that had once been on any of his furniture was now strewn across the room. He hadn't had much decoration on his walls, some posters that came with the bed set he had purchased, and those were torn off the walls and now resided on the floor.

The nightstand was toppled to the side, drawer open, contents spilled carelessly. The lamp next to his bed lay broken next to it. His mattress was pushed to the side and looked like it had even been cut to search inside. Feeling his heart pulse as he took in the destruction around him, Drake felt under his bed. He searched blindly, fingers walking along the wood until he found what he was looking for. Sucking in a breath of celebratory relief, he pulled his Glock 26 from where he had taped it. For the amount of damage they caused, and searching as they did, Drake was surprised that they hadn't found the gun. Of course, it was possible that they had found it and they hadn't cared, since they obviously weren't looking for his weapon.

Releasing the clip, Drake checked his rounds before sliding it back home. Making sure the safety was on, he tucked the weapon into the waistline of his jeans. Once the gun was secure, he pulled his shirt over his head, hissing as the cloth tore away from his skin. Shit. He hadn't realized how torn up he had been. He winced as the shirt pulled newly scabbed flesh and coagulated blood along with it. His back stung, particularly where his shirt and his skin had been ground together enough to feel like they were fused. Since removing his shirt appeared to be in line with picking off a scab, Drake wasn't surprised when he felt a new tingle of blood as it dripped down his skin. Sucking breath in through his teeth, he threw the shirt to the floor and inspected his wounds with tentative fingers.

Adrenaline, the masked mistress. It always proved a double-edged sword. Sure, the hormones raged enough to keep you alive, or pull a car off a kid, or whatever it was they did. But the hormones also masked the pain and the fatigue. It kept them at bay until suddenly it wore off, slinking back into the night and leaving behind only the devastation in its wake.

Seeing his wounds made everything more real, and now that the adrenaline was wearing off, Drake began to feel the pain, the throb of his skin and the ache in his abused muscles.

Grabbing another shirt randomly from the floor, he managed to pull it on, very aware of each movement, feeling every ache and pain. Grunting softly, he settled the fabric into place over the gun still wedged in at his waist. Darting another look around, Drake longed for a drink. He searched the floor hoping that one of the items flung to the floor was a bottle of scotch. Unfortunately for him, he made it a point not to leave the bottle in his bedroom because once the bottle was next to the bed, the ability to deny being an alcoholic diminished.

Giving up on that dream, Drake turned to his closet. The door was open, the clothes pulled from the hangers and strewn around his feet on the floor. Boxes of keepsakes, not that he had much, just clutter he'd managed to pick up through the years, were littered along the floor. Holding his breath, Drake stepped into the small room and looked toward the wall that housed his family. The wall was bare; only the nail that had held the frame was there. Drake's breath hitched and he dropped to his knees, feeling along the piles on the floor for the frame.

A light flared to life inside the room and Drake's heart almost burst out of his chest. He spun on his knees and faced the doorway of the closet.

"Come out, come out, wherever you are," Natasha sang with a childish lilt from inside his bedroom. "I've been waiting for you."

Closing his eyes in frustration, Drake slowly stood. He couldn't see Natasha since he was in the closet, but he could almost feel the weight of the crosshairs on him. Setting his shoulders, Drake clenched his jaw and moved toward the door, hands raised to shoulder level. He should have known that they would have still been in the house. Once he had seen the wreck of his room, he should have turned and left the same way he had come in. But he couldn't do it. He couldn't just leave. No, he refused to leave them behind.

Sucking in a gulp of air and with the comfort of cold steel pressing against his back, Drake stepped out of the closet.

Natasha stood waiting, shoulder resting casually on the doorframe, her leather-clad legs crossed, the propped foot tapping against the floor impatiently. In one hand, she held a dark pistol, a silencer attached, and in the other, she held a picture frame. Drake glared at her from just outside the closet.

"Ah," she said, her red lips curling into a smile. "There you are."

When she spoke, a man, also clad in all black, moved to stand next to her. He too had a weapon, and it pointed steadily at Drake. Drake stopped his approach when the other man appeared, wary of the gun.

Natasha's smile widened and she gestured at Drake with the pistol to come closer. "Now, don't be shy," she said, waving him closer. "Ryan here isn't going to hurt you. Er, at least not yet. I won't make promises I can't keep."

"That's big of you," Drake quipped.

Natasha's laugh filled the room, causing Drake to grind his teeth as he continued his slow approach. Drake's eyes shifted between the two figures in front of him. He quickly calculated his odds if he tried to run, and though he wasn't much for math, even he could tell those odds were not in his favor. Even if he could duck behind his bed, or fling himself back out his window, he couldn't guarantee they wouldn't be able to get a shot off or two. If he tried to rush them, he would only be able to disarm one of them—that was also assuming that there weren't any other goons in the hall. For the time being, Drake was stuck.

"Natasha," Drake said, his voice steady, belying his nerves. He nodded in mock greeting. "What brings you to my humble abode?"

"Oh, Drakey, Drakey, such a handsome, brooding man. It's almost too bad that it has to go down this way." She clucked her tongue at him, leering. "We could have had such a great time."

Drake shrugged, his hands still palms up, facing outward. "Yeah, well," he said, "I just didn't see it working out between us."

Her smile seemed to brighten as Drake stopped mere feet away. She blinked at him innocently, her old act firmly in place. She sashayed around him to sit down on the bed. Drake turned with her, aware that the man hadn't moved, and now he had one in front and one behind. He watched Natasha as she crossed her legs seductively, eyeing him suggestively. Then curling her tongue around her top lip, she winked at Drake before tilting her head to indicate the frame. Drake's hackles rose as Natasha caressed her pistol along the edge of the picture. That photo was all he had left of his family from before they were ripped from him, and her filthy hands gripping even the frame was enough to ignite flames in the deepest part of him.

"Look at you!" Her gaze returned to his face, the innocent wide eyes replaced with a pitch darkness that contradicted her melodic tone. "Such a cute little boy. You were so happy! Look at that smile."

Drake's jaw clenched and unclenched as she continued to speak. It took all the willpower he possessed to keep from lunging at her. Instead he watched the gun as it traveled from family member to family member, before settling on Drake's father.

"Too bad Daddy hadn't been able to mind his own business, huh?" She laughed, then with a flick of her wrist, tossed the frame at Drake's feet. The glass cracked on impact, and Drake couldn't control his flinch. The twists of the fractures ran along his family's faces, distorting their image.

"Your father took everything from me," Drake managed through a jaw clenched so tight his teeth ached from the pressure. "Everything! Everyone I ever loved."

Drake started to bend down to pick up his shattered memory, but Natasha clicked her tongue at him and waved her gun to motion him to standing.

"Huh-uh," Natasha, still perched peacefully on the bed, showing teeth. "No, he hasn't, not yet." Her laugh sent a shiver down Drake's spine. "Your little cop is still breathing. At least he still was the last time I checked. Of course, after that little 'accident' on the road, that could have changed by now."

"You leave Scotty out of this!" Drake snarled taking a menacing step forward.

"Please." Natasha gave a derisive snort. "We've had our eye on Special Agent Adam Graft since he stepped foot in this city."

Drake breathed through a skip in his heartbeat. "You knew?"

Rolling her eyes, Natasha let her head fall back to stare at the ceiling. "Not much happens in the city that we don't know about."

A Cheshire grin split her face, and she brought her sharp gaze back to Drake. "Except for you."

Her gun, seemingly forgotten in her hand, very suddenly had him in its sights. Uncrossing her legs, Natasha sat up, elbows on knees steadying her aim. The lyrical quality of her words was gone, replaced with razor-sharp tones.

"Daddy had his suspicions, but I could never figure you out. I thought maybe you were just stupid enough to be in the wrong place at the wrong time, but then that cop came around." She stood up, her pistol never wavering. "What a shock it must have been for you two to learn about each other." Her voice returned to its teasing lilt.

"I have watched you two dance around each other for months. It was fun really, watching you, you totally unaware that he was working you while you drooled all over him."

Drake licked dry lips. "You'll have to forgive me if I don't see the humor."

"I don't *have* to do anything," Natasha snarled, razor blades back in place. "This isn't what I thought I would find when I came to your place." She pointed to the closet with her free hand. "I thought the cops had gotten to you. Sure. I thought that they'd used their little slut cop to make you work against us. But you didn't need their help, did you? You've been working against us on your own all of this time."

"I've been doing everything I could to learn about Boredega and this fucking monstrosity of an organization since I was fourteen years old. My entire life has been devoted to bringing him down and everyone around him."

"Aw." Natasha frowned mockingly, batting her eyelashes. "And you've only gotten this far?" Her smile resembled one of a spider as it watched a fly struggle against its web. "How very disappointing for you."

As the words hit him, Drake's chest deflated. Neck rubber, his chin fell to his chest. As much as he'd learned and as much as he'd seen, he knew even less. He wasn't the Punisher like he had thought himself to be.

Drake's gaze dropped to the floor, and he stared at his happy family smiling innocently back up at him. He closed his eyes, trying to rid himself of the disappointment. He didn't do it. He didn't avenge them; he wasn't going to be able to avenge them. He had failed.

Drake looked back at Natasha. He let the defeat show in his eyes, in his body. He couldn't hold it back any longer. As she watched him, Natasha's eyes glittered with triumph. She had him and she knew it, and she knew he knew it too.

"Let's just get on with it, then, shall we?" Drake asked. He dropped to his knees next to the frame. He ignored Natasha as he picked up the broken frame. Pulling off the back, Drake removed the paper photo from its safety.

"It's not that easy, Drakeybo." Natasha batted her lashes at him. "You see, when Daddy gets angry, he can be pretty scary, and right now, he is really angry and it's all focused on you."

Drake could hear the second gun behind him approaching, and he made sure that he kept his shoulders relaxed and defeated. Drake stared down at the photo, the glass and frame in his other hand. "So, what?" Drake asked. "You're going to make an example of me?"

"Something like that." The pleasure in Natasha's voice sent a shudder down Drake's spine. "Ryan, be a doll and restrain him."

"With pleasure," Ryan growled, and Drake could almost feel the man behind him.

Moving with little thought, but with decisive movement, Drake rose high on his knees and threw the broken glass and frame at Natasha. Without waiting to see if the frame hit its mark, Drake spun on his knees and lunged for Ryan's legs. Catching the man around his knees, Drake felt a moment of surprise and resistance from Ryan before he started to tumble. Drake pushed off with his legs, putting as much force as he could into his tackle. As soon as Ryan was floored, Drake rolled to the side and reached for the gun at his back.

A muted bang of Natasha's silencer sounded, and Drake dodged to the side as wood splintered in the floor next to him. Drake held his own gun back as he continued to work his way toward the door. He shot behind himself blindly, the sound thundering in the small room. Natasha cursed as Drake shot and rolled, finally landing in the hallway. Flattening himself against the wall, he took a deep breath, gun pointed at the doorway.

The hand holding the photo shook as he clumsily folded it, making sure he kept his gun trained on the open doorway. He cringed inwardly as the paper creased, creating lines in the only memory he had left of his family. Pulling himself from that dark thought, he shoved the photo into his back pocket.

"Really?" Natasha shouted. "Is this really how you want to play it? Get up, you stupid shit! Find him."

Pulling himself into a crouch, Drake figured his options. The best exit at this point would be through the front door. Since the shooting had started and no other gunned men had come out of the woodwork, Drake figured it was just the three of them in the house. As long as Ryan and Natasha were pinned down in his room, he should have a clear exit. He turned to work his way down the hall, ducking as bullets whizzed past him and into the wall.

Shit.

Firing off another blind shot, Drake ducked behind the first chair he came across in his living room. Eyeing his surroundings, he tried to judge his next move. The door was too far back and out in the open. He could make a run for it, continuing to shoot suppressing fire, but he didn't know what was outside waiting for him either.

"There isn't a point in hiding from me, Drakeybo." The teasing cadence was back in play. "You're going to die one way or another. You might as well just come out here and let me do it."

Drake laughed. "I think I would rather give you a challenge if it's all the same to you. Besides, I thought you wanted to make an example of me."

Pushing away from the chair, Drake snuck as best he could in a crouch, ducking behind an armchair. He strained to hear any movement so he could detect her or Ryan's position.

"It's hardly a challenge. I have men outside waiting to take you, even if you do manage to get past me."

"I would have been disappointed if you didn't. But, hell, how I figure it, I got this far, I might as well take a few of you with me."

Natasha burst with incredulous laughter. "You think you're good enough to take out Boredega's men?"

Drake shrugged even though she couldn't see him. "I could probably at least take out his daughter, and that's good enough for me."

"He took what you love, so you'll take what he loves?" Natasha's cackle almost echoed through the room. "How clichéd."

Drake peeked around the chair, looking for any sign of movement. The darkness of the room, while a great shield, didn't help him. "It's poetic."

"It just tells me how little you know about my father."

Using her talking as a distraction, Drake rolled out from overstuffed armchair and pushed forward toward his leather love seat. He had not anticipated a gunfight when he had decorated this room. It left a lot to be desired in the hide-and-seek department.

"He's going to take everything from you again. Even your death won't stop him now. He will kill everyone who ever came close to loving you, including your agent boyfriend. He will do it just because he can."

Peering up over the arm of the love seat, Drake perched his gun, itching to take a shot. He aimed as she spoke, and when he thought he had her position figured, pulled the trigger.

Her answering cry told him that he'd hit his target, but the angry cursing that followed told him that he hadn't hit as close to the mark as he had hoped.

"Motherfucker!" Natasha hissed. Then loudly she shouted, "Get the hell in here and do your fucking jobs!"

On the cusp of making a snarky comment, Drake stumbled back as his front door kicked in, showering him in small bits and pieces of wood and plaster. Two men, garbed in military tactical gear, burst in. Their bodies were covered head to toe in black, and the guns they held at the ready weren't any small handguns.

Drake swore as he pushed back to get as far away from them as possible while still staying out of sight. He needed to get room between them, but the only way out was through the hallway, which was completely exposed.

Drake rechecked his weapon and surveyed his options. He was a sitting duck in his current location. At this position, they could flank him and surround him. His best bet was to get down the hall.

Preparing for his next move, he hyped himself mentally, then with an internal count to three, shot to his feet. Twisting his arm so it was pointed back, he fired at the men as he ran down the hall, which seemed to have grown about three times its length since the last time he'd been down it. He laid down the best cover fire he could with the limited ammunition he had and had almost made it to his spare bedroom door when a searing pain tore through his thigh, instantly dropping him to his knees.

Using the momentum to propel himself onto his back, he shifted and continued to fire, this time aiming for Ryan, who had been able to come out from the opposite side of the black-clad men. Ryan jerked back, but Drake kept firing, letting the bullets hit home, until his gun clicked. As he fired, he shimmied his body back until his foot could reach the edge of the door. Gritting his teeth, he used as much strength as his injured leg would allow him and slammed the door closed.

Bullets continued to burst through the door, creating patterns of holes. Clutching his empty gun, Drake covered his face and rolled into a protective ball as wood splinters rained down. When the shots paused, he clambered to his feet, mindful of his leg, then groped underneath the bed.

"Come on, come on," he breathed, his hand fishing in the dark space. With a sigh of relief, he pulled a small black bag out and emptied it on the top of the bed. Frenzied, Drake clasped the second clip of ammunition. After switching clips, Drake aimed the gun at the door while backing up toward the window.

Four to one were not great odds, no matter how much firepower he could come up with. If he was lucky, the neighbors had called the police once the shooting started. If he was luckier, the police to get the call weren't on Boredega's payroll. If he was unlucky, well, then he just needed to get the fuck out of there. Drake fumbled with the window lock, and he hadn't realized that he had been bleeding until the blood smearing on the glass made it too slippery to get a good grip on the ledge. Still he managed to pull it up. He was almost through the window, his body contorted at an odd angle, when the door crashed open behind him.

"Stop!" Natasha demanded.

Drake kept moving, his motion only coming to a reluctant stop at the electrifying sound of gun hammer being pulled back. His body reacted on instinct, instantly doing as it was told.

"Turn around, get back here," she ordered. "Slowly."

Drake had to struggle with his injured leg to make the turn out of the windowsill but did it, facing her and the two men in black. Natasha stood between the two men, her curly hair in disarray. Her gun pointed at Drake loosely, as if she lacked the strength to hold it up, her free arm staunching the wound on her side.

Even with the blood loss, her presence was powerful. She glided between the two men standing only a few feet from Drake, motioning with her gun.

"Drop your weapon."

Tilting his head in question, Drake asked, "Why don't you just kill me?"

Natasha flipped her unruly hair. "I never like to take away from my daddy's fun. Besides, I still need you to tell me where you put all that money."

Drake didn't even attempt to conceal his laugh. "What? Really? You still think that *I* took the money?"

Glaring daggers, Natasha took a menacing step forward. "Don't even lie to me. Jacob showed me the account information. Now, tell me how to get the damn money. Now. Drop. Your. Weapon."

"Wow," Drake said with a smirk and shifted. He was now sitting on the sill, both feet planted on the floor, the gun held loosely in his hand. The two men flanking Natasha watched him warily as he moved. "Daddy is going to be pissed when he finds out that Jacob was the one who had the money all along."

Drake finished with a laugh and then pushed off with his feet, propelling himself through the window. For a moment, Drake was in a free fall, and then he landed hard, in the garden of decorative rocks, solidly on his back. The air rushed from his lungs, and Drake saw black on the edges of his vision. He had never been so happy to live on the first story.

"Goddammit!" Natasha screamed from inside as Drake tried to will his body to work.

Not allowing himself the luxury of air, Drake twisted, pulling his knees under him, trying to regain his footing. When he landed, the gun had fallen from his grip, and he swiped it up as he pushed himself to his feet.

He swayed, the blackness tightening in around his vision. Pushing through the fog, Drake stumbled forward, angling toward the trees. Coughing, Drake gasped in gulps of air as his lungs finally decided to work again. He quickened his pace, but a searing burn through his shoulder spun him around and brought him back to his knees.

Natasha, mostly through the window, had her gun aimed toward Drake. Drake didn't have time to react before her muzzle flashed and shocking heat blazed through his side.

Hissing from the pain but unwilling to let it deter him, Drake used the momentum of the bullet's impact to swing his other arm around. Pulling the trigger, he fired, fired, fired. Each muzzle flash came and went in short succession. Time seemed to slow, and he was able to follow each bullet on its path. One went wild, the second hit somewhere near her legs, and the third found its home in her torso, moving in with a flash of red.

As Natasha's figure fell unceremoniously to the ground, Drake didn't let his gun aim falter. Slowly getting to his feet, he observed her crumpled form. Taking a step closer, Drake watched as Natasha struggled to move. Just as when he had fallen, Natasha's gun had slipped from her hand and landed almost a foot away from her. She was stretching, reaching for her weapon, but she wouldn't have time. Drake felt the pull of his face as his lips curled into a cruel smile. Drake aimed the weapon and pulled the trigger.

CHAPTER 27

THE TASTE of vengeance still fresh on his tongue, Drake turned to make his way into the shadows. There were still two armed men somewhere. He thought they would have exited behind Natasha, but they must have gone out the front and were circling around. He needed to find cover and quick.

As he started toward the trees on the side of the building, the full impact of what he had done hit him in the chest, and he stumbled back as if taking another bullet. Clutching at his ribs, he frantically pulled in deep drags of air, but his racing heart couldn't be slowed. Light-headed, he fell against the sturdy support of tree, the rough bark scratching along his skin. Putting his hands on his knees, gun still clutched tight, he fought the threatening haze.

He had just killed Boredega's daughter. He had killed that guy Ryan. He had killed.

Killed. Him. He had.

He killed someone.

No, not just someone, but Boredega's flesh and blood.

He was finally on his way to vengeance.

But… it didn't feel as good as he had thought it would feel. Where he had thought he would find satisfaction, glee, and even relief, he found instead shock and disbelief.

He'd never taken a life before. Never directly.

Drake's lips curled in a sardonic twist. He had made everyone think he was a bad guy, and in the end, he had become one. He was a murderer. He'd started his path to hell, and now he might as well take the quick route.

He'd killed Boredega's daughter. There was absolutely no turning back now. He'd passed the point of no return going full throttle straight ahead.

Hearing shouting behind him, Drake straightened from his stunned crouch and looked behind him, where the two men were dropping out of the window, guns up.

Shit, he was so done with this.

One of the men stopped at Natasha's body. The other man watched his six. After confirming that Natasha was good and dead, the men spoke to each other briefly, too far away for Drake to hear. After a few moments, the men started a retreat, moving cautiously back toward the shadows of the building.

Drake didn't move as the men crept away, just gripped his weapon at his side. Every place his skin made contact against the cool metal of the gun tingled with anticipation. Using the pain of his wounds as a focal point, Drake gathered his adrenaline, using it to prepare himself for whatever might happen next. His panic, fear, and shock pushed aside, he watched the men as they continued their descent into shadow.

Even after the shadows had stilled and the men were gone, Drake couldn't make himself move. His body, exhausted and still suffering from the symptoms of shock, started to tremble. He didn't have time to fall apart. Most likely those men were on their way to tell Boredega the news of his daughter's demise. Once that knowledge was out there, Drake's life was forfeit. There wasn't any way he could move about the city without someone working for Boredega spotting him. He needed to act now. If he thought Boredega's reach was far when all he had done was put a dent in a few of his drug operations, there was nowhere that would be safe for him now.

No, Drake Clane needed to disappear.

Pushing away from the tree, Drake managed to take a few slight steps before his knees buckled. Collapsing onto all fours, Drake realized how shallow and frenetic his breaths were. He forced himself to take in a large lungful of much-needed air, letting it settle deep in his chest. He did it again. And again. *In, one, two, three. Out, one, two, three.* But even with his breathing under control, his limbs felt leaden and he couldn't quite lose the dizzy feeling turning in his gut.

Head dropped between his shoulders, Drake noticed a gathering of blood forming at the end of his left arm, pooling around his hand where it lay against another wound in his side. Drake laughed as the blood from both wounds mingled and spread. No wonder he was so weak. Between those two bullet wounds and the one in his leg, he was surprised he wasn't dead.

So much for his plans. Apparently, Drake Clane was going to disappear, just not in the manner he had been expecting. At least, not yet. He'd thought maybe he would get to take a little bit more of the cartel with him. But he could settle for Natasha. At least it all hadn't been in vain. He'd at least taken something from Boredega that he could never get back.

Maybe now he'd feel the pain, anguish, and rage that Drake had suffered all these years.

Even though he wouldn't be able to take Boredega out of the playing field, Drake felt better knowing the cops hadn't given up on trying to demolish the cartel. Sure, it was slow going and nearly impossible to infiltrate, but they were trying, and that's all that mattered.

Coughing, Drake cringed at the explosion of pain that radiated down his arm. Groaning, he placed the back of his hand against his shoulder wound. The skin around the hole was cold and deadened, numbed from the blood loss. Instead the aching throb traveled throughout his limb, and even his fingers pulsated in rhythmic pain.

How many bullets could a body take and still continue to fight? He was three in, not including the one from his rescue, and he wasn't sure if he could take any more.

A noise sounding to his right made him jerk and, despite his exhaustion, bring his gun up. He had been pretty certain the men had gone, but it wouldn't have shocked him if they had played him, making him think it was safe to come out in the open.

It wasn't until that moment that he saw the flashing lights. They lit the sky in a flurry of colors, dancing through the air.

What do ya know? The cavalry had arrived.

More men in black were circling the area, and Drake kept his gun poised as they zeroed in on him. While he wanted to believe the cops were the good guys and the bad guys were the bad guys, there was no way to be sure these cops weren't on Boredega's payroll. Even just one cop on the dark side was enough. He could just as soon be shot trying to "flee" as he could be arrested and tossed in the back of a squad car.

Anxious shouts of "drop the weapon" filled the air, but Drake ignored them, searching the surrounding flock for a familiar face. Anyone he could trust.

Adam broke through the circle, gun limp at his side, his other hand held up, telling the men to stand down. They only half complied, weapons still at the ready.

Drake's shallow breaths became even shallower as Adam cautiously approached. He was banged up from the car crash earlier, but Drake was relieved to see him, to know that he was okay.

Drake lowered his gun as Adam came forward. Keeping the weapon at his side, he achingly got his feet under him. The men anticipating action brought their guns up, following his sluggish movements.

Swallowing a lump in his throat, Drake drank in the magnificent view of Adam, all power and glory, commanding the troops around him, his golden hair and light eyes a welcome contrast to all the violence and the men in black.

Adam stopped about five feet from Drake, one hand held up like he was trying to calm a spooked animal. His gaze wandered quickly over Drake's body, probably assessing all his wounds, sizing up his physical and mental state as he did so. Drake wondered what he saw when his eyes widened in alarm—most likely the currents of blood flowing out of him.

"Hi," Drake said, uncaring about the armed and alarmed men enveloping him.

Adam's lips tried to turn up into a smile but failed. "Hi," he said instead, his voice breathy, but whether from fear or relief Drake couldn't tell.

"I'm tired," Drake said with a shrug. The left side of his body protested loudly, but he ignored it.

Adam nodded, creeping a little closer, arms still upraised. "I know. I know you are, Drake." He moved his hand in a placating gesture, his gun still not pointed at him. "Put the gun down and you can get some rest."

A smile sneaked its way onto Drake's lips. It was the second time he had gotten to see Adam in full cop mode, and damn, he was cute. He wished he had gotten to see him in action more often. Maybe in a different life, they could have had time together.

"You're a good cop, Adam. You know when the fight is over."

A light dimmed in Adam's eyes as Drake's words sunk in. There was a moment where Drake was sure Adam was going rush him, fling his body over his, cover him, and will them away to a faraway land, but instead he swallowed, pursed his lips, and followed his procedures and his training.

"Put down the gun, Drake. The fight *is* over. We won."

Drake's wan smile faded even more. They hadn't won, not really. Maybe they could claim victory to a battle, but the war was far from over. This was a crusade that would only end once the head of the serpent was eradicated, and that couldn't happen until Boredega was good and dead. No, all they had succeeded in was poking the beast. Boredega had a long reach. No prison or protection program would keep him from finding Drake.

Drake gripped the gun, his fingers tightening. The men around him grew anxious and twitchy. Adam's palms shot up, keeping the men from reacting, trying to keep Drake from making a move.

"Okay, okay, look, I'm putting up my weapon." Adam slid the gun into his holster and held up both empty hands. "Stop this, Drake. It's over."

"Don't put your gun away, Adam. You're going to need it."

Adam's eyes closed briefly, his lips twisted in helpless grief. The uniforms, already twitchy, edged closer, some already pointing their weapons at him after his softly spoken threat. Adam's gaze returned to Drake's face, and that light that had gone from his eyes now glowed bright with determination.

"We can make this work!" His voice was firm. "There has to be a way."

Drake shook his head, dropping his gaze. He couldn't stand to see the hope alive and desperate on Adam's face. No matter what happened from this point on, Drake was a dead man. At least this way it was on his terms.

"I'm so tired, Adam."

"I don't care!" Anger now. "You don't get to take the easy way out of this!"

Drake smirked. He thought this was easy? "I'm sorry."

Furious, Adam took a step forward, his hands outstretched like he was going to grab Drake. But as the man moved, Drake raised his arm with the gun. Even though it was raised, he couldn't bring himself to point it at Adam, but it was up nevertheless.

Within seconds, the uniforms were in combat mode, weapons up and shouting for Drake to put his gun down. The only thing that stopped

Drake from getting pumped full of lead was Adam's crisp tone demanding that they hold fire.

"Don't come any closer." Drake said it softly. He wanted nothing more than to be in Adam's arms, far away from all of this but... that was all. But.

Adam stopped his edging forward, but his once-determined face was pinched. "Please, Drake." Drake had to close his eyes against the plea, shaking off the desperation.

Not wanting his last conversation with Adam to be one filled with yelling and hate, Drake let his gun drop back to his side.

"He knows about you," Drake said, meeting Adam's gaze and holding it. "Natasha said they knew who you were the moment you walked into the club. She knew your real name."

"Okay." Adam nodded his understanding.

"Don't you get it? There is no surprising them. There is no getting in to take them out from the inside. They know everything. They are everywhere."

"They didn't know about you."

Drake huffed, "Yeah, well, look where that got me."

"Please," Adam whimpered. "Please, don't do this."

"Adam," Drake whispered. He wasn't sure if it was loud enough for Adam to hear, but he said it anyway. "I killed people today."

Pain filled eyes met his. Adam nodded swallowing hard. "I know."

"I've never done that before."

"I know."

Drake's eyes closed as a wave of exhaustion trembled through him. He tried to breathe through it. He forced his eyes open. "I passed the point of no return. Nothing can save me now."

Shaking his head vehemently, Adam took another hesitant step forward. "No." He had his hands out again, both reaching for Drake while also showing his surrender. "That's not true. I can. Let me help you."

Piercing hope tore through Drake at Adam's words, but it wasn't enough to quell the incapacitating defeat. He wished he could let Adam help. He wished they'd had more time together. He wished that he'd had the courage and trust to listen to Scotty when he'd begged him to go to the police the first time. But of course, he didn't, they couldn't, and he wouldn't.

There was no place left to run. He'd hit the end of the road. Taking one last deep breath of fresh air, Drake let the cool oxygen fill his lungs.

He wished Adam's scent would travel on the breeze. What he wouldn't give for just another breath of musky cologne.

"There is no help for me."

There was the briefest of pauses before suddenly, everything happened at once. Adam cringed at the words, shouting a desperate plea, and with desolate abandon, reached for Drake. Drake's arm, almost too heavy to lift another time, struggled up, taking aim. And the uniforms surrounding them no longer took heed of Adam's commands. Their weapons up and ready, and as Drake's weapon came to a stop, not quite pointing at Adam, the air filled with a deafening roar.

None of it took longer than a few seconds, but to Drake it felt as if time had stopped. The gunshots and the yelling melted into one long continuous rumble. After what felt like eternity, Drake realized he was flat on his back staring at the dark sky.

He wanted to laugh at his luck. He had been shot again, he didn't have a clue how many times, and he was still breathing. He didn't know how many shots a man could take before he called it quits. And now his body was so filled with pain or completely void of pain, because all he was aware of was a fuzzy white feeling swimming around his vision. That and cold.

His breath hitched and liquid spit from his lips. He tried to take a moment to think of how water had gotten into his mouth when the suddenly overwhelming coppery flavor registered. Blood, yes, that made sense.

Rough hands grabbed Drake, turning him to the side. The white fuzz flared to life in deep red, searing his body in agony. The pooled blood spilled from his lips in a dark puddle.

"You are such an asshole." The anguished words were whispered into his ear before Adam raised his voice to shout for an ambulance.

Using the last of his strength, Drake shifted so he could make out the hunched form above him. His body started a fine tremble and he gasped, clutching at Adam's arms, trying to steady himself.

"Can't... help... it," Drake managed through clattering teeth. He had never felt so cold in his life.

Adam made a sound between a gasp and a sob. "No, you never could."

"Back... pocket," Drake tried to speak, but his words were hardly louder than a breath. "Keep it safe?"

His body was shifted slightly again while the contents of his back pocket were removed. The sound of folded paper being flattened filled his ears, and he could breathe a little easier knowing that his family was in safe hands.

A new wetness dripped onto Drake's cheeks, and he marveled at their warmth. Adam, the picture delicately held between two fingers, dropped his head onto Drake's chest. "Don't do this. Please, please, don't leave me."

"Sorry," Drake breathed. He tried to lift a hand to sweep his fingers through Adam's light hair one last time, but the act was too much.

"I love you," Adam sobbed, sitting back so he could peer down at Drake. "I need you to know that. I never lied about that. You hear me?" His voice cracked. "I love you." Adam's tears flowed fast and steady, dripping off his cheeks, the flashing lights in the background catching a tear here and there and brightening it with a spectral show of illuminations, creating a halo around Adam and encasing him in an ethereal glow. Drake thought it was the most beautiful thing he'd ever seen.

He wanted to put a hand to those sparkling morsels, but his body just didn't have anything left. Not even the gratification of touching Adam one last time could force his limbs into motion. Instead, he sighed out a shallow breath, his last confession, and hoped that it reached Adam's ears.

"Love...." His word tapered off with his fading breath.

Adam's lip trembled slightly, before he willed a soothing look onto his face, his lips twisting into a semblance of a smile. Putting a hand to Drake's cheek, he caressed his fingers along Drake's cold skin, and to Drake's amazement, he could feel the warmth of Adam. Relaxing into that touch with words of love surrounding him, he let the threatening darkness envelop him. His senses still mostly aware, filled with Adam, he sank slowly deeper and deeper into the abyss.

EPILOGUE

THE HOT stove crackled and popped with the overheating fat as Adam flipped the oversized burgers. Sweat beaded on his brow as he worked, moving the finished burgers to waiting buns while the others continued to cook. His body ached from being on his feet for the last eight hours, rarely moving from his place in the bustling kitchen.

Finishing the plates, adding the small flourish that helped him get through the day, a sprig of parsley here, a decorative splash of ketchup there, he placed the plates on their warming tray for the servers to deliver.

Getting a moment of reprieve, he stepped back from the hot stove feeling wet sweat sitting on his skin. Running a hand across his forehead, he wiped away the stagnant liquid. He was washing his hands in the sink when Debbie, his favorite manager in the small downtown diner, perched her elbow on the ledge of the warming rack.

"Josh, honey, you've been here longer than your shift. You should take off." Her Southern twang was complete with the smacking of her gum.

Adam smiled at her as he washed his hands. "Yeah, I just have a couple more things to prep, and then I'm out of here."

Debbie raised a mom eyebrow at him, then smiled. "As long as you're back there, if you could whip up some of those banana pancakes for Mrs. Dorty. She says she can't eat them unless you make them."

Adam smiled. He liked Mrs. Dorty, the old woman who lived down the street from the diner. Her old age made her a force to be reckoned with, always willing to speak her mind. As soon as he had arrived in town, he had taken a liking to her and her to him after he had made her a plate of homemade banana nut pancakes.

"Sure thing."

The quiet town that he now was beginning to think of as home was slowly growing on him. It was definitely a change from his old life, but its slow pace and hardly ever changing atmosphere made it the perfect place for him to hole up. The people, all natives of the small town, were leery of the newcomer at first, but after a while, especially after he took the job as a cook in the local diner, they had started to accept him as one of their own.

Because their town was small and because there wasn't any major traffic coming or going, it was the perfect place for Adam to hole up while he waited for the Boredega cartel to be officially dismembered. Unsure of whether it would happen in his lifetime, he was glad that he had found a place where at least the people were friendly.

He had spent so much of his life pretending to be other people that it seemed fitting that he would spend the remainder of it as someone else. Out of all his aliases, the one he had most wished to remain was Scotty Harden, the quirky bartender. But that was impossible. Just as remaining Special Agent Adam Graft had become a death sentence.

No one knew who was and who was not on the Boredega payroll, and to keep breathing, Adam had agreed to enter WitSec. There were only three people in the world who knew he was in witness protection, and of those three, only two of them knew where.

The short stack of pancakes, the last task of his day, was finally finished and sent on its way to the little old woman waiting patiently in her usual booth. Adam slipped out of his apron. Saying his goodbyes to the other cooks in the kitchen and waving to Debbie and Kristy, the other server working the floor, he stepped out through the back door.

The chilly air created goose bumps on his flesh, and he hugged his arms around himself as he made the long trek back to his small two-bedroom home. He always took a varying path back to his home and never traveled the same pattern. It was his way of making sure that everything remained the same, that there were no new cars or unfamiliar faces.

It was during these walks, where there was nothing for Adam to truly think about, that he fell back into thoughts of his past. Thoughts of Drake.

After the gurney had disappeared down the hospital corridor, Adam had never seen the man again. He'd waited at the hospital for hours, his time split between pacing the halls outside the intensive care unit Drake had been rushed into and the private room Craig was quickly recuperating in from his earlier injuries. Craig had tried to distract him, tried to help him think of the best and be logical about the outcome, but he'd only been able to imagine the worst.

Even though he had been expecting it, dreading it, coming to terms with it, the news that Drake had been pronounced dead six hours after he was taken through those double doors knocked the wind out of Adam. It had taken him another couple of hours to scrounge up the will to move.

As the days had passed and Adam's life was turned upside down and inside out, he tried to conjure all the possibilities in his mind. He held fast to the idea that Drake hadn't died that night, and instead he'd been whisked away by federal marshals who had already changed his identity. After all, death was a standard procedure for entering witness protection. People didn't usually waste their time actively hunting for the deceased. Adam refused to believe that Drake was gone. He knew that if Drake died, he would feel it in his bones. Their relationship hadn't been long, but it had been powerful, and he had to believe that somewhere out there, Drake was confessing his own sorrows to a bottle of scotch, lamenting the love he'd lost.

The picture of Drake's family, the only possession Adam had had of Drake's—the real Drake—had been taken from him unceremoniously during his debriefing. You could appeal to get evidence back, but no matter how many times he asked, how many forms he filled out, the picture had never been returned to him. It had been boxed up with all the other photos and clippings that had been taken from Drake's condo and put on a shelf. Or so he was told.

The absence of the photo that Drake had specifically asked him to care for hurt. Not only because it was the last request Drake had ever asked of him, but also because it was the only thing Adam had as a real memento of Drake, of his real life and his real self. The man behind the curtain.

But no one could grieve forever, and before Adam knew it, his name had changed, his belongings were boxed up, and he was shifted to a quiet corner of the American South.

Adam rounded the corner of his block as the sun began its descent below the horizon. The glittery twilight was a beautiful thing in the quiet town, and nightfall even more spectacular with the thousands of twinkling stars lighting up the dark sky.

The silhouette of a man stood at the edge of Adam's front porch, and Adam's pace faltered at the unexpected sight. His mind whirred, quickly shuffling through his options. Did he continue to walk past his house as if it wasn't his, assuming who was waiting didn't know what he looked like? Did he turn around now and go back to the diner? Or did he just continue to his house and see who and what was waiting for him?

He missed the days when a shadow from the corner of his eye didn't have him checking over his shoulder. But he knew what he was getting into when he'd signed on. His job was dangerous and could have deadly consequences.

Pushing his flash of panic aside, he continued to walk steadily toward his house. The man standing at his porch didn't move, but as Adam strode closer, the man's bulky physique became more apparent. Adam felt a meager burst of something resembling happiness flit through his system. It had been a long time since he'd seen a familiar face; he hadn't been sure he would get to see one this familiar so soon.

Craig stood tall, his elbow resting leisurely on the railing edge. Adam smiled, quickening his pace. Their hands met in a tight shake that Craig pulled into a hug.

"Hey, man, it's good to see you."

Adam hadn't realized how lonely he had been, even with a town full of people. But now that Craig was here, someone who knew him, someone from his past, he could feel the sadness of solitary.

"You have no idea how good it is to see you." Adam grinned, his cheeks burning from the neglected act. "What are you doing here? Is everything okay?"

"Everything's fine, or at least as fine as it can be. I can't stay long because I'm doing this off the grid, but I had something I wanted to give you. Can we... uh?" Craig nodded at the house.

Adam followed his shrug and fumbled for his key in his pocket. "Of course, right! Yes, come inside."

After opening the door, Adam led the way into his small cottage home, the house seeming even smaller as Craig's large frame filled the entryway. Craig followed Adam into a small sitting room big enough only for a couple of chairs and a small table.

"Off the grid, huh?" Adam asked, smiling at the ridiculousness of it all. Craig and he had been working together for better than five years. Adam had been undercover and Craig his point of contact. They'd found ways over the years to contact each other "off the grid."

Craig sat in one of the small chairs, leaning forward, his elbows on his knees. "The cartel has been a mess since both Natasha and Jacob have been out of commission. Boredega has recruited a shit-ton of new dealers and enforcers, and the word right now is that there is a very hefty fee for any information regarding the whereabouts of you and any knowledge regarding Drake."

Hearing Drake's name out loud after so long made Adam flinch. He thought about him constantly, could still see a clear image of him in his mind, but he never spoke his name out loud. His heart missed a beat, stealing a breath. He placed a hand over the spot he could feel the palpitation and let the sensation roll over him.

"If the danger is so high, why would you risk coming here?"

Shifting uncomfortably, Craig dropped his gaze to the floor. He was silent a few moments before bringing his eyes back up to meet Adam's. He pulled his jacket open to reach a hand in to rummage in the inside pocket. "Because your appeal finally went through, and I wanted to give this to you in person."

He pulled out a plastic-wrapped square of glossy paper and Adam's heart sped up uncontrollably fast as it was handed to him. Reaching out tentatively, he took the photo from Craig. Swallowing to prepare himself, he looked down and found a very young, innocent Drake smiling up at him, his eyes bright with love and laughter, snuggled securely in the arms of his family.

"I—" Adam began, but his voice came out in an emotional waver. He cleared his throat. "Thank you," he managed, still staring down at the dark brown eyes that he'd fallen in love with.

Craig shifted again, but Adam didn't look up; he couldn't. Now that he had an image of Drake, even if it was a time before he knew him, before he'd become the man Adam knew, he couldn't look away.

"I, uh, I also have this for you," Craig said, holding out a small dark object.

Still unable to look up, Adam reached for it blindly. He positioned it so it was adjacent to the photo so he could see it without looking away from the smiling faces. He frowned, turning it over in his hand.

"What's this?"

"It's a burner phone. I know you have some from your transition and that you probably bought some to have just in case, and you know that if you have trouble you can call me anytime, right? Right?" He waited for Adam to nod before continuing. "Well, I wanted you to have one without any connection to you whatsoever. There is nothing to tie this phone to you, no paper trail, nothing."

Adam frowned, finally gathering the nerve to look up at Craig. "Why would I need that?"

Hesitating for just a moment, Craig seemed to deliberate in his head, but he'd made the trip out here and he'd gone through all the work to give him whatever else it was he had, so the debate didn't last too long. His face hardened to one of determination, and he reached back into his jacket pocket for another piece of paper.

This one was small, hardly larger than a sticky note. Adam cocked his head as Craig offered it to him. He took the paper cautiously, only noticing that his fingers were shaking when he tried unsuccessfully to take the slip from Craig the first time. Looking down, he saw an unfamiliar combination of numbers. There was nothing else. No name. No note. Nothing but a ten-digit phone number.

His mouth went dry as he stared at the black writing that seemed to jump out from the pale sheet. He fingered the piece of paper and then looked at Craig in confusion, too scared to hope.

Craig stood, straightening his clothes. "I shouldn't stay any longer. I still have a long walk back to my car."

Adam, overwhelmed from the entirety of the visit, nodded, his face unable to express a single emotion and his tongue too dry to speak.

Craig headed toward Adam's back door, turning back to face him as he reached to pull it open. He smiled warmly. "Take care of yourself, okay? And remember what I said about calling me."

"Of course," Adam stammered, clutching all the items Craig had brought him to his chest.

Craig gave him one last up and down before nodding and opening the door. "See you around, partner."

"Bye," Adam managed as the door shut with a soft click.

Silence stretched around Adam, and he sat in his chair with the picture, phone, and slip of paper cradled in his arms. Slowly, as if all the items would disappear if he moved too quickly, he set them each on the table.

His breathing hard and shallow, his heart pounding, he picked up the small piece of paper. The excitement, fear, and anticipation raged through his limbs. He was suddenly having an out-of-body experience, as he no longer felt as if he controlled any aspect of his limbs. He watched as trembling fingers gingerly picked up the phone, turning it so they could dial. The numbers from the paper lit up the screen as they were entered, and he stared at them a moment before finally pushing Send.

The buzzing in his ears was practically deafening as the phone rang. Once. Twice. Three times.

Finally, there was a click and pause as someone answered the phone. A deep, gruff voice answered, sending Adam's already thumping heart into super overdrive. So surprised to hear the voice that he'd thought he would never hear again, he didn't say anything.

"Hello?" the voice intoned again, this time curter than the last, and Adam couldn't control the euphoric smile that took over his lips, even as his eyes released a myriad of tears.

Suddenly, everything was back in its place. His heart back in his chest, the ocean out of his ears, the fog out of his head, and his tongue back in his mouth. The world was once again solid around him.

"Hi," he said softly, imagining what the man on the other end of the line looked like as his own voice filtered through the phone.

There was a short pause, and then a hiss intoned through the phone as if a sharp inhalation of breath was taken. Then finally, with a voice filled to the brim with emotion, came the familiar response.

"Hi," Drake responded.

CHRIS E. SAROS lives in the beautiful Mitten State, surrounded by the exhilaration of the Great Lakes. In her free time, she enjoys swimming, reading, ministering to her cats' needs, and watching TV. An avid traveler, she loves immersing herself in different cultures, discovering new foods, and meeting new people. Always game for a new adventure, she covets stimulating experiences such as working on locally filmed movies, coaching students in after-school activities, and spending time spoiling and sugaring-up her nieces and nephew to keep her status as "the fun aunt." Though ideally an optimist, Chris E. is intrigued by the darkness life has to offer. Using writing as an outlet for her darker nature, she loves constructing characters and tossing them into dangerous situations, just to see what happens.

Reach out to Chris E. Saros through email at chrisesaros@outlook.com or visit her on Facebook.

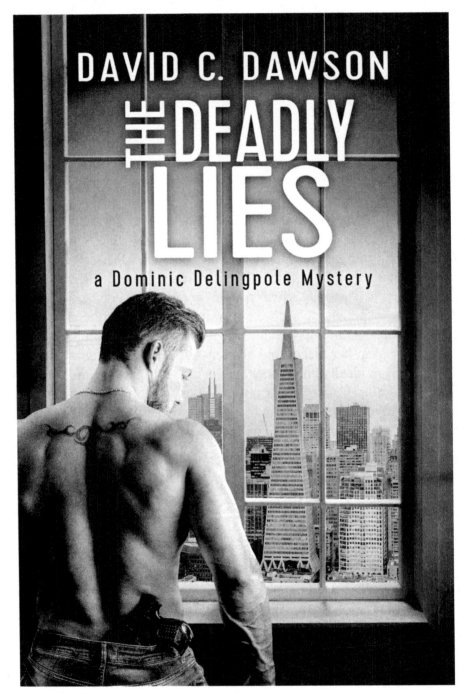

Sequel to FAPA Award-winning *The Necessary Deaths*
The Delingpole Mysteries: Book Two

Dominic and Jonathan are on their romantic Spanish honeymoon, and things are perfect... except Dominic has kept a secret from his husband. He's failed to tell Jonathan that he plans to meet his former lover, Bernhardt, who is speeding on his way from Germany to present Dominic with a mysterious gift.

But Bernhardt is killed in a suspicious car accident. Shortly before he dies, he sends Dominic a bizarre text message that will take the newlyweds on a hair-raising adventure.

Lies upon lies plunge Dominic and Jonathan into an internet crime that could destroy the lives of millions of people. What is the mysterious Charter Ninety-Nine group? And will their planned internet assault force Dominic to choose between the fate of the world and the life of his lover?

www.dsppublications.com

CPSIA information can be obtained
at www.ICGtesting.com
Printed in the USA
BVOW11s1009120318
510355BV00031B/1327/P